"Sharp, witty, perceptive."

—Bookreporter.com

"Refreshing . . . *My Little Blue Dress* is rife with hilarious anachronisms and provides a delightfully wry antidote to too much Jane Austen and epistolary novels, while at the same time elucidating Gen X angst and parodying Manhattan theme restaurants. With dry wit Maddox propels the reader through a whirlwind tour of historical misinformation until past and future meet." —*The Baltimore Sun*

"Lively and ingenious . . . cheerfully pessimistic . . . perversely enjoyable." —*Kirkus Reviews*

"In his first novel, Maddox concocts a hilariously off-the-wall satire of the memoir. . . . Brilliantly funny . . . Maddox's writing is purposely uppity, but the kitschy, honest overtones communicate a very witty take on love and life."

—*Publishers Weekly*

"Hilarious" —*The Seattle Times*

"Both great fun and very funny . . . *My Little Blue Dress* is a minor classic in a world of its own."

—*The Independent*

PENGUIN BOOKS

MY LITTLE BLUE DRESS

Bruno Maddox was born in 1969 and raised in London. A Harvard graduate and former book reviewer for *The New York Times* and *The Washington Post*, Maddox took over the editorship of *Spy* magazine in 1996, elevated it to within spitting distance of its former glory, then accidentally drove it out of business after two short years. He lives in London and New York.

My Little Blue Dress

A Novel

BRUNO MADDOX

Penguin Books

The author would like to thank John Brockman, Adam Lehner,
Brenda Maddox, John Maddox, Jake Michie, and especially Cintra Scott for
their crucial contributions to the writing of this book. Cintra Scott, especially.

PENGUIN BOOKS
Published by the Penguin Group
Penguin Putnam Inc., 375 Hudson Street, New York, New York 10014, U.S.A.
Penguin Books Ltd, 80 Strand, London WC2R 0RL, England
Penguin Books Australia Ltd, 250 Camberwell Road,
Camberwell, Victoria 3124, Australia
Penguin Books Canada Ltd, 10 Alcorn Avenue,
Toronto, Ontario, Canada M4V 3B2
Penguin Books India (P) Ltd, 11 Community Centre,
Panchsheel Park, New Delhi – 110 017, India
Penguin Books (N.Z.) Ltd, Cnr Rosedale and Airborne Roads,
Albany, Auckland, New Zealand
Penguin Books (South Africa) (Pty) Ltd, 24 Sturdee Avenue,
Rosebank, Johannesburg 2196, South Africa

Penguin Books Ltd, Registered Offices: Harmondsworth, Middlesex, England

First published in the United States of America by Viking Penguin,
a member of Penguin Putnam Inc. 2001
Published in Penguin Books 2002

1 3 5 7 9 10 8 6 4 2

Copyright © Bruno Maddox, 2001
All rights reserved

THE LIBRARY OF CONGRESS HAS CATALOGED
THE HARDCOVER EDITION AS FOLLOWS:
Maddox, Bruno.
My little blue dress / Bruno Maddox.
p. cm.
ISBN 0-670-88483-9 (hc.)
ISBN 0 14 20.0048 5 (pbk.)
I. Title.
PS3563.A339444 M34 2001
813'.6—dc21   00-043596

Printed in the United States of America
Set in Stempel Garamond

My Little Blue Dress

To B.M.
Thanks for everything.

CONTENTS

1950–1959—FIFTIES
postwar prosperity; moves to America; finds self awash in
vacuum cleaners; home-movie cameras; ice-cream machines, etc.

1960–1969—SIXTIES
beatles warhol dylan etc.; then hippies

1970–1979—SEVENTIES
oil crisis; orange trousers

1980–1989—EIGHTIES
wads of money; cackles while smoking cigar and talking on
cellphone the size of brick

1990–1999—NINETIES
cellphone much smaller; computer everything; millennial
foreboding

2000–present—NEW YORK
life in Chinatown; nice young man; i would like to die
now please

PART I

Coming of Age

1900–1909

THE RIGHT SORT
OF BEAUTIFUL

———

LIKE A LOT of little girls back then in that part of the world I viewed the future with a certain lack of enthusiasm, though for a different set of reasons than the rest of them.

The problem for all the other little girls was that these were the early years of the Twentieth Century and we lived in a particularly rural section of England where, even by the standards of the day, people held very fixed and depressing ideas about how a little girl's life was supposed to unfold. Unless you were bedridden with polio or some other disease they would generally allow you an idyllic country childhood—lots of daisy-chain making and cramming berries in your mouth as fast as you could pick them—then even a fairly languid and sun-soaked early teenage, but if by *seventeen* years old you weren't married to a farmer, hiding his wage packet in case he drank away its contents, then you were officially declared a Spinster and you had to go start work immediately in the windowless village dairy where the hours were long and the wages microscopic.

If this all sounds familiar to you, I can't say I'm surprised. It does sometimes seem these days as if every other book that gets published is an old woman's memoir that begins exactly like this one is beginning: back in the gaslit, horsedrawn days of yore with the author complaining about how tough it was to be a little girl and I would be reluctant to add to that steaming pile of volumes if I didn't feel that few of them have even come close to capturing the true horror of what it felt like to wake up every morning in an unheated house to the knowledge that your future was a) set in stone and b) bleak. It was one of the worst feelings you can imagine.

Or so I gathered. Thanks to a fluke of genetics I wasn't personally faced with either of the grim scenarios outlined above but was destined instead to be elected "Queen of the May" at our annual village "fayre" after which, if tradition held, the world would essentially be my oyster.

————

IT WAS ALL due to happen in 1905, when I would be five, my first year of eligibility. For two weeks that May, after my coronation at the opening ceremony, I would strut among the various tents and stalls of the fayre in a phalanx of local dignitaries, snipping ribbons, awarding prizes, posing for line drawings and then, after declaring the fayre officially closed, retire to a chair in our living room where I'd spend the rest of the summer listening to pitches from people who wanted to adopt me and/or give me money.

There'd be a lot of them, if tradition held: rich old women craving companionship, distinguished local artists begging to set me up in a cottage and use me as a "muse," savvy local businessmen offering me largish annual sums to endorse their emporiums . . . and the choice of a benefactor would be entirely up to me. This wasn't one of those situations like in an old English novel where the gorgeous little yokel girl gets set to live with the evil rich family so that her real family can buy food. My parents were relatively well off, owing to me da being foreman of an enormous crop-processing device known as a "fangle," and they had no other children. According to me mam they "just wanted me to be 'appy," which by any sensible reckoning I probably would be. I mean, think about it. I was going to be rich, at six, living a life of unrelenting comfort and leisure that was entirely of my own choosing.

But did this prospect excite me?

No. It depressed me. As stated, I viewed the future with a certain lack of enthusiasm. For the reasons I just explained I'd been an object of extreme resentment to all the other little girls in Murbery since the moment I first ventured down the hill in my perambulator, to the point that by the tender age of three I'd developed a crippling case of social anxiety.

Down at the schoolhouse every day I'd slump low in my chair and pray that I wouldn't be called on to answer a question, because every time I did there'd be dirty looks. When playtime came I'd spend as much of it as possible playing with my only friend—Karen, the daughter of me mam's best friend who had been forced to bond with me during the crucial first few weeks of life—and then either hide in the bathroom or stand at the edge of a group of girls, smiling tightly and hoping nobody felt like punching me in the face. Little girls can't punch very hard, famously, but when you are one yourself, when the muscles and bones in your face are as puny as the muscles and bones in the arm of the little girl who's punching you, it can feel like a block of pure concrete.

And the Queen of the May thing was just going to make it all worse. To start with there'd be the fayre itself, everyone looking at me and making comments on my appearance for two weeks, and then there'd be the rest of my life which, no matter how I ran the numbers, seemed certain to carry me even further away from my only real ambition, which was to one day experience the feeling that had eluded me all my life: the feeling of simply fitting in, of belonging, of being accepted as normal. If I were to leave Murbery, by letting myself get adopted into the aristocracy, then I'd be a permanent, wrong-fork-using oddity, but even if I stayed, as I planned to, and married an only reasonably prosperous local man—as me mam had done after winning the Queenship—then I'd never be free of the other little girls, whose resentment of me, one could just tell, was likely to deepen rather than wane.

Not that me mam's contemporaries resented *her*, particularly. But that was because me mam had won Queen of the May in the usual fashion, after the usual hard-fought and suspenseful contest. In 1905, everybody knew, there wasn't going to be any suspense, nor even any reason for any other little girl to enter. No one else had even a prayer of winning.

The problem was my looks. Not only was I far and away the most classically quote unquote "attractive" girl in Murbery, even as a three-year-old, but mine also happened to be the exact brand of doll-like English beauty that the judges of the contest had historically rewarded, featuring: a snub little nose; a slim, athletic build; and a cloud of golden ringlets that bounced behind me when I walked.

What really clinched it though was my size. The whole point of the village holding a springtime fayre in the first place was to celebrate the return of the Lifeforce after the long cold months of Winter. Consequently the Queen of the May, whose job it was to be the fayre's symbolic figurehead, was always either a) what was known as a "Slut," an alluring and voluptuous fifteen-year-old to symbolize fertility and bumper harvests etc., or b) an "Infant," meaning a little golden-haired angel child like myself to symbolize birth, and freshness, and that whole other side of the Lifeforce.

Nowhere was it *written* that some medium-sized eleven-year-old couldn't waltz along and scoop top honors; it just never, ever happened. Queen of the May was always either an Infant or a Slut, and in the years the judges elected an Infant they invariably went with the smallest one available, which in 1905 looked set to be me by about eight inches. The Sluts weren't going to be anything special that year, it was widely accepted, so even if I'd been normal height I think I would have still had victory in the bag. But my size put the thing beyond doubt. Barring a freakish growth spurt or a disfiguring facial accident Murbery's Queen of the May for the year 1905 was going to me, yours truly, the author of the memoir which you are holding in your hands, and there was absolutely nothing I could do about it. The whole situation was like one of those deceptively toothless Chinese curses: "May you be gorgeous and rich and live happily every after!" Sounded great until you thought about it, and then you realized it was actually a nightmare.

So I tried not to think about it, distracting myself as much as possible with the traditional joys of rural childhood, and I'm glad I did because that really was a fantastic time to be a toddler in the English countryside. Some evenings even now, when the sunset fills my apartment and makes my possessions go all pink, I find my eyelids fluttering shut, my heart rate decelerating, my mind detaching from its moorings and floating up ... away ... away from New York and this high-speed modern world ... floating back in time ... over decades and decades and decades ...

... and suddenly it's me and Karen, just like it used to be, tearing over fields in the hours after school, splashing through streams, probing into caves, punching little-girl-shaped holes through the hedgerows as we tried to outrun the dusk and squeeze as much juice from the day as possible before that soul-crushing moment when the voice of your mam came floating over the hills and called you home for your tea. Reader, there was nothing worse, nothing worse than that moment. "That were *your* mam, reet?" you'd say, turning to Karen, straining to ignore the fact that it was *your* name the voice had called ... but Karen would shake her head, leaving you no choice but to hurl your last egg in disgust at Wee Lickle Davey, the school's smallest boy, whom you and Karen had tied to a tree, and set off on the long plod home. With the earth between your feet going all shimmery and invisible in the fading light, the breeze off the ocean beginning to buffle in your ears, you slowly made your way back toward Murbery. Suddenly *whoosh*. Miles away down the coast you watched the gaslamps of Hughley flame on for the night, followed in quick succession by those of Clee ... then Waxford ... then Bliffington ... and finally Froom: until it was like someone had taken a string of burning pearls and laid it out along England's ragged coast, the beauty of which made you sadder than ever.

But then there was your house. And there was the hearthlight wiggling in the windows, and you picked up speed in spite of yourself, trotting as you hit the slope of the Hill, then sprinting up it, and then eventually just *erupting* through the door of the kitchen to dive at your mam's legs. "Oh look at the state o' thee!" she'd squeal as you hugged her, and with her tutting her exasperation you would break away, peeling off your muddy brambled pinafore as you tore up the stairs, then scrambling instantly back down again in flannel pajamas to find the table already groaning with thick-cut slabs of ham, crusty rolls of water bread, a jug of lemon cider with the anti-insect piece of burlap still stretched across its mouth, dumplings, and gravies, and salads, and pastes, authentic local cheeses in coats of greasy greaseproof paper and a great tureen of steaming turnip with the little flecks of wild walnut winking at you from deep in the pale green depths . . .

Yes, those were magical years to be a tiny little girl, growing up in the depths of the English countryside.

But then, of course, boom.

All of a sudden you were five.

———————

THANKS TO SOMEONE'S sense of drama, my Queen of the May preinterview was scheduled for the last possible day, the fourth Saturday in April 1905, and I remember the dread descending that morning before I'd even opened my eyes. I tried to will myself back to sleep but my eyelids snapped open of their own accord and I lifted my head to glumly regard the simple but expensive white pinafore that me mam and I had picked out months before at the Fancy Shop up in Bliffington. It hung coldly from the back of my desk chair, like a funereal shroud, if there is such a thing. From the kitchen below wafted up a distressing lack of odor, that I knew to be emanating from a bowl of complexion-friendly mixed berries rather than my usual deep-fried platter. "As tha roused thaself, lass?" came me mam's cheery voice up the stairs. "Is tha ready?"

No, I wasn't, and I mouthed as much into the frigid air of my bedroom. "Aye, me mam! Just fixin' me ringlets!"

After several deep breaths I tumbled out of bed to confront my destiny.

ON THE STREET outside the grocer's, me mam squatted down to give me a final hair and face check.

"Is tha nervous, lass?" She smiled.

I shook my head. I wasn't nervous. The streets were deserted and there was no one around to hate me. I just felt numb. On complete autopilot.

"Well, *I* were," she confided. "April o' me Queenship t'were a terrible 'umid climate in these parts, an' me ringlets all frizzed up rotten like an 'eron's nest. Oh, it were awful!" She chuckled at the memory. "But oh lass ..." Her voice tailed off. She plucked a loose ringlet from my cheek and tucked it gently behind my ear. "Oh me smallest lass tha's more comely than I *ever* were. Lass, tha's *beautiful.*"

I gave her hand a squeeze. She was having a bittersweet moment, I could tell, and I was pretty sure I knew why. In the summer following her Queen of the May victory, a few weeks after she'd married me da, a haberdasher had come to our house from all the way up in Bliffington to offer me mam a whole guinea if she would quickly stand amidst bolts of cloth in his emporium while an artist made a drawing for a handbill. It had been a really awkward scene, apparently, according to Karen, who got the story from her own mam. A full thirty minutes the haberdasher had stood there on our kitchen floor, making his pitch to me da while me mam did the dishes and pretended not to care. Me da heard him out, apparently, never saying a word, then politely showed him to the door and closed it in his face.

And he would not now be back, that haberdasher, not for me mam at least. Though still only in her late twenties she was no longer much to look at. Every once in a while, if you caught her in the right light, you might catch a *trace* of her former beauty, flickering beneath her skin like the bulge of a fine antique being carried to market in an old leather bag— but then tilt your head even slightly and *boom.* It was gone.

"Thanks, me mam. Thanks for everythin'."

"Oh lass," she said huskily. "Best o' luck and I'll see thee back at 'ome." We hugged carefully so as not to wrinkle my outfit.

THE PREINTERVIEW ROOM, I discovered when I poked my head around its door, was spare and dusty, with the classic feel of a dance studio or rehearsal space. In the center of the floor was an *X* made of silver duct tape, and behind a trestle table against the facing wall sat the three members of the preinterview committee, their heads bent over their paperwork.

The only one I recognized was the man in the middle, our butcher, a gigantic and amiable man with a huge mustache and a perfectly spherical bald head. He was flanked, as the village constitution insisted he had to be, by two randomly selected representatives of other villages to ensure impartiality. To his left sat an impassive old man from Clee (according to a piece of folded cardboard in front of him) with a disconcertingly massive pile of hair that looked like a loaf of bread with the crusts cut off and to his right, representing Hughley, a tall and rather debonair young man in his late twenties with a wide mouth and a square jaw weaving a three-piece brown woolen suit the exact same shade as his sideburns and his longish hair.

I tapped on the door. All three looked up. The butcher, who'd seen me before, beamed broadly. The other two were stunned. "Hail there lass," the butcher said softly, as if a magical little fawn had just appeared in a woodland clearing and he didn't want to scare her away.

"Hail, our butcher," I replied. "Is tha ready for me now, or shall I bide me time out 'ere in t'vestibule?"

"Nay, nay lass." He beckoned me in with both hands. "We're more'n ready for thee. Bring thaself in. Nowt to be frit o'."

I walked erectly to the X and smiled at my evaluators. The two non-Murbery judges were still gawping at my beauty, especially the young-looking Hughley man, who had slumped low in his chair and was now positively *leering* at me, like I was a barmaid in a seaport town rather than an innocent little five-year-old girl. I flashed him a mouthful of baby teeth, trying to shame him into showing some respect, but all he did was raise an eyebrow.

"Reet then," said the butcher, obviously flipping through his clipboard. "Why doesn't tha start by tellin' us about . . . oh 'eck." He tossed his question list aside and creaked back happily in his chair. "Jus' about why it is that tha wants to be Queen o' t'May. What appeals to thee about it?"

"Why?"

"Aye."

"Alreet. Well, that's a reet fair question," I began. "An' I think I'd 'ave to say that t'*main* reason that I've come down 'ere this mornin' is not because I 'ave any kind of," I deepened my voice satirically, "*obsession wi' bein' Queen o' t' May* than that I'm keen to simply . . . what's t'word . . . *participate*. Oh, it would be reet nice to win t'thing, don't get me wrong." I flashed a smile. "But far more important, to me at least, is jus' showin' up an' takin' part. Ever since I were a lickle babe, I've been aware o' a sense in which . . ."

"An' 'ow old is tha now, lass?" asked the old judge from Clee, his quill pen hovering above his clipboard.

"Five, sir. I am five year old. At t'moment."

"Carry on, lass."

"Aye." I cleared my tiny throat again and readdressed the spot on the wall. "I were sayin' that ever since I were a tiny babe in me crib I've been conscious o' t'extent to which it's rituals like Queen o' t'May, an' the springtime fayre as an 'ole, which bind us together as a village. I mean after t'long, col' months o' winter. To be able to all gather together in t'same place an' turn to one another an' say," I jabbed my finger, "'*Alreet!* Winter's *over!* We made it through! We survived! An' now let's begin t'cycle again, an' let's prove to ourselves that we know it *is* a cycle by 'oldin' t'same celebration we 'eld *last* year,'" I gestured over my shoulder, "'an' by once again electing a queen'. Does tha know what I'm sayin'?" There were nods all round. "It's annual rituals like Queen o' t'May that serve as . . . almos' as t'*heartbeat* o' a community. Because a community . . . an' people get this wrong all t'time . . . a community is a great deal more than just a bunch of people 'oose 'ouses are quite close by each other, it's . . . it's an *organism*."

I tailed off not entirely comfortable with how I was sounding. None of this was coming out right.

"Lass?" inquired the butcher.

"Sorry. All I'm sayin' is that I want to be Queen o' t' May because I love t'village o' Murb'ry an' I want to do whatever I can to 'elp it thrive."

There ensued a lengthy pause, during which all three judges stared at me.

"Well!" said the butcher eventually. "Them's a selection of reet satisfactory answers, lass. On be'alf o' t'committee I'd like to thank thee for thine time and express to thee 'ow much we're looking for'ard to thine appearance at Queen o' t'May competition proper, two Saturdays hence, on t'inaugural afternoon o' Murb'ry Fayre. Thank' ee, lass, an' . . ."

"Wait."

It was the lanky, dissolute judge from Hughley. He was tapping his teeth with the end of his pencil and peering at me intently.

The butcher covered his eyes with his hand. "Please, Jack. Not again."

"Aye," said Jack aggressively. "Again. I believe if tha consults t'constitution o' t'Murb'ry Fayre Committee tha'll find that t'judges from surroundin' towns are entitled to ask any question o' a candidate that occurs to 'em."

Creaking back in his chair the butcher stared at the ceiling.

"Does tha 'ave a question for me, sir?"

"Aye, lass. I do," said Jack. A very simple one. Me question is this." He paused dramatically. "Does tha really *want* to be Queen o' t'May, lass? Or is tha fakin'?"

I went cold.

"Oh, now." The butcher surged forward in his chair. "I

warned thee, Jack. I warned thee about 'arassin' t'contestants. Don't know 'ow tha's been accustomed to be'avin' down in 'Ughley Town but 'ere in Murb'ry tha'll keep a civil tongue in thine 'ead whilst addressin' our girlfolk or tha'll be tastin' me belt an' no mistake."

Jack's gaze never left me. He smiled gently. "I'm not 'arrassin' thee am I, lass? Tha's not in an 'urry to leave, is tha?"

I dumbly shook my head.

"Well, then?"

"Yes," I said, "I do want to be Queen o' t'May."

"Reet." Jack nodded. "O' course tha does. An' tha knows o' course what bein' Queen o' t'May entails, doesn't tha? Tha's aware that for two 'ole weeks this springtime season tha'll 'ave ev'ry eye in Murb'ry upon thee, evaluatin' thee an' scrutinizin' thee, listenin' to thine words as tha declares t'Fayre officially open, an' congratulates t'winner o' t'Best Three Carrots competition on 'is triumph?"

"O' course," I said weakly, pretty sure I was about to vomit.

" 'Cause wi' all due respeck, lass." Jack steepled his fingers. "Wi' all due respeck it seems to me that tha may not be necessarily very *suited* to them types o' acktivity. As I lissen to thine words I find meself struck by a certain . . . 'ow shall I put this . . . a certain *fanciness* in thine mode o' speech, lass. For a lickle five-year-ol' lass from a tiny village like Murb'ry, tha talks . . ." he scratched his cheek, "funny."

BOOM! The butcher pounded the trestle with both palms. "Reet. Tha's crossed t'line now, Jack." He stood and fumbled at his buckle. "Tha's jus' earned thaself a thrashin' o' biblical proportions. I 'ope tha' likes t'flavor o' Bliffin'ton leather because . . ."

"Stop."

This was me.

I didn't feel cold anymore, and I didn't feel sick.

Far from it.

All of a sudden I was having what I think people call an "epiphany."

This Jack person, it occurred to me in a great rush of warmth, was absolutely right. I *did* talk funny. I sounded freakishly worldly and sophisticated.

But my epiphany didn't stop there, reader. Not by a long chalk. It got deeper, more profound. In fact, it stopped even feeling like an epiphany and started to feel like a memory, a memory, believe it or not, of an old man's finger, gnarled and stained . . . tracing a patient, tender course across a great white expanse like a bedsheet or a piece of paper or the sail of a ship . . .

And I was also remembering a voice, a voice rather like my own, though even shriller and more feeble, if that were possible: a clear voice, a supple voice, a voice of great range and adaptability which, as I stood on that duct-tape *X* in the grip of my great epiphany, sprang suddenly forth within me like a clear mountain stream bursting through a sheet of old gray rock!

"Just stop," I heard myself say, looking the butcher straight in the eye. "This guy here." I gestured. "This Jack guy. He's utterly and totally right. I do talk funny. In fact, I talk funnier than any of you realize. *This* is how I talk, do you see?" I pointed at the air in front of my mouth. "Like *this*. I've only just realized it and to save you asking, no, I have no explanation. But I do know one thing. Like Jack says, I am the absolutely last person you want serving as the symbolic figurehead of your springtime fayre. All that stuff I said before? About the gluelike importance of ritual to rustic communities? I stand by those words, if not by the voice in which I said them. I'd make the worst Queen of the May in history and so for everyone's sake I am withdrawing my name."

Jack looked flabbergasted, as did they all. I walked to the trestle and laid my hand on his. "Thank you," I said. "Thank you for seeing whatever it is you just saw in me."

And with those words I exited, leaving a golden but unwanted future that I had never been without to bleed itself dry onto those dusty floorboards, and stepping into a life I knew nothing about—except that with any luck it might involve me one day finding out what the hell had just happened to me.

WHICH DIDN'T TAKE very long, as it happened. Halfway up the hill toward home, still feeling utterly surreal, I spied me grand-da through a thin patch of foliage in the hedgerow and decided to pay him a visit. A little human contact might steady my nerves, I reckoned, and like many retired sailors me grand-da wasn't the sort of person who felt the need to fill the air with idle chatter.

The old man was sitting on the wall of the retired animals' enclosure in the lower slopes of our sprawling garden, smoking his pipe and staring into space.

"Hail, me grand-da," said I, approaching from the side.

"Hail there, me lubbly," said me grand-da, never shifting his gaze from the distant hills as I clambered up on the wall beside him. " 'Ow were thine preinterbiew for Queen o' t'May?"

I blew out my cheeks. "Alright I suppose. Slightly bizarre. I don't know."

I was still talking funny, I realized, and there was nothing I could do about it. For a while we sat in silence, watching Mrs. Featherface the old hen as she pecked for some reason at a puddle. "Why's she doing that?" I wondered aloud, turning to squint up at me grand-da.

He was crying, or seemed to be. He'd pulled his cap down over his face, but I could see his shoulders shaking.

"Me grand-da . . . ?"

"Oh what a *fool* I am!" he wailed suddenly, menacing the sky with a fist. On his cheek I saw a single tear, nosing its way down his wrinkles like a mouse in a scientist's maze. "What an old stupid *fool*! *Why* Lord? Why didn't Tha stop me? Why did Tha let me do what I did? *Oh*, me lubbly. Oh me poor tiny lass. Oh me *smallest* lubbly . . ."

"Yes?"

"Me lubbly . . ."

"Yes?"

"Me lubbly . . . it weren't no 'preinterbiew' tha attended this mornin'."

"Um, yes it was."

"Nay, lass." He grimly examined his cap's interior. " 'Ere in Murb'ry Billage, t'phrase for what tha went through jus' now is 'first quick checkin'."

I frowned. "Well, *some* people call it that, me grand-da, but . . . I thought the two terms were interchangeable. You can say *preinterview* or you can say *first quick checking*. Right?"

"Nay, me lubbly. Wrong. Tha only knows t'phrase 'preinterbiew' because o' what I did to thee as a nipper."

I turned and stared up at him. "Excuse me?"

"Me lubbly . . ." He shifted round to face me. Our eyes locked. "Me lubbly I used to *read* to thee."

"What do you mean?"

"Oh, I nebber meant to *'arm*," he grimaced. "It were reet around the time tha were birthed an' I were just back from t'sea wi' the wound in me leg. What wi' me a cripple and tha still a tiny babe, t'pair o' us would pass our days by t'fire in t'main room, readin' from some o' t' bollumes I'ad left ober from when thine mam were a lass. Jus' standard infant material to start wi'. Tales o' pixies and fairies and animal fables etcet'ra. But oh me lubbly! Me lubbly tha showed such *aptitude*! Wi'in a few weeks tha were readin' the stories *all by thaself*, wi' no promptin' or assistance! Those lickle blue orbs o' thine . . . scurryin' 'cross the pages . . . I'd nebber seen 'owt like it! Quickly tha exhausted me tiny bookshelf an' so I whittled meself a cane an' made a journey up t'coastal road to Bliffin'ton, the booksmiths there, where I loaded up me satchel wi' t'mos' *difficult* books I could find, lass: dictionaries, instruction manuals, works o' reference by scientists and professors and t'like. But did it slow thee down one single iota? Nay lass! Tha tore through thine new librey in less than a week!"

My head was spinning. "And *that's* why I talk like this! Because you read to me as a kid and . . . and . . . inculcated me with a massive vocabulary!"

"Aye," he said resignedly. "An' then one day thine da came 'ome early from work. I were fixin' meself an 'ot drink in t'kitchen. The pair o' ye exchanged greetin's an' t'next thin' I knew 'e were reet up in me face screamin' that I 'ad ruined 'is only lass, made thee all 'fancy.' "

"Jesus."

"I tasted thine da's belt that day, me lubbly. 'E served me up a beritable *feast* o' t'thin'. An' when 'e were done I begged 'im to let me taste it sum more, I were that awash in *guilt*, lass, but 'e dragged me into t'main room and stood ober me while I burned all t'books in t'fireplace. Tha bawled thine tiny eyes out, lass, and from that day for'ard, tha nebber spoke a word. I'd' a' gibben me reet arm to undo what I did but t'were too late, lass. T'damage were done. An' it were only a matter o' time before this day arribed an' me trangressions were exposed. I've made o' thee an oddball, lass." He buried his face in his hands. "So does tha 'ate me now, lass? Now that tha knows?"

I didn't answer him.

On top of the wall I had curled into a fetal position and had begun to weep myself, in the grip—if you can believe it—of yet another epiphany.

The social anxiety and the crippling self-consciousness that had plagued me all my life . . . I understood it now. The Queen of the May thing, the other girls' resentment, had been minor factors compared to the secret I'd been harboring all my life:

That I wasn't just better looking than a normal little Murbery girl.

I was also *far more articulate.*

KAREN WAS THE first one I told. Late that afternoon, drowsy from play and the springtime heat, we two girls lay on our fronts by the millpond, watching the ducks drag their Vs across the cold black skin of the water.

Bong. Bong. Bong. Bong. Bong.

Over in the village three judges would be exchanging helpless glances in that dusty room, or maybe Jack would be tasting the butcher's belt.

Preinterviews were over.

And the strongest Queen of the May candidate in several centuries hadn't survived them.

"By 'eck!" Karen sat up. "I forgot to ask! 'Ow were thine first quick checkin'?" Her voice set off a fresh round of sobbing from Wee Lickle Davey, who was fastened to a spruce on the far side of the millhouse.

"Fine. Fine-ish. I don't know. Look, Karen, I've decided not to go through with the whole Queen of the May thing."

"Eh?"

"I'm not a candidate for Queen of the May this year. I withdrew my name."

"Nay! Tha's messin' wi' me!"

"I'm not. I was down there this morning at my preinterview, and I was standing there and . . ."

"Thine what?"

"Sorry, my first quick checking." I jerked my head. "Up above the grocer's, and I don't know. I was standing there in my little white pinafore and my shiny little shoes and suddenly . . . I don't know. Suddenly I felt like a piece of meat. A cow or something. Off to the slaughter. So I told them I'd changed my mind and went home."

Karen's mouth fell open. "Jesus bless me eyes, I can't believe it! Tha was sure to win!"

"What can I tell you? I guess I've got better things to do than stick leaves in my hair and be ridiculous."

"Aye," she murmured admiringly. "I reckon tha must do!"

I turned to look at my friend, sweet simple Karen Travers, with her nut-brown pigtails and her smattering of freckles, her hand-me-down floral-print pinafore and her tanned, sturdy calves, and felt a pulse of gratitude. Any other little girl in Murbery would have taken the pretentious-sounding announcement that I had finally Found My True Voice as an excuse to punch me in the face. Should I tell her the rest? Could she handle it?

"Karen?"

"Aye?"

"Have you noticed anything strange about the way I'm talking?"

She blushed. "Aye. I 'ave a bit. I weren't gonna say any-thin'."

"Karen, I've had the *weirdest* day."

"Oh aye?"

"Yeah, it started at my first quick checking. One of the judges accused me of talking funny and when I opened my mouth to speak the words came out . . . well, like this. All chatty and sophisticated, like you say. I had no idea what was happening. To tell you the truth that's why I walked out. I was panicking, pretty much."

"*Aye* . . ." said Karen thoughtfully.

"But then it was all *fine*! I went and talked to me grand-da and he explained he used to *read to me* when I was very, very young, from these *incredibly* difficult books, and it gave me this huge vocabulary and that's why I speak like this!"

"Really?" Karen scrunched up her nose. "Jus' because thine grand-da read to thee from books it's given thee an entirely diff'rent accent and . . . style o' speakin'?"

"Yes."

"Well *that's* reet queer."

I sniffed and looked out at the water.

Karen didn't have a point, did she?

Perhaps she did.

It made no sense that I wouldn't have a Murbery accent, just because me grand-da read to me.

The huge vocabulary, yes.

But not the lack of a Murbery accent.

And what about the casual turns of phrase? The *okays* and *yeahs*? The sheer informality?

The more I thought about it the more I came to doubt me grand-da's story. It wasn't just the holes in his logic. It was the way he'd shaken his fist at the sky in that bogus, theatrical manner. . . . That single squeezed-out tear . . .

"I've got to go," I told Karen, scrambling up.

"Jus' use t'bushes."

"No. It's not that. I've got some unfinished business. I'll see you tomorrow."

"Alreet then. 'Til t'morrow."

ME GRAND-DA WASN'T in the garden, or down on the cliff tops staring out at the ocean. That meant he was in his bedroom. No one answered when I tapped on his door, but I pushed it open anyway.

The stench was overpowering in that gloomy box of a room: pipe tobacco, mildew, and exotic foreign spices. The carpet was entirely laundry and on the desk a tower of coffee mugs was strung with spider webs like rigging. I didn't see him at first, but then a spluttering caused me to zero in on a flat gray shape beneath a blanket on the military-style cot.

"Me grand-da?"

He spluttered again and his eyes popped open. "Oh . . . hail me lubbly."

"I need to talk to you."

"Oh aye?" he yawned. "Come set thine tiny flammocks 'ere." He patted the bed beside him.

"This isn't a social call." I pushed the door shut behind me. "It wasn't true, was it? What you told me earlier about reading to me as a kid."

We locked eyes, then the blood drained from his face and he slumped back onto his pillows.

"Me grand-da?"

He didn't speak, just lay there, eyes helplessly searching the ceiling.

"Aye . . ." he said sadly, "it were *true*, lass . . ." He trailed off.

"But?"

"Me lubbly, don't make me do this. There's sum thin's in life that an old feller's best off 'oldin on to rather than un-burthenin'. Terrible thin's. Thin's that once learned can't be so easily *un*learned."

"Yes? Such as what?" I didn't sound as scared as I felt. "For God's sake, me grand-da, what do you expect me to do at this point? Say, 'Oh okay, me grand-da knows something terrible about me but he doesn't want to tell me what it is, so why not just forget the whole thing and go to bed'?"

The old man sighed. A sigh alarming in its length. For second after second the air hissed from his long old nose until my instincts were screaming at me to clamp his nostrils shut with my fingers and yell for me mam to go fetch Dr. Proctor.

Then it stopped.

"Berry well, me lubbly. I *did* read to thee as a nipper, but only so I'd 'ave sumthin' to tell thee if this day ebber came. If tha ebber came to me askin' to know why tha talks t'way tha does."

"Yes? So why do I?"

"Is tha sure tha wants to know?"

Not really, but it was too late to back out now. "Yes."

"Berry well. The truth, me lubbly, is that tha speaks in thine distinctib way because tha's *allergic.*"

"Excuse me?"

"Tha suffers from an allergy, lass."

"An allergy? To what?"

He flapped his hand at the window. "An allergy to all this."

"What are you pointing at?"

"Take a closer look, me lubbly."

I hesitated, then trotted to the window and pressed my face against the glass.

An epic sunset was in full effect over Murbery. It looked like the sky had tilted, making all the colors of the day run together in a big fluid bruise of orange and yellow and purple and red above the ocean. On the air you could hear the *cawing* of crows, the *tink* of the blacksmith's hammer, and ever so faintly, if you strained to listen, the clopping of the friendly old carthorse as he trudged home in the thickening dark from Dubford up to Bramley Forge. Then with a visible *whoosh*, the gaslamps of Hughley flamed on far away down the coast . . . then those of Clee . . . Waxford . . . Froom . . . Bliffington . . .

I turned away, and as I did there came a great choir of women's voices, gliding in formation across the landscape as they scoured the terrain for little lads and little lasses, with cheeks as red as apples, and pockets full of frogspawn, calling them home for their tea . . .

"The *Past*, me lubbly. Tha's allergic to the *Past.*"

WHEN I CAME TO, me grand-da was still talking, not having noticed that I'd fallen over.

"... an' that's why tha talks so diff'rently to all t'other lickle lasses in Murb'ry. Because at thine core tha bain't be from round these parts. Tha comes from *t'Future,* lass. A faraway age berry diff'rent to t'one we in'abit, where all folk speak like thee."

"Sorry, can you say that again?" I requested from the floor.

"It's true me lubbly. I knew it t'first moment I laid eyes on thee. 'Cause I'm allergic meself. That's why I spent me life on t'sea, 'cause no matter 'ow I tried I could nebber *fit in* round 'ere in Murbr'y. An' that's why I tried to shield thee, lass, why ... why is tha givin' me that partickular look?"

"Because what you're saying makes no sense. A person can't be allergic to the past. Because ..." I looked out the window again. "Well, it never *is* the past. As far as anyone can tell it's always the *present*. It just makes no sense."

"I'm speakin' as plainly as I know 'ow, lass. Tha's allergic to t'past. An' if tha needs further proof, why don't tha fetch me old seaman's locker from 'neath me bunk? Should be unlocked."

I tugged the rusty old trunk out from under his bed. The lid gave a scraping sound and then there it was, on top of all the silks and sword canes and shrunken pygmy heads: a sleek gray cardboard box with an oriental character embossed into one corner. "Open it, lass. It's a gift for thee."

Reader ... the little blue dress was a *cornflower* blue, with ruffled burgundy trim around its hem and its square-cut neck. Jouncing it in my hands I found it much *lighter*

32

than it looked like it should have been, and when I peered closer . . . well, it was the weirdest thing. The fabric was *entirely smooth*, without discernible pores or fibers.

"Modern, i'n't it?" me grand-da said rather smugly.

I held the dress up and examined it.

Modern?

Was it?

I could *sort* of see what he meant. The fabric was certainly of ingenious weave, perhaps the product of some new machine, and the design of the thing was markedly . . . eclectic. If you only stared at one small area you could kid yourself that you'd seen its like before, in a magazine or shop. But then when you held it at arm's length . . . well, then it was like the dress, rather than *copying* those other styles, was . . . was sort of *quoting* them, ironically, as if all the other dresses in the history of the world were slow, stupid, ugly people at a party and the little blue dress was the cleverest, possibly drunkest person there, mimicking their voices, aping their mannerisms . . .

"Yes," I said simply. "It's modern."

"And so is tha, me lubbly," the old man continued warmly. " 'Ow that dress appears to thee reet now is 'ow *tha* 'as allus looked to t'simple folk o' Murb'ry. Diff'rent. Strange. Belongin' to another world. Because tha *does*, lass. Tha belongs to a world that's far more sophisticated an' . . . an' *worldly* than this simple rustic region. Oh, but me lubbly . . ." I heard him smile. "It'll all come good in t'end. It's too late for an old feller like me but *tha* lass . . . thine time will come. A moment will arrive when these quaint surroundin's will drop away and both tha and thine new dress will be t'norm, rather than t'exception. An age in which a person can speak and act 'owebber 'e wants wi'out no fear o' censure. I'm speakin' o' t'future, lass, though I don't know when it'll arribe. Could be a year, could be an 'undred year . . ."

"Okay, stop." I shoved the dress back in its tissue paper and wobbled to my feet, suddenly exhausted. I'd had long days before, reader. Long like you couldn't imagine. Interminable slabs of buttery country fun where literally about ninety minutes seemed to pass between each *tink* of the blacksmith's hammer. But nothing like this. Nothing ever like this. Since tiny foot had met chilly floorboard that morning I had: washed and dressed myself to a very high standard; submitted myself to the scrutiny of a three-judge panel; had an epiphany; renounced the only future I'd ever envisioned; climbed a hill; talked to me grand-da; had *another* epiphany; enjoyed a full session of playing with Karen; gone to see me grand-da again; and been made privy to a theory so mindbending and counterintuitive that I had actually *fallen over.* It was time for me to go to bed.

"We can talk about it more tomorrow. Thanks for the dress. It's certainly very pretty, and . . . me grand-da? Are you okay?"

The old man's eyelids were fluttering like two trapped moths, and his breathing had a gurgle to it. "Aye, me lubbly. Reet as rain. We'll speak on it more tomorrow."

EXCEPT WE DIDN'T. Because by morning me grand-da was dead, of a conniption in the night according to Dr. Proctor.

At his graveside funeral I wore the little blue dress beneath my black funeral pinafore in the preposterous hope that as it departed this world, bound for wherever it was headed, me grand-da's dissipating spirit might pass briefly through my brain and impart the concrete, intelligible version of the nonsense he'd been feeding me on the evening he died.

But no such luck. The coffin went into the ground, the soil went on top of the coffin, and as we walked to the inn for the reception I lagged behind the other mourners and faced, for the first time, the fact that I would probably now never know what he'd been trying to tell me: why I spoke the way I did.

But at least I had the dress.

Despite the obvious untrueness of me grand-da's theory that I was "allergic to the past," the fact that he had even felt able to *make* a diagnosis on that surreal afternoon, and that to corroborate his claim he had given me an actual *object* with which I did, in truth, feel a weird sort of kinship, both suggested strongly that somewhere out there in the world there was a *rational explanation* for my strange style of speaking and thinking. The little blue dress was conclusive proof that, contrary to appearances, I was not an implausible freak but in fact a *real person*, and with that knowledge, I found, I was able to carry on.

QUEEN OF THE MAY that spring was a strawberry-blond Slut named Sophie Fairlop and after closing ceremonies I wrote her a long, thoughtful letter explaining how in my opinion she might possibly be the best May Queen in the entire history of the region; and later that summer, after her honeymoon, Sophie's carriage drew up at the edge of the green where I was playing with Karen and she beckoned me over to tell me that reading my letter had made her cry. Coming from me, Sophie said, it really meant a lot. She'd even persuaded her husband to buy her a silver frame so she could hang the thing in her dressing room next to her mirror. I was glad, I told her. I'd meant every word. And Sophie leaned out of the carriage window so we could hug.

That was a good day. A real turning point.

Hey, who knew?

Maybe there was even a future in it.

1910–1919

ME AND THE GLOBE AFLAME

———

ALL I CAN really remember about the years 1910 to 1913 is that when they were over my best friend Karen and I were easily the two most attractive girls in Murbery. Puberty had treated us both very kindly, especially Karen, who had mutated under its influence from an averagely pretty, rather gangly child with pigtails into a stunningly curvaceous brunette who wore her nut-brown hair in a ponytail. My own metamorphosis was subtler. Though I became taller than I had been, and my ringlets relaxed enough for me to also wear my hair in a ponytail, my womanly form, when it finally arrived, was of the slender, birdlike variety. I was willowy, reader, and lithe. Facially, though, I was still spectacular and taking everything into account I reckon I would have stopped easily as much traffic as Karen, had there been any.

The whistles and stares we attracted as we sashayed arm-in-arm through the village made Karen feel uncomfortable, but to me they were heavenly balm. For eight long years I'd been keeping a low profile, biting my tongue, fearful that at any moment I might open my mouth and blurt something out that would expose me irrevocably as being . . . well, as being every kind of freak it was that me grand-da had accused me of being on that weird afternoon.

But the arrival of puberty changed all that. All of a sudden I *was* something, something people understood, namely a gorgeous teenage girl, and as long as everyone was staring glazedly at my chest, I realized, the chances of their catching a glimpse into my soul and rejecting me for what they saw there were thrillingly remote.

It was Karen who found a boyfriend first, however. She fell madly in love with the first guy to ask her out, one of the drover's apprentices, an ordinary-looking lad named Greg. But I wasn't jealous. Happy as Karen visibly was in her relationship, and though my desk every morning was inches deep in love notes when I got to school, I felt I owed it to myself to be more discriminating. After the difficult time I'd had as a child, I reckoned my teenage self deserved nothing but the best.

———

THE SUMMER OF 1913 was the sort of long, slow, sticky summer that you just don't tend to see anymore, when the streams and the rivers seemed to bubble with sap, and the sundial's shadow was as long and as straight as the Roman road from Meanly up to Narpenceser. At that year's Summer Fair—another of the annual rituals without which, in my private opinion, our community would probably disintegrate—a local manufacturer of horses' harnesses had sponsored a tree-trunk-pulling contest on the village green, and one sweltering Sunday I found myself down there, spectating from a deckchair in the shade of a willow as Murbery's menfolk took turns dragging an old knobbled tree trunk down a fifty-yard track with a jar of premium whale-oil saddle cream for the fastest time. That was how the contest was supposed to work anyway. The whole thing was thrown into chaos by this one big lad I didn't recognize who literally made the tree trunk look like it had an engine in it. Again and again and again the young lad roared across Murbery green, shaving seconds off his record each time as he perfected his technique, until gradually the other males stopped even trying. The contest was supposed to last all day but at the stroke of noon the officials threw up their hands, gave the winner his jar of saddle cream and started folding up their paraphernalia. I sat there in the shade, watching the big lad walk away . . . and realized all of a sudden that I didn't *want* him to walk away. As the massive chap was joining some smaller friends at the corner of the green I stepped out of the shadows. "Hail," I hailed him. "Congratulations. That was really . . . omigod. *Davey*?"

"Aye?"

It was! It was Wee Lickle Davey, the former smallest boy in school, the one Karen and I used to tie up to trees! No one I knew had seen hide nor hair of Davey since 1911, when he'd left school to start a cartwheel-making business with his brother, or maybe . . . or maybe people *had* seen Davey and just failed to recognize him, because to be perfectly frank the proposition that this . . . this raging slab of muscle, oozing sweat into a too-small shirt, had somehow evolved out of Wee Lickle Davey McCracken was one that simply hurt the brain.

"D-Davey," I stammered, feeling faint, "it's me. Do you

remember? From school?" I fanned my face with my fingers, simultaneously indicating it and cooling it.

His forehead furrowed, then an earthy smile split his giant brown face. "Oh aye! I remember thee, lass. Tha were that lass 'oo were goin' to be Queen o' t'May, but 'oo changed her mind at t'last minute."

"Exactly." I beamed.

"But . . ." He touched a finger to his lips and blinked at my breasts, the tops of which you could see over my low-cut neckline. "But tha wert smaller back then, lass. Tha's . . . tha's been *burgeonin'*!"

Someone snickered but I tuned them out and beckoned Davey closer. "Davey . . ." I hissed up at him with some urgency. "You're no small chicken yourself. Davey, I've *missed* you."

For a second his face was adorably blank, but then the subtext of my words hit home and his eyes sprang wide. Nothing more needed saying. With a jerk of his sandy head we set off across the village green, then away over the fields to the river. With tall stalks of mustard rising up on either side we traced the banks of the quiet Mur as it curled its lazy way through the sun-soaked lowlands of prewar England. With Davey in front, me behind, the jangle and parp of the fayre grew fainter . . . fainter . . . until there was nothing to be heard but the *zoom* and *plink* of dragonflies, the rustle of our feet in the long wet grass, and the forceful subsonic streaming of the water. Hopping first on one foot and then the other, I peeled off my sandals to feel the coolness and the wetness of the grass between my toes because I knew in my gut that I would never be this young again.

We ended up in a place that Davey seemed to know, a natural cathedral of elder trees cradled by the river's elbow.

It was peaceful in there, and very, very green. I just stood there for a while, drinking it all in.

" 'As tha ever' ad relations wi' a feller before?" Davey asked me presently, cutting straight to the chase.

Still admiring the foliage I hesitated, then came clean. "I haven't in fact. But why do you ask?"

He shrugged. "A lad allus likes to know. If it's thine first time well then it be'ooves me to really make it special."

I turned to face him. "You think I'm scared?" I raised an eyebrow.

"Um . . ." Davey was taken aback. "Well, it's nat'ral for a lass to be nervous o' 'er first takin'. An' t'lad 'as a responsibility to be gentle wi' 'er."

"Hmm." I frowned, peeling my frock over my head and letting it drop to the leaves. "But what if she doesn't want it gentle?"

I began by letting Davey suck my tits from a kneeling position. Even at thirteen I had the kind of nipples that would chug themselves stiff at the slightest stimulation and which, when they were fully engorged, given the smallness and pertness of the breasts that supported them, seemed disproportionately large, like a baby's head, in a way that Davey seemed to find particularly affecting. He moaned and he groaned, and tore at his clothing as he suckled, and pretty soon after that we were "off to the races" as people used to say in those parts.

How long we lay together that day I couldn't tell you, for under the almost industrial pounding of Davey's massive hips my perception of the passage of time simply crumbled apart, like the venetian blinds always do in someone else's house whenever you try to adjust them. Maybe it was an hour, it could have been ten minutes, but eventually orgasm hit me like a rock in the head and I fell dry lipped and breathless into the papery embrace of the leaves.

That was all very nice but the deepest joy for me came later, picking my way back to Murbery alone with my sandals in my hand. When the spire of Murbery Church appeared over the top of the crop I experienced a surge of adrenaline, and felt suddenly less like a small-boned thirteen-year-old who'd just been forcefully ravaged in a clearing than like a ravager myself, a swaggering conquistador returning in triumph after some famous victory.

Which was pretty close to the actual situation, if you thought about it. After my long years of exile, my lonely wander through the wilderness of Not Quite Fitting In, sex with Davey had finally validated me as an actual, plausible person. Such is the nature of the act. Any scientist will tell you that one of the surefire ways of determining whether two organisms are members of the same species is to lock them in a room and observe whether they copulate. A dog won't mate with a cat or a fish—well, he may *try*, but in the final analysis he will come away unsatisfied. And Davey McCracken, as pure a specimen of genuine local stock as you could imagine, had come away from our coupling *extremely* satisfied. In other words, we were the same, he and I, real authentic Murberyites.

———

DAVEY AND I met for lunch the next day, a Monday, after I'd spent a pleasant morning tormenting Karen with my silence. With her surveilling me from the lunchroom window I snuck faux-furtively across the playground and rendezvoused with Davey at the foot of the steps. He was in the same clothes as the day before, but with a small wicker hamper strapped to his back.

"Hail." He smiled shyly. "My queen o' the afternoon."

"Hail," I said, looking him up and down. "How are you?"

"I'm 'appy, lass. 'Appy down at me core."

"Great. Me too. Yesterday was really fantastic. *Really* fantastic."

"Oh aye?" He blushed. "Tha enjoyed thaself?"

"Yes. Immensely. Especially the sex." I also blushed and looked away.

"Is tha sayin' tha's in love with me, lass?"

I thought about it. In the distance, in the drover's yard down by the clifftops, a man was unloading something from a cart. "Yes," I said eventually. "That's what I'm saying."

"Well, I'm reet chuffed. Because t'fact o' t'matter is I'm in love wi' thee too."

"Great."

We set off walking, several feet apart, our knuckles brushing from time to time, and ended up in the little spinney of poplars near my house, where we had a picnic.

Davey's hamper turned out to be stuffed with local delicacies of the absolute highest quality, including bronzed Cornish ham, some deviled heron's eggs, a paper screw of waxy mustard, a brick of good cheese and a powdered lozenge of crumbly sulphor bread. For drinks we had a stoppered flask of ice-brewed orange cider, and for afters there were six gleaming baby quinces, plus thruppence-worth of candied violets, also wrapped in a paper screw.

"Does tha know what I love most about thee, lass?" Davey asked as we lingered over the quinces.

"No."

"I love thine *energy*. Thine *verve*. T'way that if tha wants a thin' tha just *seizes* it."

I sucked at my straw. "Wow," I said. "Thanks." He was still squinting at me, though. The ball was still in my court.

I cleared my throat. "Well, look, I really love the way you *carry* yourself, Davey. Your whole *stance*."

"Oh why thankee, lass." He sounded pleased. "And dost tha know that when tha's not wi' me I 'ave t'image of thine face swimmin' in me 'ead? At all times? P'raps it sounds daft . . ."

"No, not at all."

It did though.

It did sound daft.

In fact, it sounded ridiculous. This was rapidly turning into the most mawkish and excruciating conversation of my entire young life. Was this love? I found myself wondering to my own dismay. Thrashing about in sun-dappled clearings, fumbling for abstract nouns? Scouring one's heart for emotions one might or might not be feeling?

I rather hoped not.

Because it didn't feel like something I was good at.

"Listen, Davey." Emphatically I slurped the last of my cider through my straw. "Do you know of any reason why I shouldn't duck behind that tree over there and quickly slide out of my panties?" I winked at him.

"N-none at all, lass," stammered Davey.

"Well, I do." Setting down my cup I rucked up my skirt until its hem was at my hips, and then I looked at him. "Because I'm not *wearing* any panties."

———

IT WASN'T ANY USE, though. As the summer wore on, while the sex remained fantastic, I was forced to face the fact that my relationship with Davey McCracken was missing some vital element—you could call it love, I suppose—and I had no clue why. Was it me? I would wonder most nights, lying anguished on my bed in bra and panties, behind a locked bedroom door that since my thirteenth birthday had had a Do Not Enter sign on it. Or was it him? Or was everything actually fine?

It was him, I decided. Sometime around the end of August, after searching my soul pretty unflinchingly, I'd come to the conclusion that I wasn't a homosexual. I liked sex with men too much to be any kind of closet lesbian, which was lucky, because these were still the early years of the twentieth century and bigotry was rampant. Gays in that era were beaten senseless every time they went to the shops, and had such a quantity of human excrement shoveled through their letterbox every day that I suspect they probably ended up reading some of it.

No, the problem, I reckoned, lay with Davey, but for my own peace of mind I needed to be sure.

During physics one morning at the end of June, I finally put Karen out of her misery. We were running a current through a nugget of metal to measure the voltage, and between readings from the voltmeter I confessed to her that Davey and I had been more than just friends for some time. She squealed with excitement and hopped from foot to foot.

"'As tha *been* wi' 'im, yet?" she whispered, leaning close.

"Excuse me?"

"'As tha . . . 'As tha *lain* wi' 'im?"

"'Lain'?" I frowned, torturing her. "What do you mean? You're going to need to be more clear."

Karen by this point was red as a tomato and extremely flustered. "Tha knows! Tha knows worr'imean! 'As tha . . . 'as tha . . . *ackquiesced* to 'im yet?"

"*Oh . . .*" I nodded. "No. Not at all. Though the other day I *did* let him fuck me with his cock, right in the vagina."

In a cloud of snorts and giggles Karen vanished beneath the workbench, eventually resurfacing with an entirely purple face. And who could blame her? My remark had been amusing.

"Oh that's reet good news! So when can t'four o' us go out, like? Double datin'?"

I adjusted my goggles. "Well, I wanted to talk to you about that, Karen, actually. I think I need your help. As great as things are going between me and Davey—and they are going great—I'm starting to suspect that there may be something *wrong* with him. The sex part is fine but *afterwards*. All the talking. The staring into each other's eyes. Well, to be perfectly honest it makes me want to claw my own skin off and then take a hot bath."

"Nay!"

"Yes."

"But . . . that's not 'ow a lass is s'posed to feel when she's wi' 'er feller!"

"I know. That's what I'm saying. And what I was thinking was that maybe if the four of us went out together you could take a look at Davey and tell me if you think there's something wrong with him." Grimly I bent to the experiment. "Because if there isn't, then there's something wrong with *me*."

KAREN THOUGHT MY plan was a great idea and that Thursday the four of us went out: me and Davey, Karen and

Greg. On the green we threw horseshoes until the brink of dusk and then went for chicken-in-a-basket at the inn.

Davey had really made an effort, I noticed as we studied our menus. He'd borrowed a white shirt and a pair of clean trousers from his brother, and when he thumped his wallet on the table it occurred to me for the first time that there was a sense in which he owned his own business. I hoped Karen would be able to see past these irrelevancies and discern the true horror that was Davey. Personally, I found it pretty easy. All through dinner, and as we lingered over ices, my heavily muscled boyfriend lectured the table about his plans to open a chain of mechanized cartwheel shops, all across the region, and funnel the profits into a hospital for orphans that he was going to build down in Hughley. I glanced at Karen to see if she was finding him as nauseating as I was, but her eyes gave nothing away. Or rather I *wished* her eyes gave nothing away. In fact, they were shining. She seemed to be *lapping up* Davey's drivel. "Oo, that's a reet philanthropic scheme o' thine, Davey," said Karen during one of his infrequent pauses for breath and all of a sudden I simply could not take it anymore.

"Karen!" I bounced to my feet. "I'm going to the bathroom now, Karen!"

Bound by the Girl's Code, Karen rose also. "Aye. Me an' all."

"Well?" I demanded, once we were alone, flattening myself against the ladies' room door to stop Karen from escaping. "What do you think?"

Karen fished her lipstick out of her bag and turned to the mirror.

"'Bout what?"

"Don't mess with me, Karen. This thing with Davey is literally killing me. Tell me what you think of him."

She stretched her mouth wide and started applying the makeup. "What if tha won't like what I 'ave to say?"

My chin began to quiver. "So it's true. You *like* him, don't you? There's nothing wrong with Davey at all, is there? It's me. I'm a cold fucking fish and I will never know love."

Karen smooshed her freshly painted lips, as one does, then straightened to admire her handiwork. "Aye. There's sumthin' *badly* wrong wi' thee." She smartly recapped the tube and smirked at me. "Tha's jus' wasted an 'ole week o' thine young life on the soppiest an' most irritatin' lad 'oo were ever born o' woman! That 'ospital for orphans?" Karen mimed vomiting. "I nearly lost me chicken reet back into me basket when 'e were on about that."

Twenty seconds later, after I'd nearly hugged the life out of Karen, I dragged her into the stall, and started whispering. "God yeah that hospital thing was *awful*. And that's how he is *all the time*, Karen. If he's not actually inside me then it's just . . . well, he's just spewing that soft, sensitive *crap* into my ear. Feelings and emotions and just anything that's on his mind, no filter at all."

Karen shook her head in sympathy. "Oh, tha poor lass. 'E's a fine-lookin' clump o' man, though. 'T 'as to be said."

"Yeah I know. And he's hung like Guy Fawkes. But . . . I don't know. I just don't think I can take it anymore. What do you think I should do?"

"Well . . . if I were thee I think I'd satiate myself on what 'e's got in 'is trouser an' then give 'im 'is papers."

"Find someone else?"

"Aye. Find thaself a feller 'oo fills thine 'eart with as much blood as 'e does thine privates. There's nowt like love, lass. Nowt in t'world."

THE EVENING ENDED down on the clifftops with two flasks of apple wine. Davey and I were lying on a big flat rock while ten feet away Greg was still fucking Karen behind a crag. The moon was on the ocean and above the crashing of the waves the night resounded to Karen's stifled moans, the swish of her hair on her shoulders, the tiny little clicks from her wetness.

I nudged Davey. "Do you want me again?" I was in a strapless floral halter top and a pair of hessian karate trousers.

"No," he said, not looking at me. "I want thee to tell me that tha loves me."

Oh God. Here we went.

I cleared my throat. "I love you."

Davey turned, his eyes glittering with resentment in the deep blue evening. "Well then why when I'm wi' thee do I allus feel so alone?"

Cooing playfully, I rolled over and tickled his mustache with my finger. "'Cause you're a weirdo. 'Cause you're a crazy, kooky dreamer who's always got some kind of crazy . . . *thing* going on in his head."

"Tha's mockin' me. Why does tha allus 'ave to mock me?"

I hovered over him, smile fading, then with a snort of exasperation scrambled away to the far side of the rock where I drew my knees to my chest and glared out at the noisy black water. "You know, Davey, I really wish you'd warned me that you wanted to have some Big Conversation. I really thought we were here just to fuck and have a nice time. I'm just not in the mood for one of your . . ." I deepened my voice and made it go all stupid, ". . . 'Tell me 'ow tha feels about me, lass' discussions."

"Oh aye?" I heard him prop himself up on an elbow. "And when is tha ever, eh? When is tha *ever* in t'mood to do owt but 'ave relations? When do the pair of us *ever* get to talk about 'ow we're *feelin'*? Oh aye," he scoffed, "tha comes on all soft and nuzzly when it's time for fleshly union, when tha craves t'feel o' me 'ardness inside thee. But then after? When an ordin'ry lass'd be askin' me 'bout me dreams an' me fears, me plans for t'future? Alls I see is the back o' thine form as tha disappears o'er t'dale, thine pony-tail reet near 'orizontal wi' t'speed o' ye. It's like tha's . . . like tha's *frit*, lass. Frit o' intimacy or summat. Either that or tha 'ates me."

"Yeah, and what makes you think I *don't* hate you, Davey? You know they say the simplest explanation is often the best."

These were harsh words, I knew, and sure enough Davey started to cry. Karen's worried face appeared over the crag. "I've just dumped him," I mouthed, making a slashing gesture at my throat. She nodded and disappeared.

"Lass?" sniveled Davey eventually. "Lass, please don't leave me. *Please*. Tell me tha's not leavin' me."

"I don't know," I lied. "I haven't decided. I don't like how things are between us."

"Oh *please*, lass! Gi' me one more chance. I'll be better, I swear it. I'm so in love wi' thee I can't *stan'* it! What tha's lookin' for I 'ave reet here! Tha'll never find another lad as good as me!"

"Don't be so sure," I said.

But he was right.

Suddenly I knew he was right.

Or that he might be.

I mean think about it.

If I *did* jettison Davey and find another boyfriend, and then found myself running into the same emotional blockage . . . well, then I'd be in trouble. I'd have no choice but to admit to myself that my deepest fear was a reality, that there was something wrong with *me*, something profound, maybe a fear of intimacy like Davey was saying. Maybe something worse.

Damn.

"Look, I'm tired," I told him truthfully, getting up. "And I'm drunk. Davey, I'm not going to leave you, but I am . . . I do need some space and some time to think."

"I unnerstan', lass. Take all t'time tha needs. I want nuthin' more than for thee to be 'appy. For thee to be 'appy wi' *me*," he added.

You know, reader, the Chinese have a saying: Be careful what you wish for, because you just might get it. Little did I dream that evening, as I trudged miserably up the hill from Murbery, that within a few short hours I would get more "space," more time to think than I could shake a stick at— and from the unlikeliest of sources:

Germany.

"Where's me da?"

I was nursing a coffee in my pajamas at the kitchen window while me mam finished cooking my breakfast. In the field below our house the large piece of farm machinery that me da worked on, the fangle, was unstaffed and draped with a black tarpaulin, which made it look a lot like a giant, folded umbrella.

"Why 'e's gone off to war, lass. Battlin' the Germans and keepin' us safe."

"The Germans?" I blew on my coffee. "What did *they* do?"

"Doesn't tha know?" said me mam, expertly shuttling kippers from the oven to a large white plate that was already heaped high with mushrooms and fried bread and baked beans. "P'raps tha's been too busy with a certain young gentleman to keep abreast o' world affairs!"

"Oh me *mam*!"

While I ate, me mam explained about the political situation in Europe: the man who'd been assassinated, the role of the French . . . It was scintillating stuff, but the big news as far as I was concerned was that the army had put out a call to essentially every male in England to come and help them with the fighting. Would that mean Davey? I wondered. He was only fourteen, of course, but the size he was he could probably pass for about forty-five, if he chose to . . .

My thoughts were interrupted by someone calling my name at the end of the path. I craned my neck.

It was Davey.

And he seemed to be wearing some sort of uniform.

———

"So this'll be good," I told him, reaching up across the gate to straighten his soldier's lapel. "For us. You know . . . I didn't mean the things I said last night, Davey." I squinted up at him in the bright morning sun. "I was drunk and I was tired. I really *do* care about you. But, like you say, I do need to do some growing up. Which I can do while you're away at war."

Davey smiled. He looked tall and noble in his new green uniform and was clearly feeling very virile and mature. Whatever dents I'd put in his manly façade the night before had been popped right back out again by the news that his country needed him to go kill people. "Aye lass," he rumbled philosophically. "It's mornin's like this that really put things in perspective."

"Yeah, you're right." I nodded sagely. "Anyway. Look. You won't do anything stupid over there, will you?"

"Not wi' thee to come back to, lass. For thee I shall keep meself safe. They're saying it'll all be over by Wednesday any'ow."

"I'm sure they're right. Well, look . . . Bye."

I squeezed his hand, let him kiss me on the forehead, and then off he went: Davey McCracken, my first boyfriend, marching inexpertly away down the road that would carry him to Murbery, and then to the train station in Hughley, and beyond that, obviously, to the battlefields of the First World War. *O England,* I somberly extemporized, *Thy daffodilled lanes do yea o'erun this morning with doomed and dismal youth,* and scuttled thoughtfully back inside to my cooling breakfast.

The First World War was a really black time for me. I rose late. I never bathed. Every once in a while, at me mam's insistence, I went for a walk so halfhearted that from a distance it probably looked like I was checking the house for structural damage, and the rest of the time I spent in my bedroom with the curtains drawn, staring numbly at the radio with an ashtray on my tits until unconsciousness came to claim me. Karen stopped by a few times, but she rarely lingered. It seemed we had nothing in common anymore. All

Karen wanted to talk about was how much she missed Greg, and all I wanted to talk about was when she was going to leave so I could return to the bucket of beer I had stashed beneath my bed.

———

DESPITE THE GRISLY reports filtering back from the War, I had a strong, inexplicable feeling that Davey was going to survive it. Sooner or later he'd be back, possibly injured, possibly fine, and when the next spring turned to summer I would drape myself in white and become his bride, willingly condemning myself to a life of excruciating intimacy and stilted conversations with a sweaty hulking man I had no feelings for. I had no choice. I was tired of fighting the system, and too terrified of finding myself at odds again with the rustic world around me and this time having no grand-da to bail me out.

To the extent, that is, that he *had* bailed me out. More than a decade had passed since that hallucinatory afternoon when he'd given me the little blue dress and informed me that I spoke the way I did because I was "allergic to the past," and I was still no closer to understanding what he'd been talking about. Not that it mattered. The nonsense me grand-da had spewed had all been focused on why I said "okay" instead of "alreet" like a normal Murberyite. He hadn't mentioned anything about my not being able to feel love for a man.

———

SURE ENOUGH, IN December of 1918 the 'phone rang. The thing had just been installed and it took me a second to remember which was the mouthpiece and which was the earpiece.

"Hello?" I said eventually.

"... (lass?) ..."

"Davey? Is that you? Are you okay?"

"... (nay) ..."

The line was faint and crackly, but Davey's voice triggered an avalanche of memories. I could practically taste his mustache down the 'phoneline as he spoke.

"Are you ... are you injured?"

"... (aye) ..."

"Badly?"

"... (aye) ..."

"Well, you're alive. That's the main thing. You're coming home, is that right?"

"... (aye) ..."

"Well that's fantastic news. I'll see you at the station."

Davey croaked me his details, I hung up, and turned to find me mam standing right there at the foot of the stairs. "Mam!" I said, pumping my fist. "Fantastic news! My Davey's alive and he's coming ..."

But all was not well, I saw. Me mam's face was white and her own fist hung slackly at her side.

Me da wouldn't be coming home, she told me.

What? Why not?

Because he'd been killed by the Germans.

I broke down and wept, for what had to have been an hour, but then I stopped. The time for self-pity was past. Now was the time for me to be strong, a rock, the glue that held the family together. I glanced at the grandfather clock in the hallway. Now was the time for me to go meet Davey at the station.

THEY UNLOADED DAVEY from the rear of the train with the freight. He didn't look well: completely unconscious and plastered and bandaged from head to toe, with one arm propped bizarrely away from his body by a metal rod. It was a horrible thing to think, I chided myself, but he looked like the sort of invalid one came across in funny cartoon strips. You kept expecting him to wake up and say, "Doctor, Doctor, do I have a large intestine?" and for some white-coated medic to appear out of nowhere and shoot back something hilarious over the top of his wire-rimmed half-glasses.

In fact a doctor did appear: Dr. Proctor, our family physician from Murbery, and he took charge of the whole situation. He gave me a sheaf of prescriptions to fill at the apothecary's and told me to meet him back at the house.

The mood was firmly upbeat when I finally got there. In my bedroom, which I'd agreed to convert into Davey's sickroom, me mam and Dr. Proctor were drinking tea around my writing desk while Davey lay on my bed, supported by a mound of inflatable orthopedic cushions. And it seemed that he was conscious, because with his one free arm, the one without the metal rod, he was scribbling away at a large white block of writing paper.

"What's he doing?" I whispered, helping myself to tea.

"'E's writing poetry, lass," said Dr. Proctor. "Don't worry, tha won't disturb 'im. 'E's lost in t'world o' 'is memories. This is standard treatment for lads returning from t'front. We've found that recov'ry times are slashed in 'alf if t'poor lad is gi'en an outlet for 'is feelin's."

"And how *is* he feeling?" I sat down on the windowsill and blew on my tea. "Did he say?"

Proctor had a chocolate biscuit in his mouth and so I had to wait for a response. Finally, he swallowed. "We won't be able to speak wi' 'im until he's fully unburthened 'imself o' all 'is trauma, lass. Ev'ry particle o' it."

"Wow." I looked over at Davey, the pen in his hand was jiggling away like the needle of a seismograph. "That could take a while."

———

ACTUALLY, IT DIDN'T take that long. About a week. That Friday morning as I was emptying Davey's feces-and-urine bowl curiosity got the better of me and as he dozed, I tip-toed up and slid a poem from beneath his plastered hand.

"Noooo!" he roared, waking up. "Don't tha be readin' that! Don't tha be readin' that!"

"Why not? What is it?"

"It's not *finished* is what it *isn't*. Lass, please . . ."

The title of the poem was "Caveat Emptor." I cleared my throat and started reading aloud. " 'Mud and gas?' " I playfully declaimed. " 'May as well be *gud* and *mas* for all the difference I perceive between them. They are both brown. I *hate* them both. Both substances have found their way into my special soldier's bag and have permeated my belongings . . .'"

"Lass, please . . ." Davey croaked. "Tha's tort'rin' me . . ."

I read on in silence . . . and, actually wow! "Caveat Emptor" was the best poem I'd ever read! Despite his lack of formal education Davey had somehow managed to capture the entire experience of being a soldier in the First World War in occasionally rhyming couplets that were as vivid and moving as anything I'd ever read. For instance, in one sequence Davey was crumped awake by a falling bombshell in the early morning and stood with some friends gazing blearily over the edge of the trench at this patch of weird smoke that was just sort of hanging there. Then a breeze picked up and the smoke blew slowly away to reveal:

The leg of a dead horse
Cold, and stiff, and
Sticking straight up.

Jesus, I thought, impressed, and read on agog as one of Davey's friends, a young, scared private who evidently viewed Davey as something of a father figure, had his head blown off by an enemy sniper, at which point their commanding officer—an effete, upper-class type—minced over and announced that it was "rather a jolly development" that their friend was dead because it meant the Germans were wasting ammunition on mere infantrymen as opposed to officers or equipment. There was a lot more stuff like that, all of it incredibly powerful, and upon reaching the final stanza I found I'd been literally pushed back against the ironing board by the sheer force of Davey's poesy.

So then caveat emptor, quote unquote "Sir."
A simple phrase from Latin that I'm told means
    "buyer beware."
If you buy, as you seem to, the inherent worth-
    fightingness of this war,
Then please beware the day when it's over that I
    turn up on your door
Step. I'll be looking very different,
In casual weekend gear,
Come for a peek at the other junk you've doubtless
    bought over the years.
Because the things you think are good
The lads and I think are bad.
And this is without a doubt the worst birthday I've
    ever had.

"Unnerstan', lass. This is nowt more than manure at this stage. It's basically just a first draft like . . ." I silenced him with desperate flaps of my hand.

Because I was suddenly having a vision . . . a vision of us, of me and Davey, twenty, forty, even *sixty* years down the line . . . as a happily married couple, a poet and his wife . . . him in the shed at the bottom of the garden, outside which I would leave his meals, me up in the main building eating meals of my own, dreaming my own dreams . . .

A thing like that could really work out.

SOME TIME AFTER that I ran into Dr. Proctor at the apothecary's where I was buying Davey some medicated antidandruff shampoo and asked him what he thought the chances were that Davey would continue to write poetry once his recovery was complete.

"Oh aye, lass!" he said with a lusty flare of the nostrils. "If me data are correct 'e'll only become *more* enslaved to his rhymin' craft as t'years roll by. An' it's not just thine Davey! Out o' the mud o' that terrible war 'as sprung a great fountin' o' progress, rainin' down on all o' Western culture. Tha's 'eard about the great Viennese psychiatrist Sigmund Freud and 'is controversial theories o' 'uman be'avior?"

"A bit."

"And all the goin's on in Paris? T'French capital? Oh lass, it's sheer *bedlam* over there. Folk takin' their clothes off, drinkin' each other's urine, sellin' each other toilet bowls for millions of pounds in the name of art, struttin' around doin' whatever they choose . . . Why even 'ere in the Isles of Britain we've got authors writin' books wi'out *any punctuation at all* as an attempt to render the workin's o' the 'uman mind in all its burblin' grandeur! Why it's as if . . ." he removed his tortoiseshell half-glasses and polished them on his shirt. "Almos' as if the war brought so much un'appiness to this formerly pure an' unreflectin' land that it forced us for t'first time to acknowledge 'ow much o' a role our mental lives play in our . . . lass?"

I wasn't listening.

I was staring past him out the shop window, absently fingering the edge of a bag of lozenges that was next to me in a wire stand . . . lost in thought . . .

ME MAM COULDN'T really process the news that I was upping stakes and moving to France. The information jammed her brain. Rather than question my motives, or try to talk me out of it, or ask me what the hell she was supposed to do about the hulking form of one Davey L. McCracken currently filling up pads of paper and porcelain bowls at the top of her house, she immediately started twittering, "But we haven't any suitcases. What'll tha do for a suitcase?" I told her I'd use some of the old hatboxes we had in the attic. She countered that it wasn't "proper" for a girl my age to travel in Europe with more than one hatbox, and quickly what should have been a tear-sodden mother-daughter hugfest degenerated into a stupid argument about money belts and working visas and insect repellent. Somehow she managed to shut up long enough for me to instruct her on caring for Davey, and after squabbling some more briefly, I made my escape up the stairs to the sickroom.

I found him scribbling away as usual, and in the doorway I toyed with the idea of just slipping quietly away without saying anything. Perhaps by this point he was wrapped up enough in his rhymes and his symbolism and his imagery that he would never notice my absence, that he'd been able to keep telling himself that I was somewhere nearby, watching over him . . . In fact I did more than toy with the idea; I executed it.

That just left Karen. As I neared her house I heard laughter from her garden. Reaching her gate I saw that she had wheeled Greg out into the sun. He was mocking her gently as she tried to erect a deckchair for herself to sit. She was heavily pregnant, I saw also.

"Hey," I called. Karen turned, gasped and came waddling ecstatically down the path. We hugged across the gate.

"*Oh*, tha's looking well," she said.

"So are you." I nodded down at her belly. "Though you may want to ease up on the candied violets."

My best friend ever gave a tinkling laugh and fondly stroked her bulge. "Any day now says Proctor."

"Wow. Can I?"

"Aye, o' course."

I laid my hand upon the bulge. It was warm and round and wholesome, like a beachball after a day at the beach . . .

But I wasn't here to feel bellies. I was here to say goodbye. "Look, Karen." I pulled back my hand and focused on a button of her burlap maternity dress. "I've got news. I'm leaving Murbery. I'm going to France to study art."

"Tha's never!"

I looked up. Karen's eyes were sparkling.

"Yeah, I am. I love Murbery. I love you . . . and Davey. But . . . Well apparently things have gotten very loose over in France socially and, as you know, I've never found it particularly easy fitting in here in Murbery. I think I need to go somewhere where people don't judge you for how you talk or act or 'seem' and I think Paris may be the place."

"Oh that's reet *fantastic* news," said Karen. "I'll miss thee sumthin' rotten o' course but tha's definitely makin' the reet decision. Tha was allus meant for bigger things than just Murb'ry."

I shrugged, embarrassed. "Well . . . you've got a life as well now, Karen. Greg, and the baby . . ."

"Aye," she looked over at Greg in his deck chair, lifting his pale scarred face to the watery sun. "Tha's right. I do." She faced me again. "Reckon we've both grown up, tha and me."

"You're right." I took a deep, deep breath and let it out, determined not to cry. "Look." I laid my hand on her swollen belly again. "Promise you'll tell little him or her all about me?"

Karen giggled again, a bright peal of laughter defying the gravity of the moment. "Oh 'ow could I not? Though I may 'ave to water it down in parts just to make it believable."

We hugged one final time and then without another word I pulled away and strode quickly off, making it per- haps twenty feet before I heard her call my name. I turned. She was still at the gate, fingering the ironwork with her face contorting. "Thanks . . ." she said, then had to look away. I followed her gaze. On the village green some children were playing, little girls and little boys, laughing and shrieking and chasing each other . . . "Thanks."

"For what?"

Karen sucked a breath and swallowed. "Thanks for bein' lasses wi' me."

I nodded, turned, and jogged away. She was utterly, ut- terly welcome.

1920–1929

A DANCE TO THE MUSIC
OF JAZZ

———

ONE OF THE astounding paradoxes of foreign travel—and there are several—is that nobody does it with quite as much composure and surefootedness as an untraveled yokel from a tiny little village. Contrary to what you might expect, such a figure does not get swamped by feelings of insignificance the minute she leaves the world she knows. No. So clueless is she as to the true size of the world that at least for a while as she travels she's able to continue sticking definite articles on the things she sees, adding them to her index of the familiar as if this is merely the other *half* of the world that she's exploring, as opposed to the other hundred percent. That's how it was for me on the way to Paris. I did not realize that there was a woman like that in every carriage of every train in all the world. On the boat I memorized a list of observations about the snack bar, under the assumption that everyone I was about to meet would have their own set of feelings about it. And in Paris itself I was initially very pleasant with my surly cabdriver, genuinely scared that if I wasn't he might bad mouth me to the entire city.

By four in the afternoon, though, I was feeling frazzled and overwhelmed. Over the 'phone from Murbery I'd rented a set of lodgings through my art *collège* and by some combination of my imperfect French and the even more imperfect 'phone technology of that long-ago era (my French was actually pretty good, I'd discovered, thanks to me grand-da's early tutelage) we seemed to have gotten the directions garbled. Down boulevard after boulevard my cabbie whipped his tired horses, contemptuously flicking another handful of beads across on his abacus every time I sprang out, had a conversation with a veil-wearing concierge, and returned disappointed. By the time we eventually found the place, nestled away in a narrow, twisting boulevard some distance from the Eiffel Tower, I was literally on the brink of tears. From the street my building was dark and ugly, and although the concierge was very friendly, hugging me like a daughter and hefting all six of my hatboxes herself, she then proceeded to lead me up about eleven steep flights of rickety stairs that smelled of snails and old croissants. As she unlocked the door, I braced myself for the worst.

But, reader, it was love at first sight.

Located at the very top of the building, the *apartement* I had rented consisted of one large room, dark and homey, with paneled walls, a sloping ceiling, overstuffed armchairs, and a large bay window with a cushioned seat that gave onto a lovely old church across the road and then just an endless roofscape of cupolas and minarets and terra-cotta tiling. In the rear, behind a curtain, was a tiny little kitchen and on a table by the door sat a child's ballet shoe filled with potpourri. It was, I decided as I threw myself onto one of two freshly made single beds, the most comfortable and inspiring place to live I'd ever visited. Decades later I would find myself reminded of it very strongly by the cozy, slightly louche set of rooms shared by Sherlock Holmes and his friend Dr. Watson in one of the filmed adventures of that world-class detective.

"No," said the concierge nervously.

"I'm sorry?"

"That bed is being the sleeping place of your room-friend, Miss Eloïse."

She spoke in French, but for the purposes of this narrative I shall follow the convention of translating all foreign dialogue into English, using awkward grammar and word choice to indicate that the speaker is saying something potentially annoying.

"What do you mean?"

I had a roommate, she explained, a girl of about my own age who'd been living there a few years. Why hadn't I been informed of this over the 'phone? I inquired. Because it wasn't relevant, she told me. Eloïse lived an almost entirely nocturnal existence. If I could refrain from sitting on her bed during the day while she was actually sleeping in it there was a good chance the two of us would never meet.

This was nonsense, patently, but I was far too tired to argue. I merely heaved myself up, tipped the concierge, showed her to the door, and dragged myself over to the other bed where I found a packet of registration materials from the *collège*. I kicked off my shoes and lay down to study the curriculum.

The program for that first year looked pretty daunting. In three short months I was expected to learn how to render objects in the distance by painting them smaller than you would have done otherwise, how to do birds in a seascape by making a little M-shape with your smallest brush, how to whittle a piece of charcoal so you could use it as a pencil . . .

When I awoke the light was different, and someone nearby was sobbing. I lifted my head. There on the cushions of the window seat, silhouetted against the day, was a compact brunette in a red satin bathrobe, face pointed out the window, shoulders shaking. She also had an expensive-looking "bob" hairstyle, I noticed.

"Oh hail . . ." I racked my boat-lagged brain. "Eloïse, right?"

The eyes that swung to meet my own were huge and black and haughty, spewing forth great gouts of mascara down the smoothest and whitest cheeks I'd ever seen toward a delicate, quivering chin. "*Bastard,*" spat Eloïse, with venom, in French.

"Me?"

"No. Not you."

"Who then?"

She turned away with a snort. "It does not matter." From her sleeve she fished a square of lace, parped her nose on it, and seemed, for a second, to be pulling herself together. Then she lost it again. "*Styves,*" she wailed.

"Who?"

"*Who is Styves?*" Eloïse turned and glared at me like I was the stupidest person in the whole world. "Why, Styves is *nothing*. An awful *banker*. A purveyor of financial *instruments*. An executor of such *monies* as are due the under-signed."

"Um, I'm sorry to hear that. Look, do you want some wine? I've got some duty-free in one of my hatboxes."

This was the right thing to say, as it turned out. A hundred and eighty seconds after making that remark I was nestled in the window seat with a crystal goblet of Pinot Grigio, my knees resting against hers, and bantering away like we'd been friends all our lives. Hardly pausing for breath, I jabbered out the entire story of my life and then Eloïse told me hers. The only child of Middle-European aristocrats, she had spent her youth in a bizarre succession of mountain-locked boarding schools, lakeshore finishing schools and girls-only fencing academies before settling in Paris to pursue intensely sexual affairs with anguished young sculptors, famous American novelists and various rich old kinky world travelers that she only had sex with, apparently, because they reminded her of her father. To sustain herself she sold volumes of her diaries to an old Parisian publisher, with whom she was also sleeping, and twice a week she took her clothes off for the Senior Life Class at my *collège*, though she wouldn't let them pay her because apparently nobody paid the starving kittens in the alleyways of Paris for *their* nakedness, which made a crazy kind of sense, I supposed.

"We two girls shall be friends," said Eloïse eventually, tossing the last of her wine down her throat like a peanut. "You and I. And I shall consecrate our friendship by telling you a secret."

"Okay."

"Styves..." she hissed, her mouth to my ear. "Has a long smooth penis! As hard and as flawless as if it were carved out of wood by a master craftsman!"

Across the street the sun was setting, a bubble of cosmic pink plasma throwing the jagged molding of the church's old spire into razor-sharp black relief. And all of a sudden I wanted to cry. I wanted to wrap my arms around this new friend of my mine and release the great ocean of tears I'd been storing up for the best part of fifteen years. I didn't know who Styves was and I didn't care one whit about his penis, but the very fact that Eloïse had felt free enough to even *say* a thing like that, a thing that outrageous, a thing that inappropriate ... well, it was proof that coming to Paris had been the right decision, that I had finally found a home.

"Eloïse ..." I said, about to try to give voice to these surging emotions.

"But come," she said, standing and extending her hand. "The evening lies before us like a saucerful of freshly drawn cream before a pair of thirsty kittens. There is no time to lose."

WHAT DID WE do that evening, reader? We did it all. We painted the entire city a flaming, garish red. At a place called the Black Bongo in the bowels of the old city we slipped our fingers into castanets and cut a clacking swath across the dance floor. We sniffed powdered cocaine with the famous writer Henry Miller in his living room, then piled giggling onto the back of his bicycle for a wobbly ride down some alleyways to a whorehouse. We drank champagne with the whores, then absinthe with Eloïse's hermaphrodite friend Mathilde in an abandoned, roofless church, and finally whiskey with a dwarf on a houseboat. The rest is pretty much a blur. Sometime around threeish I think I remember watching a trembling Czech nobleman peer at Eloïse through a monocle as she squatted and peed on a mirror, and though I know it sounds unlikely, I swear I remember two entirely separate instances that involved Eloïse and me knocking for ages on the door of a brilliant young sculptor's studio, only to learn from the neighboring artist that the young man in question had hung himself that very afternoon after falling in love with one of his own statues. It was a wild night. We must have taken about fifty cabs. It was *classic*.

FIVE IN THE morning found us down on a footpath by the river, leaning against a fancy wrought-iron railing as we watched the water slide by, all gray, silent and corrugated in the luminous, decadent predawn. To the best of my recollection, I was about sixty percent asleep at the moment the bells of St. Hunchback's sent their sad tune rolling over the roofs of the sleeping city. *Bong bong bong bong bong*, they went, and I surged back to consciousness. Five in the morning, it occurred to me. That was pretty late.

I yawned and shoved back from the railing. "Thanks for an utterly classic evening, Eloïse, but I think I should probably zonk. I have to register for school in . . . four hours."

"I love your body" was what Eloïse said, not even looking at me.

"Er . . . thanks."

"A woman's body, I have always thought, is like the bottle of her soul. Do you not agree?"

I yawned again, loudly.

"And in your case, my new English friend . . ." Finally she turned. She had a smile on her face, a smile that spoke of imminent misbehavior. "I have come to suspect that your cork has not yet been removed."

I wasn't a fool.

I knew what was happening.

These idle musings by Eloïse were the opening pawn moves of what she clearly hoped would become a full-blown lesbian chess match—involving actual naked sex, most likely—for which activity I had neither the energy nor obviously the requisite sexual orientation. To be sure: like every ingenue I had come to Paris to find myself, but not through *trial and error*, not by randomly trying on new selves like cheap sunglasses in a pharmacy until I found one that suited me. I'd been down that road already, and discovered that it didn't really lead anywhere.

"Eloïse . . ." I began uncomfortably.

"It is like with wine, no?" She took a step in my direction. "The men, they gouge at the wine bottle with their corkscrews. Usually their gouging is successful. But once in a great while . . ." She took another step toward me and lowered her voice. "Once in a great while a bottle comes his way whose cork will not so easily be removed. Oh, it will yield up its exterior, its exposed upper surface . . ."

From within her black velvet cape appeared a tiny white hand. It gripped the belt of my shapeless tweed house coat and tugged. I didn't resist, for some reason, and now our faces were mere inches apart. I could feel her hot breath, and Eloïse still wasn't finished with the wine thing.

"But still there remains a plug of cork lodged deep in the bottle's neck, upon which his corkscrew can achieve no purchase. The man he grows outraged. He stamps his foot and shakes his fist. He tears at his hair and his mind it is filled with the most *outlandish* schemes. Should he push the plug of cork down into the bottle with some thin, pencillike object?" I felt lips on my throat. "Should he cut it to pieces with the tip of a knife and then strain the liquid through a piece of muslin in order to remove the suspended detritus?

Oh, how . . ." Suddenly her hand was on my stomach, foraging south toward my panties, "oh how will he taste of the sweet, sweet, wine?"

I twisted away. "Eloïse . . . Eloïse . . . look, I'm really, really sorry but I just really can't do this. I'm not a homosexual, or even a bisexual or whatever. There was a time in my life when I thought I might be but . . . well, I decided that I wasn't one."

I ran a hand through my ringlets, conflictedly, and gazed up in anguish at the barely lightening sky.

"Do you know where I was this afternoon before you arrived?" said Eloïse, turning back to the river. A used croissant floated by on the water, puffy and pale as the moon.

"Were you . . . were you out having sex with women?"

"No," said Eloïse. "I was several boulevards away, delivering a letter to my lover and good friend Ernest Hemingway, the celebrated novelist. Ernest was not at home, unfortunately, and so I was forced to leave the envelope in the custody of his building's concierge."

"Oh."

"And now I have a question for you, my new English friend." She turned again. The fact that I delivered a letter today . . ." Eloïse cocked her tiny head. "Does that make me a postman?"

I bit my lip and looked at her.

No.

It didn't.

It didn't make her a postman.

And right then I fell to the ground and had an epiphany. There was nothing wrong with me, and there never had been. All my life I'd been desperately trying to solve the equation

71

frantically trying to determine X, why I was the way I was, why I spoke the way I did, why I had no feelings for Davey and all of that nonsense. Never had it occurred to me that there might be no X, that I just was the way I was because I was. Twenty long, difficult years I'd been searching for a *category*, a little social slot labeled "Was Read to as a Child" or "Allergic to the Past" or "Sexual Orientation Number Four" that would account for all my oddities, when the truth of the matter was no such category need exist. Just as Eloïse delivering a letter didn't make her a "postman," just as me kissing her—and I did, I wobbled to my feet and slid my tongue into her hot, tight mouth—didn't make me a "homosexual," my talking funny and having trouble relating to men didn't mean that I was necessarily any particular type of freak.

I was just me.

Nothing more, nor less, than that.

Disentangling my face from Eloïse's, I mumbled something like "We need just one more cab," and shortly after it was all just warm skin and clean sheets and tiny little strangled cries.

———

THAT WAS THE only time we ever made love (as far as I know; masked balls were all the rage) but quickly we were closer than lovers, more like sisters, sharing every detail of each other's lives, helping each other deal with the endless logistics of being a woman about town in 1920s Paris.

Like Eloïse with her diaries, I threw myself into my painting and ended up making some really quite serious money. My final project for that first semester at the college was a piece called *Bachelor Pad* (1921), a medium-size gouache of a man with both eyes on the same side of his nose peering hungrily into a fridge containing nothing but a box of baking soda and a lime, and it sold for U.S. $10,000 to a major French bank that wanted to hang it in its Main Conference Room.

Buoyed by success, after taking the summer off I devoted the next year and a half to a far more ambitious and conceptual piece called *The Living Experience*. *The Living Experience* (1923) was a set of four high-quality colored clay and papier-mâché dioramas mounted in glass cases depicting the various facets of human life. *The Quest for Nourishment* showed a farmer and his son hand in hand in a field beside a skinless cow that had the different cuts of beef labeled while crops surged from the ground all around, and in the top right corner in a patch of vivid blue felt ocean, a jubilant sailor was sitting on the prow of this ship waving a pineapple that he was importing. *Oh, What a Feeling!* featured seven roommates, in an apartment that looked a lot like the one I shared with Eloïse, each standing and reading a newly delivered letter and reacting with a different facial expression: grief, irritation, joy, amusement, curiosity, awe, confusion. *The Life of the Mind* depicted the famous author Charles Dickens hard at work in his book-lined study, scribbling in a pad while in a thought-bubble attached to his head by a wire, a giant lizard did battle with a giant monkey, and in my favorite, titled simply *Sport!*, every face of a city marathon's starting pack was turned to watch England's most famous cricketer, W. G. Grace, lob a rugby ball at Sir Roger Bannister, the famous sprinter, who seemed unlikely to catch the thing because he was thirty feet in the air, pole-vaulting. It was witty, it was weird...there was a poignancy there somewhere . . . It sold for U.S. $50,000 to an American rubber magnate who told me, postcoitally, that he would install it in his foyer.

Much of the rest of the decade is a blur. For I was having fun, and therefore time flew.

THE LAST TIME I saw Eloïse was December 31, 1929. She was heading home to Bavaria to spend the New Year with her father the count. An urchin had just carried her trunk down to the street and she was putting on her cape, getting ready to leave. I was in the armchair with an absinthe.

"I wish I had a dad," I announced, watching her fiddle with the chin strap of her gray cashmere traveling helmet.

She snorted. "You do not wish you had *my* father. We have no relationship. We sit at opposite ends of a very long table. He is a man."

"Still. You're lucky to have a dad."

"Lucky?" She pouted. "Oh what a monster you are. You know that I am not lucky, that I inhabit a world constructed entirely of pain. Only *very* occasionally, on those rare, rare nights when the music races high and fast, when the wild beat of the bongo takes the place of my own heartbeat and I am whirling, *whirling* . . . entirely given over to the dance . . . a flame of flesh licking at the twig of life . . . only on those rare, magical nights would I say I was 'lucky.' "

"Oh, come now," I chided her, standing to help with the chin strap. "Are they really so rare, Eloïse? Those nights?"

She tutted. "Well, then you are lucky to have a mother. Why do *you* not go home to Muffington and visit her? Do you not think she misses you?"

A bell clanged down in the snowy boulevard.

"There's your cab. And it's Murbery."

"You are scared, I think." She narrowed her eyes. "For all that you have become, for all the happiness you have found here in Paris . . . some part of you is haunted by the memory of childhood awkwardness. You feel you do not deserve your successes and your joy. You suspect that if you were to return to Mubford they would strip you of your finery, expose you as a fraud and you would once again find yourself to be a lonely little girl who does not belong."

"Eloïse, the place is called Murbery. And I don't want to talk about it."

"Oh. So you will go?"

The cabbie's bell rang again. "That remains your cab and no. I am absolutely one hundred percent not going back to Murbery." I shoved her out the door, slammed it playfully in her face.

"That is a large number of percentage points for someone who is not one bit scared," came her voice through the oaken slab. They were the last words I would hear her speak while "Bye! Safe journey!" were the last she would hear from me.

ELOÏSE'S PARTING WORDS had certainly had the ring of truth to them, yet at the same time she could not have been more wrong. I wasn't *scared* to go back to Murbery. I just didn't *want* to. In a few short days I would be thirty years old and I was impatient to move on with my life, in a mood to *free* myself of old attachments, before I entered my life's next phase. Youth had not been easy for me was the fact of the matter, and I couldn't help feeling that the best thing to do was to make a clean break. With a big white piece of paper torn from my old student sketchpad I headed downstairs to get a drink and make plans. The restaurant next door was deserted but for the barman polishing glasses.

"Hail. Where is everyone?"

"Hail. It's New Year's Eve. Sometimes we do do something here, but this year the owner's away on business so . . ."

"Look, is it okay if I just drink? I mean do I have to order an appetizer, or . . . ?"

"No, no. That's fine. Have a seat. What'll it be?"

"Mm . . . brandy."

At a table by the window I sipped thoughtfully from a tumbler. Snow was still falling in the street outside, the flakes so fat and heavy it seemed absurd that they should hit the ground and make no sound. A year was ending, a decade too, and the barman sat at a table by the fire with his own little glass of something, totaling columns of figures in a big parchment ledger with a quill pen that he filled from an inkpot. The flames of the fire fluttered, the pen scratched hypnotically . . .

. . . and suddenly I was in the function room of a cheap hotel, a guest at a surprise party to welcome in the Nineteen Thirties. Every other guest was a decade. The Twenties were there, in a floppy jazz hat and a string of pearls, dancing crazily while trying not to spill a little glass of absinthe . . . The Teens stood erect and apart in military fatigues, sucking on the end of a pencil while they worked on a poem about life in the trenches . . . The Zeros were off to one side in Victorian garb, basking in their own personal downpour of new-century optimism . . .

Suddenly footsteps! I dove for the lightswitch and we stood in the blackness with thumping hearts as the footsteps

crescendoed, the squeak of the handle . . . SURPRISE!!!!! we
yelled at the figure in the doorway, a . . . a nondescript man
in a white T-shirt . . . with hair of ordinary length. I looked
at him harder, the veins in my forehead popping out.

He mumbled something I couldn't hear . . . in a voice I
couldn't describe . . .

"Hey! Hey!" The barman stood above me in a raincoat
and a fedora. "You were shouting."

"Where are you . . . where are you going?" I didn't want
him to leave. Not yet. Not now.

"I'm going to a party."

"No, please, I . . . not alone. Please." I wrenched apart
the front of my blouse and invitingly cupped my breasts.
"Don't leave."

It was no use. The man sensibly ignored me. "There's a
set of keys on top of the register. Lock up when you leave.
Happy New Year."

With that the barman departed.

And boulevards away, a drunken crowd began the New
Year countdown.

Ten.

Nine.

Eight.

I wasn't *ready*. I wasn't *ready* for the thirties.

Seven.

What would they be like? What would the world be like?
Six.

Five. I fell off my chair, felt my face crash where the
floor met the wall.

Four. I . . .

I . . .

[jesus fucking christ what the fuck is a slope of foreboding? hmm?"

you MUST know something else.

thirties thirties thirties, come on THINK

if you can survive not sounding even faintly like an infant or a yokel or a girl of any description you can wing it through the thirties despite total gaping ignorance

time now is
27 AUG--7:53 P.M.

a.k.a. only 30 yrs done in nine hours—half of it wasted on typing word "eloïse" a million times. Did she HAVE to have an umlaut? MÖRÖN?

fucking only ten hours left so TYPE LIKE THE WIND— and also obviously like an incredibly old woman recalling her life in the 1930s.

stakes = INFINITELY high

and delete all notes to self when finished, obviously

27 AUG--7:54 P.M.]

Three.
Two.
One.
"Happy New Year."

1930–1939

NEW INTERIORS

———

[27 AUG--7:54 P.M.]

To start with, reader, I really thought I was fine. The
ceiling of the *apartement* looked the same as it always had.
Checking my body with my hand I felt no blood, wet or dry,
and when I swung my feet to the floor and sat up, I felt no
sharp, stabbing pains. Greatly relieved, I commenced my
usual morning routine: get to feet, pull on bathrobe, kettle
on stove, *tick tick whoosh* of gas, go to bathroom, sit down,
urinate, stand up, back into main body of room, activate
radio with hand . . .

An announcer was reading the news. Unbidden, my
right hand scrabbled for the off switch.

Silence.

I looked at the hand, then ran to the bathroom to be sick.

Something was wrong with me.

Hunger forced me up again at twenty past eleven. Obviously it would be about a decade before I could show my face at the restaurant downstairs, but there was a new crepe place a few boulevards over that I'd had my eye on. I slung on my poncho, grabbed my keys, and started thundering down the stair. I made it as far as the final staircase.

Somebody was on our doorstep, some sort of news urchin, waving a rolled-up newspaper at passersby and urging them to buy it.

I felt sick again, and I remember thinking to myself, Oh dear. If he's going to insist on standing there and shouting that . . . stuff, then I shall not be able to leave the building.

And I went back upstairs.

UPSTAIRS, USING THE 'phone at the end of the hall, I put a call through to the crepe place and ordered a delivery, then I hurried back to bed and pulled the covers over my face.

My crepe arrived very quickly. I sprang up and ran to the door to receive it. My voice didn't sound like my own when I said:

"Hail there. How much do I owe you?"

"Hello lady!" The delivery boy was of ethnic, possibly Algerian, origin with kinky hair and had a big toothy smile. "How you today!"

"Sorry, *how* much?"

I could see my bag of food dangling right there at his side but the boy wasn't even *trying* to give it to me. "Oh lady!" he exclaimed, eyebrows shooting skyward. "You hear about office workers in America?"

I winced.

. "Look, can I . . . can I just have my food, please? I have the money right here."

"They all suicide themself. Issin all da papers!"

"Look . . ." I felt myself flushing red. "Look, you *have* to give me the food. I ordered it and it's mine and . . ." Falling to my knees I scooped a dripping bouquet of notes and coins out of my handbag. It looked like a head of lettuce dipped in mercury. I thrust the money at the lad, grabbed for the bag, and slammed the door.

Inside, on my bed, despite not knowing what was happening at all in my life anymore, I successfully unwrapped my spinach and crabmeat crepe and tipped it onto a plate. Hell, I even managed to hack off a little piece with my fork and get it in my mouth . . . but then the food sort of fell back on the plate again because I was crying and my mouth wouldn't chew.

Whatever it was hadn't gone away.

In fact it was getting worse.

In the same way that some people's digestive systems can't process milk, I, for some appalling reason, had *lost the ability to process information.*

———————

IT WAS AN *insane* thing to have happened, an *unbelievable* thing.

But happened it had.

Nowadays in the twenty-first century, of course, we're a lot more evolved in our understanding of the human mind than we were back then. These days we accept without question that not only *can* conditions like information-phobia suddenly cut people down in their prime, but that it happens all the time. In fact, let me quote to you briefly from *The Caregiver's Bible* by Dr. Steven Hearne.

> As weeks turn to months, increasingly the caregiver and care receiver find themselves inhabiting a sphere of lonely isolation. Curtains are drawn, newspaper subscriptions canceled or allowed to lapse, as the caregiver seeks to obliterate all evidence that an outside world even exists. At best the outside world is of no use to her, at worst it may even contribute to the chaos within the home against which she wages a daily battle.

Obviously Dr. Hearne is talking specifically about information-phobia as it afflicts *caregivers*—a caregiver being a person who spends their days looking after another person who is terminally sick or elderly (hello!)—but I offer it here as evidence that from time to time people genuinely do find themselves in the same situation I was in on January 1, 1930. I have a caregiver myself, like most people over a hundred, and he has it himself. Although he doesn't draw the curtains (we don't *have* any curtains) he rarely leaves the apartment if it isn't absolutely essential.

Back in Paris, though, of course, at the dawn of the nineteen thirties, not only had I never heard of anything like this happening to anyone, I had no idea what might have caused it. Could it be Eloïse? Had I suffered some weird delayed reaction to her leaving? That's how the ends of relationships tend to work, after all. You feel euphoric for forty minutes, delirious at having successfully extricated yourself with zero pain . . . and then boom. The forty minutes expire and you spend the next three years drinking beer and not shaving.

Had the shock of losing Eloïse unhinged me . . . ? Or maybe the shock of turning thirty . . . ?

I didn't know.

But it didn't matter.

The key thing was to work out what I was going to do about it.

———————

I HAD TO get out of France, that much I was sure of. I loved the French, loved them like brothers, but they were famously prone to all sorts of obscure cultural upheavals and revolutions in which even people cloistered away in garrets would be expected to participate, and I couldn't afford to take that risk.

England.

I wanted to go back to England. As alien and foreign as the whole universe had suddenly come to seem, some places were less alien and foreign than others, and the more I thought about England, the more I found myself rehashing the plotline of one of my favorite childhood books, this book about some children and their nanny and all the fun they had indoors without ever going outside.

Should I do that? I wondered. Go be a nanny.

Or should I do something else?

———————

I COULDN'T THINK of anything else.

———————

MR. MONTGOMERY GREETED me at the foot of the steps that led up to his large terraced house in a formerly grand residential district of London. He looked just as I'd imagined him on the 'phone: tall and stooped, in bowler hat and threadbare suit, with long soft eyelashes and peaked angular features that betrayed the strain of the last few months. His wife had just died, they had told me at the agency, of a long complaint, leaving Mr. M to raise their two children: Veronica, six, and Peter, four. That was where I came in.

"You encounter me in a state of some urgency," said Mr. Montgomery, using the clipped and proper tones of the English upper classes, "I was anticipated at the bank in the ante-meridiem period and it is now the post-meridiem period. Please make yourself at home. Peter and/or Veronica will show you to your quarters while Cook shall prepare for you a nourishing sandwich," and with that he was off, expertly pumping his umbrella as he stalked to the end of the street and out of sight around the corner. Tilting my head I admired the tall white house, its peeling paint, its faded grandeur, then dragged my hat boxes up the steps and through a heavy front door that I hoped I wouldn't have to see the other side of for at least ten years.

"*You're* not our mummy," a high voice echoed around the spacious marbled foyer. I looked for its source. The only figure visible was a bust of Beethoven, but then I raised my gaze and found two kids staring down at me through the bars of the banister, as if this were a zoo and I were a polar bear.

"You must be Peter and Veronica," I said amiably. "Good to meet you. I'm your new nanny."

"Well, we think you're just *beastly*." It was the girl who said this. Her features were sharp and pinched just like her father's.

"You won't ever leave uth will you, Nanny?" squeaked

the boy. "Not like Mummy?" Veronica jabbed her brother in the ribs and glared at him.

I thumped myself hard between the tits with my fist. "Clear as a bell, Peter. I'm not going anywhere. Now which of you little scamps is going to show me to my quarters?"

Veronica ran and locked herself in her bedroom. Peter tumbled down the stairs, hugged my leg like a man being winched out of the sea by a helicopter, and then led me up the stairs to my palatial suite of rooms.

This dynamic persisted for several weeks—Veronica resenting me and being standoffish; Peter following me around like a piece of toilet paper stuck to my shoe, his large soulful eyes growing even rounder and sadder whenever the lavatory door swung shut, separating us. Until one morning at the beginning of February when I strode into the breakfast room to find both children planted rigidly in their chairs, wide-eyed and respectful.

"Morning," I said, shaking the coffee pot. "Is something the matter?"

Both their tiny heads vibrated, then Peter nudged Veronica. "Nanny," she shrilled, "Peter says he saw you slide *up* the banister last night."

With one smooth motion I filled my cup with coffee and slid easily into my chair, cogitating furiously behind this silky demeanor. The truth of the thing was that I had nipped downstairs for a sandwich around midnight, accidentally become extremely drunk while doing so, and been forced to rely more heavily than usual on the banister's support during my subsequent ascent—but no way was I going to tell *them* that. There was an opportunity here. A chance to seize power. "*Up* the banister? Is this true, Peter? You're awfully young to be losing your entire brain."

"I'm thorry, Nanny. I wathn't thpying on you. I thought I heard a noithe and wath coming to invethtigate."

"Golly, aren't you brave," muttered Veronica without a sliver of irony. "But is it true, Nanny? Did you slide *up* the banister?"

I cradled my coffee in both hands and blew on it, letting the steam moisturize my face "No, of course not, Veronica. Who ever heard of a person sliding *up* the banister?"

And at that they both gasped.

Why, reader?

Because there on my face was a *mysterious little smile*.

I HAD NO more trouble with Veronica after that, and the magic was free to begin.

Mornings, during education, I kept things very businesslike and straitlaced, but in the playroom after lunch I would let down my hair and with a few well-chosen words unlock the doorway to a parallel universe of imagination that was visually identical to our own but with much higher stakes. The coal cellar might become a distant planet where alien creatures had laid their black, irregular eggs, and to which a team of scientists (played by Peter and Veronica) had been dispatched with teaspoon-shaped "probes," or the dumbwaiter that ran from the basement kitchen to my quarters in the attic might suddenly become the arterial system of an Important Man into which a team of miniaturized doctors (Peter and Veronica) armed with ultrasophisticated "pencil lasers" had been injected in order to track down and destroy a cushion-shaped tumor in his brain—thereby saving the globe. None of it was true—obviously—but my inventions filled that draughty old house with squeals of wonder where before there had been sighs and tears, dispelling once and for all the cold fug of bereavement that had been so palpable on my arrival.

But also there was a truth behind the lies, a lesson I wanted to teach them: that no matter how black things get in one's life, no matter how dire the situation, a little imagination can make the pain just go away. After all it had worked for me. Beyond the playroom window, the nineteen thirties were whizzing by without entangling me one iota in their complexity, and I could feel my strength returning on a daily basis, my Information gland regenerating by a few hundred cells an hour until one afternoon at our weekly meeting, Mr. Montgomery segued elegantly from congratulating me on the fantastic job I was doing raising his kids to bemoaning the fresh round of trouble we English were suddenly having with the Germans in Europe and rather than melt before his eyes into a puddle of tears and sweat, as I surely would have done just a few weeks earlier, I found instead that I was *interested in what he was saying*. Another war was looming. Another big one. Whereas the First World War had been played out entirely overseas in Europe, it was Mr. Montgomery's opinion that this terrible sequel would be a genuinely global affair, its monstrous black fingers poking into every last crevice and cranny of the Earth, from Antarctica to Zambia, touching people's lives, altering them. There would be no hiding places.

Now, obviously, to the woman I had been at the start of the thirties, who couldn't even look at a week-old racing form without breaking out in a rash, this would have been the worst news possible. But did I panic, reader? There in his study? Reader, to my own surprise and elation I did not. As my employer delivered his grim hypothesis I directed my gaze out the window and allowed my mind to be filled by a vision, a vision of myself knee deep in History alongside my countrymen, ducking bombs and cheering victories, stealing farewell kisses amid clouds of steam on railway platforms, zipping around the place in a nurse's uniform, possibly yanking people out of rubble or something and when the meeting ended I walked sedately out into the hallway, closed his study door, and pumped my fist with wild abandon.

Because, reader, I was well again.

ON THE LAST afternoon before the war the rain ran thick down the playroom windows as Peter and Veronica ventured forth on their final mission: scouring the globe (the playroom) as wildlife conservation officials for specimens of nearly extinct species (their scattered toys), which they were charged with transporting unharmed to an ultra-high-tech government-sponsored game reserve, a.k.a. the toy closet. When it was done we built a fire in the grate and sat around it in armchairs, staring into the flames and thinking our own thoughts.

"Nanny?" blurted Peter who was sitting in my lap. "Will you and Father get married?"

Reader, it was that kind of afternoon: when you just said whatever was on your mind, with no fear of embarrassment, for who knew when you'd get another chance?

"No," I responded.

"Why not?" asked Veronica. I looked over at where she sat. The firelight was dancing in her spectacles, casting shadows on her sweatshirt. She wasn't a little girl anymore, I noticed. She could probably handle the truth.

"Because I'm not in love with him."

"Why not?" Peter twisted to pout up at me.

"Well, because . . ."

And I paused.

Why *not* marry Mr. Montgomery and make a life with him and the kids?

It wasn't the stupidest idea I'd ever had. Not by a long chalk. While I'd only intended my nannyship as a temporary thing, just till I got back on my feet psychologically, the fact was I had found *stability* here, almost a form of happiness . . .

Actually, no.

Mr. Montgomery was a *man*.

Just like Davey had been a man.

I wasn't going down that road again.

"Why not?" asked Peter again.

I smoothed a prong of his jammy hair. "Oh Peter. This is all complicated adult stuff. Your father is a wonderful man but . . . I don't know. He works in a bank."

"For which he is very well compensated," said Veronica.

"Yes I know . . . I know. You're right. But money isn't everything. There's . . . companionship and . . . Look, I'm a lesbian, is the truth of the matter. I like having sex with women."

We fell to thoughtful silence, examining the demon dance of flamy shapes as they formed and intermingled in the bowels of the fire.

Presently the front door clunked shut and in walked Mr. Montgomery, looking even glummer than usual.

"It's war," he said and went to turn on the radio, a hulking brown wardrobe of a thing in the corner of the playroom.

There were some whistling noises, some static, and then the air was filled by the rich, roast-beef voice of Mr. Winston Churchill, one of England's highest-ranking statesmen at that time, delivering a speech that would change all our lives.

"Today . . ." he began, and went on to explain that the Germans, led by Adolf Hitler, had just invaded one of the countries with whom they shared a border . . .

I began to feel sick, and then suddenly . . .

POP!

The radio went dead.

"Father," Veronica straightened in her chair. "I told you the valves in the radio were corroding. Did you buy me the new valves from the ironmonger as you promised?"

He patted his pockets unconvincingly. "Ah . . . sorry, no. I've had much on my mind of late."

"If only I had the valves I could repair the radiophonograph in one instant."

"Gosh you are *clever,*" Peter said. Then he frowned, touched a finger to his lip. "What'th a valve?"

Veronica took off her glasses and polished them on her sweatshirt. "Well, think of it as a tube with a wire in it . . ."

She was right, I reflected later, extinguishing the gas-lamps in my dingy attic quarters and climbing into bed. A valve was a tube with a wire in it.

But like the dictionary says a valve was also a sort of access *hole*, an access hole that could suddenly pop open in the skin of something you thought you had all nicely sealed off, allowing the awfulness to come flooding in again.

I wasn't better, I admitted as I lay there in the dark. I wasn't better at all. Those few morsels of data that I'd been fed by Winston Churchill before the radio crapped out were still lodged in my gut like lumps of indigestible clay, making me want to vomit. My information-phobia was back with a vengeance. And on the eve of a major world war, a war from which there could be no hiding, well that was fucking bad news indeed.

"WORLD WAR TWO!" screamed the giant headline of Mr. Montgomery's newspaper as I crept into the breakfast room the next morning. I slid into my chair, poured myself a coffee with shaking hands, and downed it like a shot of whisky. I had no problem with newspaper headlines screaming WORLD WAR TWO! at me. My beef was with the material below the headline, the columns of swarming, antlike text filled with details of troop movements and strategies, and . . .

I mean: rationing.

What, for instance, was I going to do about rationing?

What was going to happen when I went into a shop and tried to buy some food that I should have known was being rationed? How would I explain myself?

And what about that thing of having to hang a heavy black cloth over the windows so the German bombers couldn't "draw a bead on" you? Would we be asked to do that in London? Or was it just for people who lived on the coast where the bombers made their landfall? There were a *million* tiny things like that, any *one* of which could trip me up.

OKAY, DEEP BREATH.

Just had to toughen up and . . .

Suddenly Mr. Montgomery lowered his newspaper. "Ah. Nanny. There you are. This morning there is to be an air-raid drill. We have been mandated by mayoral communiqué to take shelter in the local underground station. Conceivably for some length of time."

We locked eyes. I nodded.

"I'll be brave, Father," said Peter, who had just entered. Veronica was present too, all of a sudden, I noticed, a caricature of preparedness in waterproof rainhat and shoulder-slung travel bag.

"Peter, don't talk to your father while he's reading his newspaper," I said, refilling my coffee. "And will you be bringing your magnificent newspaper to the underground station, sir? I should very much like to read it. Really come to grips with where we all stand, as a nation, on this grimmest of mornings."

Down came the paper again. "No, Nanny. Sadly I shall not be. The principles of fire safety do expressly forfend the introduction of unlaminated paper to a restricted and unventilated environment such as the underground system. Nor shall there be electrical outlets for the plugging in of radio-phonographs. We shall be entirely cut off from the outside world, but we shall at least be safe."

I chewed my toast impassively and swallowed it down. "That makes sense. It's a . . . it's a question of priorities, I suppose. People should always make sure they're physically safe before they start worrying about things like newspapers."

"Well said, Nanny." Mr. Montgomery looked round at his children, hoping to imprint this nugget of wisdom on their growing brains. "As Nanny maintains, placement of the cart *behind* the horse is a vouchsafement of success in this vale of uncertainty that some wise men refer to as life."

Peter gawped at me with worthless admiration.

My chair creaked as I nodded. "When do we leave?"

"Forthwith."

The walk to the station could literally not have been more hellish. Everywhere one looked was a newspaper vendor shouting news of the war or a public information poster nailed to a tree. But then quickly we were inside, gripping the cool rubber of the escalator handrail and gliding down into what even an official cardboard sign at the station's entrance had admitted was only a Temporary Shelter.

1940–1949

THE GLOBE AFLAME AGAIN

[27 AUG--9:15 P.M.]

THE TUNNEL WAS dark and the platform very crowded. Half of London seemed to be down there, some standing, some sitting, most of them knitting or playing cards, but all of them having a visibly fantastic time. I lost the Montgomeries almost immediately—which was probably just as well, I reckoned—and thrust my way through the mob to an unoccupied square foot of platform right over by one of the tunnel's mouths where I slid to the ground beneath a vandalized chocolate-bar vending machine and commenced doing very little indeed, just sitting and breathing, not even thinking.

After some time had passed I watched a thin man with a ginger wig and a bony, misshapen face that reminded me strongly of my own ankle bounce up onto a bench, clutch his cap to his chest, and to the accompaniment of a child's toy piano being plinked by some henchman in the crowd, set the huddled people swaying with a heartbreaking cockney waltz of a sort that was fairly popular back then.

Oh, angels have taken a floor at The Ritz,

he sang,

There's a unicorn in Green Park
An' on the steps of Sain' Porl's there's a sparrer 'oo sits,
Flappin' 'is broken 'eart.

"Flappin' 'is broken 'eart" echoed a certain percentage of the crowd and I remember musing to myself, as my depression lifted ever so slightly: What a genius song. What a gorgeous, moving and utterly authentic chunk of contemporary English whimsy.

And the man wasn't finished. Once he'd soaked up the applause he identified himself as "Suggestive Bertie," announced that somewhere there was a bucket for people to put money in and then, with his chum on the toy piano plinking an awful lot faster than he had been, Bertie started striding from one end of the bench to the other while waggling his elbows and saucily passing his cap between his legs. Suddenly *boom*: we, the audience, were ears deep in a carefully worded tale of frottage and adultery amid the mossy aqueducts and leaning spires of deepest east London.

She wore it like a scarf,

sang Bertie at one stage,

> *She 'ad it in 'er marf!*
> *Oh, my massive dip-sy din-gle!*

Which struck me, actually, as pathetic.

Stupid.

In fact, I had never heard such a steaming pile of cack in all my life—with the exception, obviously, *of* my life. Because, as I sat there on the platform, reader, cowering from a war I knew nothing about, it began to occur to me that my entire life was entirely ridiculous.

Oh, it had had its moments, don't get me wrong. Like slightly paler and fractionally less stenchful pellets amidst a monstrous pile of black steaming feces, there had been sequences, incidents, that at the time had seemed like harbingers of normalcy ahead.

But they never panned out. Before you could say Jack Robinson I had invariably painted myself into another disgustingly stupid corner from which I needed to be rescued by something ridiculous happening, something random, something preposterous.

Whether or not I managed to extricate myself plausibly from this war thing, it didn't matter. The damage was already done. I had long, long, long ceased to be anything even resembling a Real Person because the tragic and embarrassing fact of the matter was that Real People didn't need their grandfathers to intervene with glistening slabs of gibberish to explain why they don't talk one iota like a tiny little farm girl and Real People's boyfriends didn't ever suddenly decide to reinvent themselves as introspective poets who never want to have another conversation and certainly Real People don't ever develop allergies to information or

[find themselves having to fake an entire old woman's autobiography in a single night? yes they do, you turd. toughen up. come this far.]

anything like that.

BOOM!

I punched myself in the face, pulled myself together.

This was no time for self-pity—though I had every excuse for feeling some. I was about to turn forty years old. *Forty*, reader. And as people, especially women, famously do around that horrific personal milestone I was clearly lashing out at myself for having drifted so far from my life plan.

But you know what? (I realized as I sat there in the London Underground on the very first day of the Second World War.)

That was just life.

Life is random. And ridiculous. And "implausible." It just is. Ask anyone.

And on reflection, reader, it was at that precise moment that I finally grew up.

———

BEFORE THE WAR the Bunley Downs Military Research Institute had been a sanitarium for rich people to visit when they had heart attacks or nervous breakdowns. Rambling over about a hundred acres of treey English countryside the vast complex of red-brick buildings and recreational facilities featured tennis courts, a golf course, a dining hall in a glass rotunda and a network of trails through the tidy woods that were color-coded with painted wooden poles according to their varying levels of cardiovascular intensity. Even now in wartime the place exuded a sort of medicinal-strength serenity and as I admired the main building's ivied exterior from the sweeping gravel driveway, hatboxes at my feet like a gaggle of children, it was the darnedest thing but I could actually feel myself becoming *taller*, as decades of tension simply drained away out of my back muscles.

At the recruitment office, down in London I had been fairly candid with the man behind the desk about my problem with Information, and the first order I received from a superior in the British Army was not to worry about it. The army understood that if they were going to recruit civilians they would have to learn to be flexible about accommodating special needs.

Besides, he told me, rustling in a file cabinet, he had just the job I was looking for: being a member of the support staff at Bunley Downs, a top-secret military research facility deep in the English countryside where the finest minds in the free world were hard at work adding a layer of purely intellectual muscle to the more conventional, soldiers-with-guns component of the Allied war effort. The focus at Bunley Downs was on breaking codes and designing new types of camouflage and thinking of tricks to confuse the Germans, which was, he explained, why the institute was situated deep in the countryside. Necessity might be the mother of invention for *ordinary* people, but for the sort of hard-core self-motivating genius they had at Bunley Downs it was apparently well documented that an abstract, low-pressure environment was far more conducive to creativity.

"You mean . . . you mean they don't talk much about the actual war itself?"

"They don't talk about the war at all. Not even a mention. We want these people following their internal creative compasses, not the headlines in the evening paper."

"You mean . . . You mean I can help with the war without actually *knowing* about the war?"

"Yes," he'd said simply, at the memory of which I'd burst into a massive flood of tears right there on the driveway. Furiously I willed them away. This was a fresh start, a new chance to be a plausible and unremarkable member of society and I wasn't going to mess it up by having my new employer's first impression of me be "oh, she's crying." I looked up at the sky, counted to ten, then seized my luggage and followed the signposts around to the servants' entrance. That door was ajar and through it I could see a pleasant-seeming gray-haired old lady who looked a little like my mother and who was folding a sheet inside. "Hail there," I said cheerily, "I'm looking for . . ." I checked the note on my hand, "Miriam. I'm the new tea lady." I looked the woman square in the face. "They told me to come here and . . . me *mam*?"

Yes.

It was me mam.

And any plans I'd had about not crying were instantly rendered moot.

THE WORK WAS really easy and I loved it. My official title was "tea lady" and all it entailed was wheeling a cart laden with sandwiches and cakes and cups and an urn of hot tea up and down the corridors of the main building. Swiftly I became an expert, tapping on an office door with one hand while pouring a cup of tea with the other and then, depending on whether the genius was bent over his sketchpad or merely looking out the window, I would either engage him in banter or quietly set down his refreshment and slink away. It sounds stupid, I know, but I really did feel that with every cup of tea I served I was inching England closer to victory in the enormous war it was presumably still fighting somewhere far, far away over the trees.

Me mam and I picked up right where we'd left off all those years before. She apologized for making such a fuss that day about my hatboxes and I told her how sorry I was for leaving her to look after Davey, who after all had been my boyfriend. Apologies were accepted, hugs exchanged, and soon we were hard at work rebuilding our relationship. At sundown each day we drank subsidized wine in the officers' mess and talked about life back in Murbery, then at night, in the servants' dormitory, after Miriam had turned out the lights, we whispered like schoolgirls until one of us (me mam) fell asleep leaving me to lie there in the darkness, warm and comfortable, listening to her breathe and thanking every god I'd ever even *heard* about for how well everything had turned out.

Was my life absurd?

Absolutely. More than ever. I'd landed an improbable-sounding job that insulated me utterly from the war, and who's the first person I run into when I get there? Me mam. Me very own mam. Reader, I was up to my hips in absurdity.

But I had learned now not to care about that sort of thing. The forces of chaos, I had learned, were only *enemy* forces if you attempted to resist them. The moment you accepted the idea that your life could, and probably would, veer off in an implausible new direction at any given moment, those forces started working *for* you. Because if anything was possible . . . well, then *anything was possible*.

A case in point: my jawdropping leapfrog of a promotion in the summer of 1942.

THAT SUMMER THE Creative Department* was torn apart by controversy. None of us in the servants' quarters had a clue what was happening, beyond the knowledge that the formerly tight-knit Creatives had staked out two separate and distinct territories in the cafeteria and were looking daggers at each other over the salad bar. One faction was led by Marc, the department head, a tall, muscular, balding man with a little tuft of chest hair in the hollow of his throat and a fondness for collarless shirts, and the other by Brandon, an intense young American who exercised a lot and who, in the days before the controversy, had always eaten alone with a large book. More than that we did not know. But we were all worried. As had been explained to me back in the recruitment office, without its light, almost giddy atmosphere of joie de vivre Bunley Downs simply couldn't function as the hotbed of creativity the Allied war effort required it to be. Wars had been lost over an awful lot less.

I found out what all the trouble was one Friday in early June. The head caterer was out with the flu and so it fell to me that afternoon to wheel the beer into the Creative De-

*Not that every man-jack of the several hundred geniuses at Bunley Downs wasn't creative. They were. But there was also a separate Creative Department, comprising the twenty or thirty most sociable geniuses, whose job it was to think up ideas en masse rather than everyone just holing themselves up in their studies and pursuing their private obsessions.

partment's Big Friday Meeting. If the mood had been sour of late in the cafeteria, it was pure *poison* in the Main Conference Room that afternoon as I carefully backed in with the beer cart.

"Has it come to this?" I heard Marc say as I laid out plates of sandwiches on the side table from his spot at the head of the rosewood conference table. "Brandon, has it come to this?"

Brandon's gaze never shifted from his yellow legal pad where he was drawing angry little boxes in the margin. "I guess it has. You've refused to take note of our objections and so . . . yeah. You've left us no choice. How can we keep on working here if you're just going to ignore us every time we make a serious objection to one of your plans."

"But *Bran*don," Marc implored him. "Brandon, Brandon, *Bran*don. But it's such a tiny *stupid* thing."

"Oh it's stupid, Marc," Brandon slammed down his pen and stared at it, "but it's not tiny. This is meant to be a top-secret facility. This is a *war*. Secrecy should be our top priority and you're acting like we're . . ."

"I know, I know. I'm acting like a member of 'The Little League,' whatever that is. Well, I'm sorry but your resignations are not accepted. We are going to stay in this room until this fiasco is resolved. Otto. You said you might have hit upon a compromise."

Otto, a thick-lipped round-headed Austrian rocket scientist with a pair of entirely spherical glasses, blinked nervously down at his notepad.

"Okay. Vell on ze front of ze T-shirt I haf ze verds 'I am being a member of ze Bunley Downs Creative Department' or vot haf you. And zen on ze rear, vich vill be seen by ze viewer," he gestured, "only after zey haf walked *past* ze person vearing ze shirt, I haf ze additional verds 'Und now I must haf to kill you.'"

There was a lot of doubt on a lot of faces, but not on Marc's. "Well, Brandon, what do you say? That strikes me as rather ingenious. He addresses your security concerns by threatening innocent passersby with *death* if they breathe a word of our existence. While he also meets *my* requirements for an organizational T-shirt," leaning forward Marc clenched his fists beseechingly, ". . . a T-shirt, Brandon, that cements the bond that everyone in this room . . ." he pointed round at them all with his pen, ". . . has with everyone *else* in this room. Maintaining esprit de corps is *my responsibility*, Brandon. Radar is yours. I don't tell you how to distinguish a plane from a weather balloon. I would prefer that you not tell me how to foster morale." He leaned back. "So how about it. We go with Otto's design and put this whole ugly episode behind us."

Brandon stood and started gathering his papers. "Marc, with all due whatever, that is the dumbest idea I've ever heard. We shouldn't have a T-shirt at all. This is a top-secret military facility, not a chain of goddam restaurants. Look I just . . . This isn't happening. Me and my people want out."

A terrible silence descended, the sound of something beautiful dying, and the next thing I knew my mouth was moving, forming words.

"Um," I said, from over by the side table. "Can I say something? I couldn't help but overhear."

Only Marc would look at me. "Please do."

I wasn't nervous. I just spoke. "Well, I just think that sometimes in situations like this it can be helpful to get some outside perspective and anyway it just occurred to me that maybe the way to accomplish *both* your goals is to, instead of a T-shirt, print up a batch of Bunley Downs Creative Department *underwear*. That way no member of the public will ever know, but you'd get the same sense of camaraderie you'd get from a T-shirt . . . in fact you'd get a deeper camaraderie because it would be like a secret you all share . . . anyway." I blushed. "I'm sorry if I've spoken out of turn. It was just something I was thinking."

No, it was more than that.

It was genius.

My memory of that next minute is a blur, but when it was over the rosewood surface of the conference room table was splattered with tears of laughter and relief, and two grown men, Brandon and Marc, were hugging each other like pandas in the zoo. I remember gripping my cart by its handle and *trying* to leave the room, but Marc broke from his embrace with Brandon and ran to block my exit.

Reader, he blocked my exit permanently.

MY STARTING WAGE as a Creative was five hundred pounds a week, an enormous sum in those days, as much as a wealthy man in a classic English novel might have in his entire bank account, and the first thing I did was move me mam and me out of the servants' quarters into a room at Mrs. Truman's rooming house in Bunley village. It was the best room she had, with a kettle and a trouser press and an *en suite* bathroom and everything. At the institute itself they gave me a corner office and a slot on the bicycle rack that no one else could use. Those were very exciting days but I was careful not to get bigheaded. On my desk I kept the small brass gyroscope the geniuses had given me for my forty-second birthday, whose polished wooden base bore the legend, "Caffeine Makes the World Go Round."

But my tea-wheeling days were done. For me the rest of the war was all about bicycling in through the air in the morning, waving to the guards, leaving my bike unlocked in my slot, how's it going, how's it going, then up the stairs and into the Main Conference Room to see what pastries were waiting on the side table. I'd get a coffee and a donut, take my seat at the table and start bantering with the other Creatives as they casually dribbled in. Sometime around nine o'clock, without any formal intervention from Marc, the conversation would smoothly turn to the subject of bouncing bombs, or bulletproof vests, or machine guns that could shoot through the propeller of a plane without hitting the blades, or how to seed the sky with little tinfoil strips to make the German radar think we had five billion planes . . . until soon the ideas would be coming to people faster than they could blurt them out and we'd all be ripping crude sketches from our legal pads and sliding them madly around the table, tossing tennis balls back and forth as an aid to concentration, swigging from little bottles of mineral water until *boom*. You thought it was still only ten past nine but in fact it was lunchtime and you had just invented a whole *plane* or something!

And that was my Second World War.

On the night it all ended, in 1945, a huge party was thrown in the officers' mess. They ordered a jazz band up from London and oh how we danced. Around eleven, bathed in sweat, I left the party and wandered off through the innards of the complex with a bottle of single malt that I had sweet-talked out of the barman. In the darkened kitchen

I danced again, alone, more gently, swaying amid the outsize appliances to the strains of the music bleeding through from the mess, then I ambled off down the corridor and snapped on the lights of the firing range.

The firing range had formerly been a squash court, and soon it would be again. At the rear, against the mattresses full of bullet holes was a bale of folded paper Germans. I sat down on them and unscrewed the cap of my whiskey.

Here was to me, I reckoned, filling my plastic glass and promptly draining it.

Here was to me for having *made it*.

From beginnings that were *worse* than humble, from *nothing*, the undeniable fact of the matter was that I had clawed my way up the pole of life, inch after terrible inch, crisis after crisis, the big black birds of Chaos and Nonexistence nipping at me incessantly with their awful beaks, to finally become an actual finished person, with a life more real and vivid than I had ever dreamed it could be. I mean look at me: sitting in a converted squash court on the last night of World War Two, the tickle of gunpowder in my nose, fresh sweat wet on my upper lip and under my arms, listening to the rumble of nearby boilers . . . the *cuck* sound my plastic glass made as I set it down on the smooth cement floor . . . the *whisper* of my blouse as I raised one fist beneath the buzzing squash-court lights and quite frankly just fucking *held it there*.

Mn?

Why?

Why did I hold my fist in the air?

Because *two* wars had ended that day, reader: The war against the Germans, whose two-dimensional paper images lay flat, docile and defeated beneath my *Bunley Downs: Britain's Best Kept Secret* boxer shorts.

But also the other war, the bigger one, the war whose first shot had been fired very quietly forty years earlier in a dusty room above a grocer's shop on a sunny Saturday morning, the War of My Becoming.

Yes, *two* wars had ended that day—not just one—and in a stunning upset *I had managed to win them both*.

[okay calm down buck

time now is
27 AUG--9:45 P.M.

45 years done in 6 hrs
8.2 years per hour.
55 years left/8.2 = 6.7073170732 hrs, call it seven which
means a finish time of about 6.13 A.M.

so ahead of sched, going very well, but NO FUCKING
NAPPING

if you have spare time then use it constructively
i.e. by fucking finding a way of expanding memoir to
explain WHY WHAT HAPPENED HAPPENED and
thereby getting self off hook.

for instance what if you made her keep a DIARY of the
summer, a diary sort of woven into the memoir, including
present day stuff featuring self.

thereby demonstrating to reader how bad everything was
for self and how none of it was self's fault.

do it.

are genius

except killing old woman was stupid stupid STUPID.

27 AUG--9:46 P.M.]

PART II

Diary of a Life Interrupted

June

June 1st—Tuesday

So I'm trying something new, reader, an entirely fresh approach to this book.

Here's how it'll work:

From this point forward, as well as being my autobiography, this book is also going to be my *diary*. Every evening between today and the end of August, which is when my publishers are coming round to collect this manuscript, I'm going to write an account of the day just ending. I'm going to tell you how I'm feeling, what I had for lunch, what the weather's like, etc., and then whenever some element of that material reminds me of an incident from my Past I am planning to "flash back" to that earlier time and deliver another installment of my autobiography, thereby weaving the two narratives—the story of my life in the Present and the story of my life in the Past—into a single narrative . . . cord.

Do you see? The *form* will be that of a diary—there'll be a day and date at the top of each entry—but the *content* will be half diary, half autobiography. For example, a typical entry might read:

July nth—Thursday

Woke up, went to the bathroom, blah blah blah. Opened a new jar of the pills I take for my arthritis and was reminded by that ball of cotton wool that's always in a pill jar of a cloud I once saw over Blahland . . .

I moved to Blahland in Blahvember of 19blahventy blah with a troupe of traveling blah blah blahs and we had the following adventures: x, y, z.

But those days are gone. Now I am an old woman whose arthritis will not let her do that sort of thing. The rest of the day passed uneventfully and now I am going to sleep.

You see? Pretty straightforward.

Now let me quickly tell you *why* I've decided to make this change.

I've decided to make this change because I'm ruining the life of my caregiver—the young man who lives next door to me—and this is the only way I can think of to even start to pay him back. For four long months, with deepening guilt, I've watched the strain of looking after me make Bruno Maddox depressed and listless, then rob him of his stamina and his sense of purpose, and eventually whittle away so much of the vigorous young man I first met back in February that there is nothing left but a nub, a lump, a wretched little stump of a man with just enough vitality left to keep me alive, but nothing left over with which to live himself.

And then, unbelievably, last week it all got much, much worse.

Bruno works one hour a day for a tiny cable television station here in Manhattan and last Thursday morning they called him up and, as far as I could tell from only his side of the conversation, asked him to attend the taping of a pilot episode for a new panel-based discussion program, potentially debuting next spring. He went and, as would later become apparent, found himself seated next to an attractive young female magazine journalist. The two of them fell to talking, one thing led to another, and the next thing Bruno Maddox knew he had a "date" for the evening, a date with a girl.

Had I known what was happening I would have tried to stop him from going. I could have fallen out of the electric bed, faked a seizure, *something*. But the first I knew of his evening plans was when he plonked a bowl of tuna mayonnaise on my swingable side table and set out whistling into the early evening.

Bruno was back in less than an hour—as I could have told him he would be—utterly destroyed, as caregivers invariably are whenever they try to reimmerse themselves in social intercourse after months of lonely caregiving. For the best part of an hour he lay in a clammy heap by the radiator, face in his hands, moaning and mumbling to himself.

Eventually, from his impressionistic mumbles, I was able to piece together most of what had happened: the taping of the pilot episode that afternoon, the girl, the bar she'd told him to meet her at, how the crowds and the noise had overwhelmed his feeble, atrophied senses, and how—most tragically—when the girl had asked him, over the din of wherever they were, what it was that he wanted to do with his life, Bruno had found himself blurting that he wanted to *live in an undersea dome and interact with the world only by computer*, prior to bolting the scene, coming home and collapsing.

I recognized those symptoms immediately, from my own experience in the nineteen thirties. It was information phobia. And having read *The Caregiver's Bible* by Dr. Steven Hearne, G.N.P., Ph.D., about nine times cover to cover, I was led to a terrible but inescapable conclusion: that Bruno Maddox had finally crossed the line from merely being depressed and exhausted by the hell of looking after me into having full-blown "caregiver's syndrome," which, as Dr. Hearne spends an entire chapter pointing out, is an actual, free-standing mental illness that people don't recover from without actual medical treatment. Even when your care recipient *dies*—which they all do, by definition—a person with Caregiver's Syndrome *doesn't get better*. In fact, they usually get worse. Caregiver's Syndrome is a truly terrible thing.

That was the evening I resolved to act, to do something. The obvious move, the only move that would actually make a difference, would be to kill myself, but sadly I'm too weak these days to even peel a banana let alone stick my head in the oven or throw myself out the window. The bulk of my remaining strength is concentrated weirdly in the two fingers and thumb with which I grip the pen that writes these words. Believe me, if I ever think of a way to kill myself that only involves those three wizened digits then I'll be off this

Earth sooner than you can say Jack Robinson. In the meantime I think the most I can do is make this autobiography into a tribute to Bruno Maddox. By keeping a daily diary I will build a permanent record of that young man's daily agonies, preserving them for posterity, so that after I'm dead anyone who cares to can pick up *My Little Blue Dress* and maybe learn a thing or two about the resiliency of the human spirit.

Here goes.

Today's lunch was vegetarian chili from a can. It reminded me, vaguely, of a chili con carne that the chef at Bunley Downs used to serve us in those lazy months after the Second World War ended, as we creative military geniuses were wrapping our gyroscopes in brown paper, disassembling our slide rules, and saying our good-byes. Those were good times, reader, whereas these are *bad* times. Though I have to say that this is possibly the sexiest and most elegant format for a memoir that any old lady has ever thought of.

So are you ready, reader? Are you ready for Part Two?
Good.
So am I.

June 2nd—Wednesday

Sad scene here this morning while Bruno was taking my blood pressure.

Just as the boy was safety pinning the cuff around my arm—which has grown too thin for the Velcro surfaces to coincide as they would on any normal person—my chest began to crackle. This happens almost every day. Bruno dropped the cuff of the blood-pressure machine, bent me forward on the electric bed, and rubbed my back in circles until I gave a proper cough, then another, then spewed a few teaspoons of dark gray phlegm into his waiting hand.

Oh God, I pulsed him telepathically.* *Sorry.*

Bruno straightened up, looked down at the phlegm in his hand and right then suffered what Dr. Steven Hearne terms a "sudden loss of focus." Instead of sprinting to the sink and washing my filth off his person the young man drifted to the window, gazed vacantly down into the street . . .

Hey, I pulsed him gently. *Hey. Earth to Bruno Maddox.*

And then, with a sigh, he absently ran the handful of phlegm through his hair.

Oh God, I pulsed as he stumbled gagging down into the kitchen. *I am so sorry. Please kill me kill me kill me . . .*

The thing you have to understand, however, about the young man Bruno Maddox is that he's a saint to his very core. I'm not exaggerating. He's a profoundly good young man. Kill me? Reader, he didn't even *hit* me. Didn't even grab me by my greasy nylon lapels and denounce me as a disgusting, effluvium-producing old bitch, which I would be the first to agree is what I am. No. Once Bruno had rinsed my dreadful goo from his hand he simply clambered back up into the living-room area and resumed checking my blood pressure in as cheerful and tender a manner as if I'd slathered his palm with gold bullion rather than lung butter. And that just made me sadder.

*I'm not actually telepathic. I just can't speak. So I pulse.

You see, reader, Bruno Maddox doesn't know anything about blood pressure. He only bought the machine last week, from this madman over on the Bowery who, if memory serves, was probably also selling a shoe, a folded square of clear plastic and a water-damaged issue of *Asian Tit Parade* from a blanket on the sidewalk, and consequently it came with no instructions.

Not that Bruno cares. He doesn't even watch the mercury shifting in the cloudy glass tube. He just stares into space as he pumps the squeezy ball in his hand. Why? Because he's a caregiver, and caregivers crave ritual of any sort, however meaningless. It makes them feel like they're "in control of the Home," according to Dr. Hearne, though the truth, of course, is that they aren't in control of anything.

So yes. All in all, today's blood-pressure incident was a very sad scene indeed.

June 3rd—Thursday

Today was the first day of summer, by my estimation. Bruno and I live on the corner of Eldridge and Broome streets, down in Chinatown, on the Lower East Side of Manhattan, one of the dirtiest, smelliest and most neglected spots in all of Manhattan. No shops, no people, just blackened shuttered storefronts and piles of reeking garbage, and from early June to late September there's a distinctive stench of fish and sewage that haunts the place, and which for the first time in nine months came floating through the window today during the Afternoon Session as we sat watching women's billiards on television.

Hey, I pulsed Bruno. *Summer's here, can you feel it? Can you smell it?*

But the boy just coughed and rubbed his face, tried to keep himself focused on the Samson Insurance Ladies Nine-Ball Challenge. I don't know what I was expecting. As a poet might say, what use hath a caregiver for the changing of seasons or the wonders of nature? None. Each day for him is like a wet, gray day in the dreariest month you can imagine.

I should have known better than to pulse him what I pulsed him.

It was thoughtless of me.

June 4th—Friday

More sad scenes this evening, reader. Some very sad scenes indeed.

Bruno got home from work at nine-thirty, two hours late, and he was visibly drunk: shiny with sweat and hiccuping at the foot of my electric bed. Rather than take me to the bathroom, however, an obvious necessity given his lateness, his first act was to stumble through the fire door to place a 'phone call.

"Hi, er . . . it's me," he slurred into someone's answering machine. "Bruno Maddox. That guy. From before. Um, sorry for calling. I just . . ." He cleared his throat. "Just wanted to offer some sort of semi-apology for, um, all that stuff that happened the other week. I'm very sorry about, um, . . . just ducking away like that. I was not . . . feeling myself and um . . . so that's what I'm calling to say. Um . . ."

There was a *thud* and a *whoosh* as he slumped against the doorjamb and slid to the ground. "I'm slightly drunk I have to say." He chuckled. "There's this *guy* at work . . . this hairy little guy who plugs in my earpiece and his *mother* unfortunately died last year and this was the one-year anniversary and so he *asked* me to go have a drink with him and well it was weird."

That's enough, I pulsed him. *Hang up. You're starting to ramble.*

"Right across from where we work there's this little *alley*way that one of the restaurants has made into a bar for people to drink at after work. They've laid down this really weird blue fake grass and got some of those little round umbrella tables and there are speakers hanging from the lampposts playing the radio . . . *anyway*, we got some whiskeys and Mark Clark—that's the hairy little guy who plugs in my earpiece—started telling me all about his mother dying and it was very sad and I tried to change the subject but then he started telling me about this ambition he has to have a newspaper column in his hometown called 'News to Me, by Mark Clark.'" Bruno cleared his throat contemptuously. "Every week he's going to round up all the wacky, offbeat stories from other papers around the nation and then sign off every time with the words 'and that's news to me. . . . ' I don't know why I'm telling you this but anyway that was in a weird way even *more* depressing than the mother thing and then more drinks came. . . ."

Okay now. That's enough now.

"Literally drinks and drinks and drinks and drinks and I . . ." Bruno's voice, which had been getting softer all this time, settled now into a hypnotic singsong drawl. . . . "I was just sort of rocking back on my chair . . . rocking back on my chair and looking up at the sky . . . the rectangle of sky where the skyscrapers ended and . . . it was all pale blue with this sort of . . . sort of yellow mist behind it . . . and I don't know, it was the weirdest, most beautiful thing. The tops of the buildings were going all peach and orange and tangerine and I was looking up at it and . . ." something caught in his throat, ". . . I don't know, I suddenly felt *bad* about sprinting away the other evening when we were together and . . . well, I tried to find a 'phone but there wasn't one and so I just came home and found one here and . . . well, now I'm talking to you and I'm going to go now in case I start . . ."

Hang up, I pulsed.

Plastic crushed into plastic, then silence.

It was over.

"Oh God," said Bruno, and may in fact have shed a few tears before stumbling out into the world to buy us dinner, leaving me here alone, desperate to go to the bathroom and feeling very, very sad, reader. Oh, it's nothing new. It's the same old sadness. The exact same sadness I feel every time it's brought home to me how much damage I've done to Bruno Maddox. Tonight, though, was particularly tough. Hearing him drool into the 'phone like that, getting all misty and gooey about the tops of high buildings, being struck by the evening sun . . .

Because he didn't used to be like that.

No, when I first met Bruno Maddox he was altogether different.

In fact, I think I'll spend tomorrow telling you all about it.

June 5th—Saturday

It was February 8 of this year. Around ten o'clock that morning I became aware of voices next door. One of them was Kevin, my Chinese landlord, who grunts instead of talking, and the other I didn't recognize. I heard the stranger use the word "radiator," and this precipitated a series of muffled, frenzied *bongs*, as of Kevin kicking a radiator . . . then suddenly *boom:* The fire door crashed open and there was my landlord, whom I hadn't seen in a year, flying through the air in his filthy jeans and his leather jacket and his yellow "SuperStud" T-shirt, and landing in the gap between my electric bed and the window where he began to clank away at the innards of *my* radiator with a metal tool that he had snatched from his belt rather impressively in midair.

And that's when I saw Bruno Maddox. Gliding through the fire door in Kevin's wake came an extremely tall and athletic-looking young man with pale skin, a wild tangle of mahogany hair, and an olive-green business suit of the lowest possible quality, a suit that I could tell immediately was far from representative of his overall attractiveness.

This young man has the Lifeforce, I remember blurting to myself as Bruno stood there inspecting my furniture, those huge, expressive eyes of his falling upon an object, extracting its essence, filing the information away, then swiftly moving on to another. He stepped down, out of veiw, into the kitchen. I heard a pill jar rattle, a knife picked up and set down again . . . and then *boom*. Suddenly there he was, right in the doorway of my bedroom, peering into the blackness, well-shaped nostrils flaring at the scent of urine.

". . . Hail . . ." I said, the second-to-last word I would ever utter.

Bruno froze. "Hello?"

Right then Kevin grunted something from the other end of the apartment to the effect that it was going to be springtime in a few short weeks, and so the lack of central heating didn't matter. Instinctively I felt a throb of apprehension on Kevin's behalf. I'd only known Bruno Maddox a few seconds, but I had already seen enough of his forcefulness, his vibrancy, to realize that Kevin Lee had just made an enormous miscalculation. Clearly, this wasn't the sort of young man one messed with or tried to hoodwink.

"Pardon the intrusion," said Bruno coolly into the stinking blackness and swiveled on his heel to lay down the law to one Kevin Lee.

Our relationship should have ended then and there, but it didn't. An hour later Bruno was back, tapping on my *front* door and waiting a full five minutes while I decanted myself out of bed, shuffled out of my bedroom and around the little promontory of cornicework, and fiddled endlessly with the latch.

"Fucking hell," were Bruno's first words upon seeing me. I wasn't offended in the slightest because the fact is, reader, that at this stage of the game I am pretty much the world's *least* attractive woman. My skin is blemished and papery, with black and silver bristles; my mouth is an irregular, lipless hole with horrible lacy edges, and my once-piercing ice-blue eyes have lost both their color and their luster. In fact, the white parts have turned the color of ear-wax.

I could go on, and in fact I think I shall: my hair is sparse and white and seems to float *above* my scalp like thin chemical clouds on some nightmarish alien planet; my body is a little knot of cartilage like you sometimes find in a stew. And on that particular day I happened to be in my least flattering outfit: a tubular smock of caramel-colored nylon, with repulsive stains around the groin.

"Sorry to bother you again," the boy continued, composure flooding back, "but I was just ducking out to the shops and wondered if I could get you anything in terms of food or supplies."

I looked at him.

Could he *get* me anything?

No, I pulsed him. *You can't get me anything. I'm trying to starve myself to death.*

And with that I turned and just shuffled away.

But I *forgot to close the door*. One of the favorite techniques of Ancient Greek playwrights, when composing their tragedies, was to have one of the characters perform some seemingly innocuous action that precipitates a whole chain of increasingly tragic events, and so it proved in this instance. Bruno interpreted my leaving the door open as a request for him to buy me a random selection of groceries, then come back and put them away for me. At the Chinese minimart around the corner he very thoughtfully bought me some half-pulp orange juice, a gallon of whole milk, a sliced loaf of seven-grain bread, but was so struck on his return by the disgusting condition of my refrigerator and, come to think of it, my apartment as a whole, that he decided out of the goodness of his heart—the genuine goodness—to spend the rest of the day cleaning the place up and generally bringing some order to my world.

So he did. He emptied the rotting food from the fridge, swept the floor and wiped the table. He lifted me out of bed, dumped me in the nasty armchair, stripped the sheets from both my beds, and took them to the laundry. For lunch he made me soup, and afterward he consulted the labels on my pill jars and made me swallow a few. When the laundry was done he remade both the beds, reinserted me into the non-electric one back in my bedroom, washed the lunch dishes in the sink, and signed off around four in the afternoon with the compassionate words: "I'm off now. Good luck. Hope I was able to be of service."

I knew he'd be back. The walls are so thin around here that by noon the next day Bruno knew—and I knew he knew—that a) I had received no other callers since he'd left me and b) I hadn't even shuffled to the bathroom or the fridge. All he had heard me do was cough, and occasionally moan. At one o'clock he was back, looming over me in my bedroom, brandishing my copy of *The Caregiver's Bible*, which had been splayed for weeks on the nasty armchair.

"Sorry to intrude again," he murmured sounding ever so slightly irked, "but I didn't hear anyone arrive and so I thought I'd better check on you. You do have a ..." He looked at the book jacket. "... caregiver, don't you?"

I tried to answer but managed only a hiss. Resourcefully, I attempted telepathy.

No, I pulsed him. *I don't. That's my book. I bought it when I was just becoming decrepit.*

"Well look. I think what I'd better do is call the health services, see if they have someone who can come and take care of you."

Just as he was turning away, making for the Yellow Pages and the 'phone, I uttered the absolute last word I would ever speak.

"... No ...".

And that was that.

Half an hour later Bruno was still pacing about the place, trying and failing to think of a way out of his predicament. Obviously he couldn't just *abandon* me. In my condition that would be murder. But neither could he in good conscience call the Health Services after I'd explicitly asked him not to. If I had in fact made the gutsy, quite reasonable decision to starve myself to death in my disgusting apartment rather than die at the hands of nurses in some soulless state-run institution, then who was he to override my wishes simply because he'd stuck his nose in where he wished he hadn't?

No, the boy was stuck. He'd got himself into a real pickle, a pickle to which there was a single, morally acceptable solution: continue to care for me until my real caregiver showed up to take me off his hands.

Which is exactly what happened.

The only problem being of course that when my real permanent caregiver did finally show up, it turned out to be him, and the *real* Bruno Maddox, the forceful, happy, motivated one, disappeared.

June 6th—Sunday

The 'phone rang today mid-afternoon while Bruno was changing the sheets on the electric bed. He let the machine take the call, as has been his policy since that fateful day last week when his office called up and made him attend that taping, which resulted, of course, in the disastrous assignation with that girl.

"Hi. This is Hayley Iskender." The girl's voice was freakishly even-pitched, like the voice they give computers in movies. "Um. I'm calling to reply to your message from the other evening. I didn't really understand it, but if you were calling to ask whether I want to go out with you again, then um, I don't think I want to so . . . Thanks."

Click.

Bruno failed to react.

He merely stuffed a pillow into its case and shook it down.

Was that really necessary? I found myself peevishly pulsing the girl through the machine. *How much more demoralized do you think this poor boy can be before he just completely . . . snaps? Hmm?*

But there was no response. Obviously.

June 7th—Monday

The heat descended with a vengeance today. Heat and extreme humidity. Less than fifteen seconds into the three and a half minutes it takes me to shuffle to the bathroom in the morning* with Bruno gripping me lightly at the elbow and waist, I realized I was sweating like a foundryman and emitting about a hundred times more old-woman stink than usual.

Sorry I smell so bad, I pulsed my gentle escort. *It's the heat. The last thing you need right now is for me to start smelling. Sorry. I can't help it.*

But "Easy does it . . . you're walking very well" was Bruno's faux-cheerful response, a classic example of the sort of upbeat verbal air freshener he uses to cover the horrible scent of old woman.

He is a gentleman, that boy. And a saint.

---

*Thirty seconds to exit the bedroom, plus a minute to cross the kitchen's checkered linoleum, plus thirty seconds negotiating the little step up into the living-room area, plus another minute and a half in conga formation as Bruno maneuvers me around the electric bed and the television set and the nasty green armchair into the bathroom.

June 8th—Tuesday

Well here we are: a week into the new format and what do you think? Personally, I reckon it's going very well.

It's bad isn't it, Bruno's life?

You may have a better imagination than me, reader, but personally I cannot even *imagine* the anguish that kind young man must be going through. To be twenty-seven years old, with the greatest city in the world humming away just beyond the window, and yet to have to spend your days trapped in an airless box with an unattractive, and now reeking old woman . . . Can you even imagine? If I were in his shoes I probably would have snapped by now and just quickly *killed* me. Wouldn't be that big a deal. I mean it's not like I'm even really alive, I'm just . . . existing.

He'd do us both a favor . . . but tragically he's far too kind and gentle.

Oh well.

Anyway, I'm pleased with the new format. I know I haven't flashed back to the past yet to give you any more memoir, but even just the poignancy of this diary . . . I reckon my publishers are in for a treat.

Actually did I tell you about my publishing situation? I probably should.

I'm under contract with a major New York publishing house to write this autobiography in exchange for the sum of one million dollars American.

Why so much money? Because of something I probably should have told you earlier, which is that I was born not just in the year 1900, but on the *first day* of that year, January 1. I didn't tell you earlier because I didn't want you thinking this was one of those . . . those *fictional* books that blind Mexican novelists write about women born on the first days of centuries and for which they are routinely awarded the Nobel Prize for Literature. This is a memoir, not a novel, and I didn't want you thinking I was any kind of "creation."

Besides, I don't actually see any of the money until I finish. Most authors who sign big contracts get some of the cash upfront, to sustain them as they write the book, but not, apparently, when they're over a hundred years old. As a centenarian and a first-time author I have apparently been deemed too much of a risk by the publisher's accountants. I'll see a penny when I finish, and not before.

If that weren't insulting enough, there is also Clause Eleven of my contract, which appeared to me to have been typed in hastily at a slight diagonal:

> Author shall additionally provide Publisher with such keys and/or passwords and/or instructions as are necessary for Publisher to gain entry to Author's residence at 133 Eldridge St., Apt. 4, on delivery date (see Paragraph 2) for the purpose of assessing the condition of the Manuscript.

By which they mean: for the purpose of stepping over my desiccated corpse and whisking away whatever fragments of memoir I've managed to generate to be completed by a snickering team of recently graduated ghostwriters and subsequently published as if I'd written it myself.

Did I sign this morbid and insulting document? Yep. Of course I did. The money was just unignorable, but as a petty gesture of defiance I keep this manuscript hidden down the side of my bed. If I do—as I hope to—die before completing this work, then when the publishers come round to collect it they're fucking well going to have to hunt around.

June 9th—Wednesday

I haven't told you about Bruno's job, and I should.

Every evening between six and seven Bruno Maddox participates on a news discussion program called *Thirty UN!der Thirty*, and if the TV is tuned to channel 79 when he leaves for work, then I get to watch him.

It isn't a very *good* television program *Thirty UN!der Thirty*. The premise is fairly basic—a panel of young people from around the nation arguing about the issues behind that day's headlines—but in order to justify the show's snappy title there are *thirty* of them, all sharing the screen at the same time. If you find this hard to imagine then you might want to try cutting thirty little faces out of a magazine and pasting them to the front of your television set, if you can fit them all in. Done it? Okay. Now imagine them all talking and scoffing and interrupting each other and occasionally making gagging gestures . . . It's overwhelming.

"Bruno Maddox in New York" broadcasts from a wooden platform some forty feet above the trading floor of the American Stock Exchange. When he makes his daily contribution—you have to make at least one comment or you can get fired—his box swells up three times its normal size and you get to see the huge vaulted room behind him with its gilded, super-ornate ceiling and these great metal towers of dusty computer screens and old stained 'phones.

The wooden platform is the Manhattan headquarters of

what I think may be the world's smallest twenty-four-hour cable news station, Channel N! The giant N! basically stands for "news," but if you actually tune in to channel 79 here in Manhattan, depending on what time of day it is you will see the N! doing duty either as the first letter of *N!ewsdesk* (7 A.M. to 6 P.M.); or of *N!ow and Then* (7 P.M. to midnight); or *N!eal Roddenberry, Horseman of Controversy* (midnight to 3 A.M.); or, between six and seven in the evening, bulging in the middle of *Thirty UN!der Thirty*.

The money isn't spectacular as you can imagine but in a lot of other ways *Thirty UN!der Thirty* is the perfect job for a caregiver. It only takes an hour a day, you don't need to have your wits about you and in Bruno's case he gets to walk to work, which I imagine must be fairly therapeutic. Ambling over to the Bowery in the early evening air, slicing southward through the hordes of Chinese into the spaciousness of Tribeca, then into the financial district, beating a path against the thin tide of secretaries and messengers limping slowly uptown in pursuit of their banker masters who are already nestled in the upholstery of their limos and spaceships and helicopters, and finally reaching shady Trinity Place. Exactly how he gets from the door of the American Stock Exchange to the floodlit wooden platform forty feet above the trading floor that is N!'s Manhattan studio I do not know, but waiting for him there, I've deduced, is Mark Clark, the small, hairy technician who has Bruno's earpiece and microphone already wired up and ready to go.

The broadcast lasts until seven and at seven-thirty he is back here, dinner dangling at his side in a white plastic bag. I have to be very careful about what I eat because I have a stomach condition called "diverticulitis"—very common among the elderly—that involves little pouches of intestinal lining bulging out into the main thoroughfare of the bowel and snagging chunks of fecal matter as they try to squeeze past, if you can imagine such a thing. The pain can be unbelievable and the only real cure is surgery, though symptoms can be kept in abeyance by following a high-fiber diet and avoiding all nuts and seeds. This evening's dinner was rigatoni with vodka sauce from a place in Little Italy: an excellent and very compassionate selection on the part of the boy.

I think I mentioned that he is an inherently good man.

June 10th—Thursday

The heat is becoming absurd. Reader, you should have seen the map of the United States the TV weatherwoman was standing in front of this morning. I'd never seen such infernal colors: horrible hellish purples and reds and oranges, like someone's terrible sweater, no pun intended—none taken, conceivably, I suppose.

It's getting really hot. Hot and nasty.

June 11th—Friday

A quiet, hot, nasty day. Bruno bought a rattly old fan from the madman vendor. The boy and I watched a documentary about two old friends reuniting decades after the drunk-driving accident that paralyzed one and left the other feeling guilty.

That's a lot like us, I pulsed Bruno. *You're the cripple and I'm the perpetrator.* But he was looking out the window, lost in thought, or in lack of thought, with his eyes pointed vaguely at the gummed-up ventilation fan of the tenement across the street. *You should kill me,* I added as an afterthought.

June 12th—Saturday

Another day. More dolor.

I'd tell you about it but it's just too depressing.

June 13th—Sunday

Okay, stop the presses. Something has happened.

Something weird.

In fact, "Can I tell you something weird?" were Bruno's precise words to me this afternoon as he returned from his daily grocery run *without any groceries.* "I was in the Kam Wo just now getting some beer . . ."

Okay, I pulsed. The Kam Wo Trading Company is one of those poky little Chinese shops where they sell medicinal herbs and great bushels of chopsticks and knobbled bedroom slippers with therapeutic magnets in the soles. The Kam Wo also sells beer, from a fridge in the rear. *Do go on.*

". . . and I ran into this girl. This girl I know who works for a magazine. I went out for a drink with her a few weeks ago . . ."

Uh oh, I thought. Not her again.

"Anyway she was there in one of the aisles, wearing rubber surgical gloves . . ." he absently held up a hand and wiggled the fingers, ". . . looking at some sort of dried *root*. I went up and said hi. Then *she* said hi. And then . . ." he frowned, well, then I just started *mumbling*. I've been mumbling a lot for some reason these last few weeks, just . . . everywhere I go, in shops and places, I've been having a hard time . . . making myself understood. Anyway I started mumbling to this girl about how *sorry* I was for having called her up drunk the other week and also for the other week when we were having a drink and I . . . I told her I wanted to live in an undersea dome and then just . . . left. Anyway I think I must have mumbled something about how I haven't been myself lately and how if she only had a chance to hang out with me for a while, a couple of weeks or something, she'd see that I was actually not the complete freak I might appear because *she* suddenly then said, 'Is that how they do things in England?' And I said, 'Is that how they do what in England?' and she said . . . I think she was smirking . . . she said, 'Is that how people date each other in England? You try them out for two weeks to see if you like them?' And I had no idea what she was talking about and so I just mumbled, 'Um . . . yes. Especially in rural areas . . . ' I didn't mean it but she suddenly then said, 'Okay.' And I said, 'Okay what?' And she said, and she wasn't smirking anymore, she just said, 'I'm not going to sleep with you but I can handle two weeks. Call me tomorrow at work,' and she gave me her number." Unfolding his fingers, Bruno revealed something whose picture could literally have appeared in a dictionary next to the phrase, "slip of paper": a slim, perfect rectangle of paper inscribed with seven neat digits, hyphen after the third, and above them the words "Hayley Iskender, come hither."*

We both stared at the slip of paper.

That is weird, I pulsed. *I tell you this city's full of complete nut . . .*

But the young man was no longer reachable. He was down on his stomach in the kitchen, scrubbing with a sponge-stick at the grime between the stove and the refrigerator.

You're not actually going to call her, are you? I pulsed him when he stood to survey his work. *Bru . . .*

But he was busy filling a bucket with hot water and detergent and was now tackling our filthy windows. I pretty much had my answer, I reckoned, and by the time dinner arrived—a can of black bean soup that has been in the cupboard for ages, garnished with specially purchased sour cream and served with a napkin that had been twirled into a decorative cone—I definitely had my answer.

Yes.

He's going to call her.

And that makes me apprehensive.

Why?

Well, for several reasons. Let me quote to you again from Dr. Steven Hearne:

> Regular breaks and excursions may be the care-giver's best weapon against burnout, but the temptation to start a "second life" outside the Home should be resisted at all costs. Contact with noncare-

---

*Before you get too excited, reader, I should tell you that *come hither,* written entirely lowercase, is the title of a fairly popular general interest magazine for young ladies in their teens and twenties.

givers may seem an obvious antidote to a deepening sense of isolation but in practice even something as simple as a weekly "card night" can be brutally demoralizing, as the caregiver finds herself reminded at every turn of how much of normal life—staying out late, overindulging—is now off limits to her, and of how little she has in common with people she used to know. Old friends can seem like strangers, and starting a new relationship is all but impossible.

"All but impossible," says Dr. Hearne, who has a Ph.D. in science, and that's under the *best* of circumstances, which you'd have to be a moron to think these were. Bruno Maddox can't function in social situations because he's a caregiver. "Hayley Iskender," if not clinically insane—having on the one hand instructed Bruno that she didn't want to see him again and on the other just agreed to be his girlfriend for two weeks—would appear at least to be dangerously impulsive. Their conversation this morning in Kam Wo Trading Company was premised on a massive misunderstanding—more a lie, really—about Anglo-Saxon mating rituals and if all that wasn't enough we're in the middle of a heat wave.

Bad feelings are the only sort of feelings you have when you get to be my age, reader.

June 14th—Monday

As predicted, Bruno did call this "Hayley Iskender" around elevenish this morning. His vocal performance was a little shaky, the inaudibility percentage rather high, but he successfully made no mention of undersea domes and came away from the conversation with instructions to meet her this evening at a fashionable-sounding place called Toast, about which, being an old woman, I know nothing.

Looking neither uplifted nor apprehensive Bruno threw himself into a full day's caregiving. Everything went normally. Meals were served. I didn't die. At five he dressed for work without any extra primping and in the same clothes as ever, the green suit, the white shirt, and had the foresight to serve me a bowl of split pea soup and a cup of water before running the usual hand through his hair and disappearing.

He just came back a few minutes ago, at the stroke of ten o'clock—a little early, perhaps, but not unduly so—and if he was suffering he didn't show it. Seemed a little tired maybe, but change is always tiring, even good change.

So maybe I'm wrong and it all went fine.

June 15th—Tuesday

I have a few little pellets of info for you today, none of them particularly telling, and all of them, I'm afraid, rather discouraging.

For instance, I am writing these words at twenty-five minutes past *nine* in the evening and Bruno Maddox is already back from the second night of his probationary relationship with that strange girl from the Kam Wo. That means he was with her, and he didn't seem well just now during the trip back to my bedroom. He kept clearing his throat and sniffing in a way that recalled for me *precisely* the way I used to feel myself after one of those intolerable evenings spent trying to have romantic conversations with Davey McCracken back in 1913. I remember that feeling very well. It was a very bad feeling.

Bruno called the girl again just before lunch and once again did a perfectly workmanlike job of saying hello and copying down directions, today to a place called "Aluminum Bertrand," but when the 'phone call was over he remained in the nasty armchair with his thumb on the plunger of the 'phone, jiggling his foot and running a crooked finger back and forth across his upper lip, not looking very content.

"Toast," I learned during the Bathroom Shuffle this morning, turned out to be a bar quite near here whose interior resembles the inside of a giant bread toaster: with walls of scorched and dented tin, sawdust "crumbs" all over the floor, and one drinks one's drink out of a beige-painted tumbler that has TOAST in gold letters down the side and a ring of darker brown plastic fitted over the rim like the crust on a piece of bread. "I have to say," Bruno chuckled flatly as we choochooed slowly between the television and the foot of the electric bed, "that I felt slightly like a piece of bread . . . sitting in a giant toaster!"

Really? I pulsed him as the bathroom door swung shut behind me. *Was it that bad? I mean, are you saying that seriously, or . . .*

The bathroom door swung shut behind me.

And that's all I got to hear about TOAST.

I get the impression things are going poorly out there in the steaming city, though I could be wrong—which obviously I hope I am.

June 16th—Wednesday

No, I'm not wrong.

The topic of *Thirty UN!der Thirty* this evening was "Does Trial by Jury Always Mean Justice?" and I'm afraid I have to report that when Bruno Maddox in New York whispered his contribution ("Yes . . . I really think it does") there was real fear in his eyes. This was about five minutes before seven, thirty-five minutes before he was scheduled to meet the girl, and the boy was white—literally—as a sheet, and then just like last night when he got back to the apartment Bruno was blinking and sniffing and swallowing in that same post-excruciating-evening manner that I was trying to describe yesterday.

In fact, I think he may be losing his mind. This morning during the Bathroom Shuffle he told me about "Aluminum Bertrand," a Belgian restaurant with a futuristic, silvery spaceship theme, in a voice that was not his own. It was all hearty and rollicking, like the voice of a happy fat man. "And at one stage," he boomed as we neared the little step, "I drank a glass of fermented beer that had the flavor . . ." Bruno half bent his left leg, steadied me with one hand and *slapped his thigh* with the other, ". . . *of an orange*. Ho ho."

Obviously, I've *read* about people slapping their thighs, reader. I think most of us have. But until you've actually seen it done in the flesh . . . well, it's not a very natural gesture and it only went to heighten my sense of terrible foreboding.

Things are not going well for the boy out there.

June 17th—Thursday

Yes. Bruno Maddox is in hell. I witnessed him there myself this evening, with my own two earwax-colored eyes.

Ten past eight there were footsteps in the stairwell and Bruno's voice apologizing to someone for the conditions. (The conditions are very poor out in our stairwell: very cramped and pungent. Back when I could walk I would always get a vision of the *a* and *e* in "fæces" being squished together into one letter whenever I used the stairs. It was weird.) Then the door next door opened and shut. "I'll just quickly find the . . ." Bruno announced in a strange, disappearing voice, then came the sound of banging drawers in his bedroom.

Then came words I couldn't make out, in the same deepish female drone that was on the answering machine that day. Hayley made two remarks in all, each with an identical rhythmic structure: a few staccato, Morse codelike syllables, and then a long stream of sound as if the Morse code operator got shot mid-transmission and slumped forward onto his equipment.

That's when I looked at the fire door and saw that it was open. And I suddenly realized I had no idea what Bruno's policy is about keeping me secret.

Had he told the girl about me? Was that why she was here? To meet me? To help facilitate my transfer to a state-run institution?

Or had he genuinely left something in his bedroom drawers that he needed to collect, and he was just taking the chance that Hayley wouldn't push open the fire door? Or was that what he wanted? For her to discover me on her own, so that the cat could be free of the bag without his having actually willfully betrayed my confidence? Or was he trying to disgust her? Trying to make her leave him alone? That made sense. For his apartment is disgusting: not just messy but depressing. It's like a diorama of the caregiving mind, with half-finished plates of food and half-finished do-it-yourself projects all over the place, and instead of a traditional bachelor-style pile of laundry in one corner, Bruno has a *ridge* of laundry extending diagonally across the carpet from his bedroom door, formed over time by the failure of each item of soiled clothing lobbed out of his bedroom at night to reach *quite* as far as the last.

No matter what his motivation for bringing the girl here, Bruno had left the fire door open, leaving *me* open to discovery, and now I could hear strange sliding footsteps and then in the window, in the wedge of light reflecting through from Bruno's apartment, suddenly there she was, in shimmering silhouette. The girl was tallish, not visibly obese, and had long, straight hair. That was all I could see. She was just standing there, not moving, semitransparent and hovering like in that detective story about the nun without a face who appears to hikers in Scotland and scares them silly.*

Come on in, I pulsed her. *Discover me . . .*

"Eureka!" bellowed Bruno. "I have been successful!"

And the girl was gone.

When they reached the street I saw Hayley Iskender properly for the first time. Her hair was long and straight and pale, her eyes were set right at the edge of her face like some

---

Damon Trent and the Faceless Nun of Abercrombie. Currently out of print.

140

sort of frog or fish and she was slouching in a certain willowy way that thin blond women often do. She was attractive, I decided, though in a musty-looking sort of way. Her skin was pale, hardly glowing with health, and her clothes were fairly drab, from bottom to top: canvas shoes, faded blue jeans and a tight white T-shirt curling up at the lower hem to bare the merest sliver of midriff. Frumpiest of all was her cardigan, grayish purple and woolly, possibly homemade. It threw me slightly, that she was wearing that cardigan. Not only was it easily eighty degrees out there in the street—though she wasn't sweating—but people in New York don't usually wear items of casual, almost whimsical knitwear, even in winter. People in New York tend to dress either grittily or glamorously, and her cardigan was neither, about as jarring against the urban backdrop as my baggy black sweater had been back in early twentieth century rural England.

And then there was her . . . bearing. Hayley and Bruno were on the sidewalk outside the blasted shell of International Buckets Inc. to discuss routes or destinations or something, and so there was no particular reason why the girl's body should have been *moving* . . . but it absolutely wasn't at all. She was perfectly motionless, inert, standing like a statue with her thumbs hooked into the belt loops of her jeans. Even in the absence of wind the tops of the tied black garbage bags were stirring more than Ms. Hayley Iskender, and it occurred to me suddenly that maybe at some point she'd been a fashion model, not because she was that attractive, but because she embodied the sort of supernatural impassivity I imagine one would need to stand in the same spot all day long being accidentally stuck with pins by homosexuals. Then I changed my mind. A fashion model would never wear that cardigan. On further inspection there *was* actually a little ripple of movement around the girl's mouth as she spoke, and every ten seconds or so a slow blinking of the large eyes, which then returned to watching . . . watching . . .

Watching Bruno Maddox, who was a complete fucking mess. As Hayley spoke Bruno was violently jerking his gaze back and forth between the rusted legs of a fire escape's ladder and the pile of black garbage bags and furiously nodding his head. Then he started tugging at his nose, again and again, as if he genuinely wanted to remove it. His back suddenly buckled as if he'd been jumped upon. He straightened it. It buckled *again*. He straightened. "Shall we go?" said the girl (I read her flickering lips), at which Bruno suddenly threw back his head and *guffawed*, like a vampire in a movie when his dinner guests ask if they can have their coats back so they can go home. While his head was thrown back I caught his eye through the window. It was terrible what I saw: a lot of plain pain, of course, but also a dreadful surprise such as coroners famously see on the faces of gunshot victims. "Why am I like this?" he seemed to be pleading. "What happened? I used to be so . . ."

Because you're a caregiver, I pulsed down at him. *And I'm really, really sorry.*

Watching him prance wretchedly away in Hayley's wake, the guilt came over me stronger than ever. A young man should never have to look the way Bruno Maddox looked this evening. *Never.*

I sign off this evening forced to entertain the idea that I may in fact be the worst old woman in the history of the universe.

June 18th—Friday

Good news, bad news, reader.

The good news is that Bruno has the weekend off. "So that girl I've been seeing has to work this weekend," he whispered around tennish, upon his return from a place called Sushi Proto-Kyoto. "So I am going to be around this weekend and . . . and . . . and I'm sorry I'm putting you to bed so early. I'm just . . . shattered."

Please don't say you're sorry, I pulsed. *Just go and get some sleep.*

In fact, he went and got some whiskey.

The bad news is that on Monday morning the 'phone is going to ring and that girl is going to drag us all through a second week of this madness, despite the torment of Week One.

Mm?

How do I know?

Because I saw it in her face. Saw it in her face on Thursday, reader. She finishes what she starts, does Hayley Iskender. She has visible inertia. She said she'd give him two weeks and so, by criminy, two weeks it'll be, no matter the human cost.

June 19th—Saturday

Today was awful. Incredibly depressing.

The boy has been completely destroyed by the last five days. His grip on my shoulder during the Bathroom Shuffle was weak as spaghetti, and after serving me my cereal he tumbled into the nasty armchair and curled up fetally, watching TV with his eyes closed.

Had he stayed there in the armchair I think he could have done himself some good, recouped a little strength, but he didn't. Periodically he would jump to his feet, clap his hands, say something brisk and no-nonsense such as "Right!" and then proceed to squander whatever smidgen of energy he'd just accrued on a pointless and symbolic act of rebirth—loading the first eighteen inches of his Laundry Ridge into a pillowcase, folding an old newspaper in half as a prelude to recycling—before emitting a shuddering groan and diving back into the chair.

It was awful. It *is* awful. I feel like one of those marine biologists who ties a lamb carcass to a rope and throws it off the back of a boat to gauge how many sharks and piranhas there are in a particular stretch of sea—Bruno being the lamb carcass, and this dreadful week just ended, the sea. Today was the day I pulled in the rope . . . and there really doesn't seem to be much of him left. If I were a marine biologist this is the point where I would be gazing into the middle distance and saying "There's something down there."

June 20th—Sunday

Better day today. There was golf on television, the final round of a tournament. From eleven in the morning the young man Bruno Maddox was able to replace the dark pictures in his head with lovely green vistas of lawn and scapes of whizzing sky, sprays of sand and bushes of azalia, wise old voices murmuring praise. . . . Lying there in the armchair, wrapped tightly in a bedsheet, he drifted in and out of sleep, looking stronger and more alert each time he awoke. By 3 P.M. he had healed enough to order, receive and tip onto plates two portions of diverticulitis-friendly Chinese bean curd, and by late afternoon he had shed his sheet-cocoon and was sitting there quite erectly in his T-shirt and boxer shorts, looking rested and ready.

Thank you, I pulsed the television set. *Thank you for being kind to my friend.*

But then the sun began to set. On the screen an old man was trudging up to the eighteenth green with a commanding three-stroke lead in the golden light of a southern evening. As he lifted his putter and touched his cap to the crowds a whimper came from the armchair. With effort I swiveled my eyes. Bruno Maddox's chin was on his chest, and drops of liquid were falling from the poor lamb's eyes to his T-shirt.

Tears, reader.

The drops of liquid were tears.

June 21st—Monday

More golf to report, believe it or not, and possibly, just possibly, some good news as well.

Bruno and Hayley spent this evening just past at a popular nightspot called The Nineteenth Hole, a bar that's been designed to resemble an upscale suburban country club. The place features plush armchairs, an actual eighteen-hole miniature golf course running all the way around the room, and sepia-tinted photos on the walls of old-fashioned miniature golfers in caps and plus-fours posing in front of mini-windmills and open-mouthed clowns, etc.

I know all this, tragically, because this morning, while on

the 'phone to Hayley, Bruno, who was using the rollicking fat-man voice again, insisted on repeating the salient features of the place with faux delight as Hayley explained them to him.

It was a pretty grim audio spectacle, but here's the thing: Bruno actually looked *okay* just now when he rolled in. Not exactly happy. Not happy per se. More like *un*happy, but he looked unhappy in a calmer, more resigned way than last week, which strikes me as fantastic news. If he can just detach himself from what's happening out there with the girl, just muscle through it like you muscle through any unpleasant task, then he might be able to avoid any more actual *damage*.

June 22nd—Tuesday

Boy continues to bear up well. You should have seen his jaw just now as he put me to bed. It was firm, and resolute, and *invincible*, reader, like the side of a mountain.

He's toughing it out.

June 23rd—Wednesday

I'm already thinking about next week. I can't wait, reader. I simply cannot wait. This madness will be behind us. However damaged Bruno is right now, it doesn't matter. Because for the first time ever I'll be watching Bruno's mental health *improve* on a daily basis, as the memory of this horrific fortnight recedes, rather than crumble apart. It'll be a time of healing, of stock taking, a chance for Bruno to make some hard, but necessary decisions: for instance calling the Health Services and getting me out of his hair, or killing me, or something. Whatever. It doesn't matter. At the risk of counting my chickens prematurely, reader, my message for you this evening is that in my humble opinion we have made it through the minefield. Crisis has been averted. Everything is going to be fine.

Just fine.

June 24th—Thursday

Look, don't panic, all right? But something appears to have occurred, exactly what I don't know. Let me give you what information I do have and maybe we can piece it together.

Four minutes ago my eyes snapped open and I found myself still lying on my electric bed, out in the main body of the apartment. It was dark outside, the TV was on, the lights were glaring down and I saw by the clock on the video that it was 3:31. In the morning, reader. Three thirty-one in the morning.

And that's when I saw the boy through the fire door.

Bruno was sitting sideways in the open window of his apartment, gazing placidly out into the night. The topmost five buttons of his shirt were unfastened and in his hand was a little plastic bottle of mineral water whose cap, as I watched, he twirled off with his long, elegant fingers. He swigged, sluiced, and casually screwed back on the bottle cap, as if he hadn't a care in the world. So stunned was I by the apparent change in him that I made an involuntary gagging noise with my throat. He glanced over. "Oh hey," he said, in a soft, confident voice I hadn't heard since that first day back in February, the day we met. "How was dinner?"

Bruno set down his water and came through. His face, it struck me, had a glow to it, an inner radiance, and the touch of his hands as he helped me down off the electric bed was like the upholstery of a luxury car. I felt safe and supported, literally in good hands. "Easy now" were his tender words as I teetered on the little step, then "Well done," when my foot found the lower surface. In the bedroom he pulled the sheet up to my chin like a mother does to a child. "Goodnight," he said sincerely.

Something's happened.

Something *good*.

But what?

Could it simply have been the climate? The moment I woke up I knew the weather had improved. The street noise of Chinatown is usually just a big tangle of undifferentiated sound by the time it filters back to my windowless bedroom, but this morning I could hear all the different sounds distinctly: every clanking metal storefront, every *eep-eep-eep* of a reversing truck, every *tumf* of a falling cabbage. The pillow of humidity had been lifted from the city's face and the sounds bounced around in the thin air all clean and shiny, like the apartment was an aviary, filled with freshly painted metal birds.

Not that Bruno gave a shit. His grip on my body was as flaccid and corpselike as ever during the Bathroom Shuffle and he spent the Morning Session curled again on the nasty armchair, repeatedly knocking his head back on the upholstery. I have been skeptical since infancy of the proposition that cooking is an art form, that you can express via food ideas, feelings that other media won't support, but then came lunch—rough-hewn cubes of cheese on a bed of moist napkins—and I was forced to rethink that position.

So no. It can't just have been the weather.

Was it the party?

They went to a party this evening. I know, because ninety seconds after Bruno left for work at five-thirty there came a message from Hayley Iskender:

"Hi, it's me," she sighed, sounding even tireder than usual, "I hope you get this message before you leave for work. I'm going to be late to the *come hither* party. Be there closer to eight-thirty than seven-thirty because I [she sighed] I have to go and interview an astrophysicist about the effects of neutrino storms and gamma radiation on the human complexion. It's stupid. Anyway, the party starts at six so feel free to go straight up to the roof and have a drink. My office is on the twenty-third floor if you want to wait there but . . . look, anyway I'll see you at eight-thirty."

Hmm.

Bruno *didn't* get this message before leaving for work, nor did he call in to retrieve it, and so I think I can safely assume that directly after *Thirty UN!der Thirty*, say at 7:05 P.M., Bruno Maddox will have been climbing into a cab outside the American Stock Exchange and directing it uptown to the midtown offices of Hayley's magazine *come hither*. At 7:20 P.M. he'll have been giving his name to someone with a clipboard, squeezing into an elevator, and a minute after that emerging onto the rooftop of a building with at least twenty-three stories, possibly a good deal more.

With a start time of six o'clock my guess is that the party will have been in semi to full swing at 7:21, and for the sake of argument let's say it was a fairly standard magazine party of the sort they feature quite regularly on the Glamour Channel: hordes of attractive young people, exuberantly dressed and milling about between giant blowup reproductions of magazine covers; white-jacketed barmen behind tables full of liquor; a band playing music ... possibly on some sort of raised dais ...

Is that as far as good old-fashioned logic and deduction can take me?

No.

It isn't.

Hayley being Hayley, a young lady burdened with a sense of responsibility so keen and inflexible that she'd rather drag three innocents through hell—only two that she knows about, I suppose—than break off a ridiculous "probationary" relationship founded on a gross misunderstanding, I bet my bottom dollar that she will have *allowed* for the possibility of Bruno not getting her 'phone message and will have ... will have, I'm almost certain, left word with one of her colleagues to keep an eye out for a tall young man in a horrible green suit who may or may not be nodding his head uncontrollably. No later than 7:30 P.M., this colleague, probably a woman, given *come hither*, will have spotted Bruno Maddox looking lost, will have accosted him, explained Hayley's lateness, showed him to a drink, engaged him in small talk, then, finding the small talk rather heavy going, will have started introducing him to other people. That much is just common sense.

Where are we now? Quarter to eight? Ten to eight ... ?

Hmm.

Okay, I'm stuck.

Maybe this is where the weather *does* come into play. Even from my filthy, low-rent vantage point down here in Chinatown I could tell it was a pretty damn magical evening out there in the World. The air was warm and light, the sky a long, drawn-out blue with a thumbnail scratch of white moon at its apex . . . Frankly, reader, it was the kind of evening that makes old ladies like me wish we could have the use of our legs back just for ten short minutes, to one final time stride out and feel the air infiltrate our clothing, the nip of evening on our naked forearms. And for Bruno? After months of claustrophobia and fetid old-woman-stinky air? To be up beneath the luminous dome of the sky with nobody needing to be fed or walked to the bathroom or have pills counted out for them, nor with any stone-faced person in a cardigan hunched across a little table from him in a bar, sucking the straw of her drink and blinking wizzically because whatever he just mumbled was inaudible or nonsensical? To be able, for the first time since arriving in this notoriously liberating country, just to talk to people without having to make any particular kind of sense, or come across as any particular sort of person . . . just to drink whiskey after whiskey without caring how it seems . . . ? It must have been fantastic.

Eight-thirty.

Hayley Iskender arrives.

So there she is, she's there by the little brick cabana that houses the elevator, looking around for him, just like he did for her, and now, like the colleague, it is Bruno's turn to go and accost.

He is ready.

He feels fine.

He feels *fine*.

Jacket and trousers moving smoothly in unison, the boy knifes through the crowd . . . and then he is with her.

"Hi," is his first line.

"Hi."

She will have studied him, at that point, studied him with her tired eyes. How could she not have done? He must have been looking so . . . so different. So let's give her a line expressing that. How about "You look . . . better."

Boy has to nod . . . but not furiously. Just once. Calm. Contained. "I *feel* better. Look . . . Hayley, I'm sorry about the last two weeks. I've been a freak."

Does she accept the apology? Mmm . . . yeah, what am I talking about? Of course she does. No reason not to.

"It's fine."

Of course she does. As bad as it's been for her she knows it's been ten times worse for him. No hard feelings.

"Sorry about before, as well. That night I told you I wanted to live in an undersea dome. I was having a tough day."

"Don't say that." She has to smile. "I liked the dome."

And what then? What next? They go to get Hayley a drink . . . ?

No.

She's too tired.

She probably just wants to go home.

And Bruno Maddox is a gentleman. He rides with her in the elevator . . . even helps her find a cab . . . and then . . . and then . . .

And then the next thing I know he's back here at three in the morning with a radiant glow and an open shirt and a little bottle of mineral water and also, if I'm to be perfectly honest, the tiniest whiff of vaginal fluid clinging to his . . .

Oh my God.

It can't be.

June 25th—Friday

But it is.

After clearing away breakfast this morning Bruno Maddox, still visibly loose-limbed and reeking of inner tranquillity, put a call through to the girl at her workplace and held up his end of a conversation that I can only describe as *unmistakably postcoital*, involving lots of quiet little chuckles and examining of fingernails.

And if further proof were needed that something sexual and cataclysmic happened last night, the time now, as I write these words, is fiveish in the afternoon, and I have already been put to bed. In other words, Bruno's out there with her again, voluntarily, and so he's not planning on coming back until morning—which I'm sure you don't need me to tell you, reader, is the characteristic behavior pattern of a Young Man Having Sex.

And I don't know how I feel about that.

I don't know what to say.

I'm just stunned.

June 26th—Saturday

I continue to be stunned by the fact that Bruno Maddox and Hayley Iskender have managed to convert their nightmarish, frigid, and doomed relationship into a steamy and fluid one that seems to be thriving—and as far as I can tell the two of them spent this sun-soaked, midsummer Saturday ambling idyllically in and out of shops—but I think it behooves me to be supportive. So I'll just state my reservation once and never mention it again.

My reservation is this:

What if Bruno Maddox, rather than being cured of his Caregiver's Syndrome, is merely in some flukish remission brought on the other night by a never-to-be-repeated convergence of drunkenness, good weather, and possibly even the altitude of the *come hither* building roof? Surely Caregiver's Syndrome isn't something you can just shake off in a single evening like a dose of the flu. What if the remission wears off? What if it all crumbles apart, as the strain of caring for a hundred-something-year-old woman once again wreaks its inexorable havoc? Reader, what *then*? I can't help but think that after enjoying this short taste of happiness, after—as the poets say—having "supped on Paradise," Bruno Maddox now has a lot further to fall should the bad old days reassert themselves. His face today was full of relief and gratitude and surprise, the same surprise that I feel at his evidently having managed to use the flimsy shovel of his genitals to tunnel his way out of prison. I just hope it doesn't turn out that he's actually dug his own grave with it.

Anyway, there. Those are my only concerns about the great wave of Young Romance that seems to have crashed down upon us these last few days, and obviously I hope they're completely unfounded. There's no denying that Bruno does seem genuinely happy. On this, what should have been the first day of his return to bachelorhood and of a slow and painful convalescence, he seemed like an entirely recovered man, a man who'd never been sick. You should have seen him when he stopped by this afternoon to feed me and put me to bed: he looked happy, relaxed and somehow even *fit*, clad from neck to waist in a glorious new item of clothing: a navy blue T-shirt with an official gold seal on the breast that says "New York Department of Housing."

Plus the boy's fingers in my flesh during the long shuffle back to my stinking care were firm and steady like I've never felt, and certainly gave no hint of any impending break-down. Time will tell, I suppose, and it occurs to me that before it does I should spend a few days giving you another installment of my autobiography, which, as you may have noticed, I have been neglecting.

No, actually, you know what? I think I'll exercise my old woman's prerogative and do that tomorrow. My fingers are hurting slightly.

June 27th—Sunday

Don't know about you but whenever someone says to me "the nineteen fifties" I always call to mind this quietly famous piece of film footage from that era involving a suburban American family having dinner. I'm sure you know it. The family has four members: a nurturing young mother—with a large, sexy bottom—standing with a plastic tray and about to serve food to her seated husband, whose hair is slicked back, her son, who has freckles and a stripy T-shirt, and her daughter, who is blond and has pigtails. All four are grinning wildly, in a somewhat sinister fashion, and over the top of the whole thing, if you're lucky enough to have sound, is a fruity, singsong voice saying: "... and *Mrs.* Olsen is happy because she has a new *vacuum* cleaner, and little *Timmy* is happy because he has a new toy machine gun, and little *Mindy* is happy ... etc." which frankly only makes the scene seem even *more* sinister.

I don't think the family themselves are famous people and yet the footage pops up on television all the time in different contexts. You can see it quite regularly on the news, for instance, under reports about the economy, and just the other day I saw it used in a promotional music video by some Negro hybrid poet-musician who was wearing a silver suit and sunglasses, and scowling into a fisheye lens that he was going to drive to white suburbia and shoot everybody. It always takes me back, seeing those few short seconds of footage, that sinister family at a table, because for me at least that's exactly how it was.

In 1948 I'd moved to London from Bunley Village with the express intention of finding an American man and persuading him to marry me—can't really say why except that I had spent the handful of postwar years in a state of increasing dismay at the deepening drabness of my homeland. The intense olive-green poignancy that had made England such a vivid place to live during the Second World War seemed to have faded away and not been replaced by anything. The country of my birth had become drab, and colorless—unknowable to me—and around 1946, I had slipped into a deep depression, a years-long black tunnel down which I aimlessly wandered until one day, at the Bunley Coronet, slumped in my velveteen seat waiting for the main feature to begin, I was exposed to a technicolor newsreel about the booming postwar U.S. economy, featuring a happy-looking family having dinner around a plastic table, and I found myself sprinting tearfully out into the sunshine with a whole new vision of what my life could be.

Americans were pretty thin on the ground, however, even down in London. Every night of the week I attended singles mixers in dusty north London church halls, guarding my handbag in the center of the grimy parquet dance floor and being pestered by scads of creepy old Englishmen sidling up and whispering, "Might it be possible . . . ? Might it be possible . . . ?" with breath that smelled invariably of sweet, decantered sherry.

And then one night, just as I had slung my handbag over my shoulder and was reaching into it to forage for my bicycle clips, I suddenly spotted the best-looking man I'd ever seen over on the far side of the room, helping himself to punch from the punch bowl. I can't recall whether I found him attractive before I realized he was American . . . though, actually, the more I think about it, he was attractive in such a way that he could have only *been* American: tanned, and tall, and muscular, wearing a neon-pink plastic outergarment with which to shield himself from the drizzly English clime.

"Good punch?" was my opening line, after essentially being winched across the parquet by the man's attractiveness.

"Not really," he grimaced, and we fell to talking. He claimed his name was Chester McGovern and that he was a nuclear-power engineer, in England on a month's loan from the American government.

"What'll you do when the month is over?"

He shrugged. "Go home I guess. Quiet little town in Wisconsin, America, try and find me a gal and settle down."

"Wow. Great. I nonchalantly poured myself a punch and sipped it, discreetly shifting my handbag over my chest in order to hide my suddenly pounding heart. "Look . . . do you . . . do you maybe want to go to a museum or something tomorrow?"

He did, as it happened, and thus began our whirlwind courtship.

For two wet weeks that winter Chester and I fed ducks in the park and went to the museums, drank coffee in cafés with steamed-up windows. We parted around fourish for propriety's sake (this was still only the nineteen fifties; it wasn't seemly for courting couples to spend all day together) but then after dark reconvened in Chester's damp, dingy lodgings where by an iridescent slab of gas heater we'd dunk chocolate biscuits into mugs of mulled cider and talk, at my insistence, of things American.

And boy oh boy did I like what I was hearing. The word picture Chester painted for me of Fordham, Wisconsin, sounded exactly like the footage that had set my heart racing at the cinema: a lush suburban idyll of automated bowling alleys and appliance stores and newly painted houses, behind each of whose façades, I felt sure, sat a grinning family of four about to nourish themselves on convenience foods served from a lightweight plastic tray—the perfect antidote to black-and-white, postwar England.

And perhaps, I realized, it also sounded like something else: the futuristic modern paradise that me grand-da had predicted all those years ago back in Murbery, on the afternoon of the night he died, back when I was a little girl. Not much of what the old man had said to me that evening had made any sense whatsoever—I had never, for instance, figured out what he meant by the statement that I was "allergic to the past" or what the significance was of that little blue dress I still had in my luggage somewhere—but what my tiny girlish brain *had* absorbed that evening was that in his opinion humankind was destined for some sort of unimprovable, ultramodern state in which people like me—whatever that meant—would finally be happy.

We were on the seventh hole of the putting green of London's Hyde Park when Chester finally asked me to marry him. Fearful of appearing too keen—this was still only the nineteen fifties; women weren't supposed to appear too keen—I trained my gaze on some distant tree and made a great show of thinking about it.

In fact, I did think about it.

Was I *sure* about marrying Chester McGovern? He was a man after all, just like Davey McCracken had been a man all those years ago—and with a similar sort of name, coincidentally. Forging and maintaining healthy, plausible relationships with men wasn't exactly my strong suit. In fact, back in the thirties, as far as I could recall, I had decided not to marry Mr. Montgomery for the sole, specific reason that he too was a man. Was I really ready to try all that again?

Oh what the hell.

"I'll marry you if we don't ever have to sleep together and you don't mind me being a little distant occasionally," I found myself blurting.

Chester's putt sailed wide. He followed the shot with his

eyes, then straightened out of his stance and fixed me with a hard stare. The intensity of the moment was suddenly too much for me, and lowering my own eyes, I bunched up the fabric of my raincoat pocket in such a way that my golf ball bulged up and *tocked* down upon the green felt tee where I distractedly tapped it back and forth with the blade of my putter.

"That's fine," said Chester eventually. "That's absolutely fine."

———

Ten days later I blinked awake in a low-ceilinged, primrose-yellow bedroom, with a vague memory of drinking too much on an airplane and, some days prior to that, having married Chester McGovern in a quick civic ceremony. Not knowing where I was, I turned my face to the light and found that I was looking through the slats of a venetian blind—a remotely controllable one, by the looks of it—at a great stretch of clean blue sky such as one never, *ever* saw in England.

In merely bra and panties, I sprang from bed, threw on some clothes, and descended the stairs of what I realized was my new home. I liked it, reader. I liked it a lot. The carpet was all swirly, the wallpaper was interestingly textured, and the spacious though low-ceilinged living room was filled with hi-fis and televisions and a great stack of brightly colored board-game boxes. Across a dividing countertop I also spied my new husband, wearing an apron in what seemed to be an equally well-appointed kitchen.

"Hey, it's me," I said. "I'm awake."

Chester whirled and held his spatula aloft like a Viking sword. "Welcome to Fordham, Wisconsin, honey!"

"Thank you. Thank you." I waved with my hand. "Are you making breakfast?"

"Sure am!"

"Excellent. Well, I'm going to take a quick stroll. Looks like a lovely day out there."

"Break a leg!"

It was more than lovely, I decided after I had walked a few blocks; it was magnificent. And so was Fordham, Wisconsin. The town was a seemingly endless grid of pastel-colored houses and manicured lawns, each of which was actually being further manicured as I passed by a friendly looking patriarch on a lawnmower, each of whom waved at me. Waving back and I gawped at the sheer variety of technology on display. There was a lawnmover shaped like a speaker's podium, at which the gardener stood erect, almost as if he were lecturing the grass to be shorter. Another was segmented into two black oval blobs, like an insect's body, one blob to cut, the other to gather the cuttings. Most impressive of all was a lawnmower that cut the grass *all by itself*, freeing its owner up to stand proudly nearby waving—in this case at a newly arrived, still quite sexy fifty-year-old English woman.

That's when I noticed something was amiss.

The man *didn't stop waving*. Five seconds passed, then ten, and still those five pink fingers were flapping at me, flapping, flapping, flapping.

I stifled a scream and sprinted back to our house.

"That was just a little spurt of false jet-lag energy," I told Chester in the kitchen. "I'm going upstairs to zonk again."

"Golden slumbers!" yelled my solicitous husband, over the insistent mechanical ping of a food-preparation device.

*　*　*

Reappearing after an uneasy nap I found our front door open and Chester standing there in conversation with a shapely young brunette, also in an apron and holding a pie.

"Oh here she is, here she *is*," the woman squealed at my approach. She handed her pie onto Chester and grabbed my wrist. "Oh, Chest! You didn't tell me she was beautiful!"

"Yes I did," said Chester quickly. "Darling, this is Betty."

"Good to meet you, Betty. Are you a neighbor?"

"Oh isn't your accent *adorable*! Yes, I live *just next door*. And I'm the head of the local *ladies* group. Oh I can't *wait* to introduce you to the other girls. We have *such* a good time."

"Oh wow. Fantastic."

". . . *such* a good time . . ." Betty repeated in a faraway voice, her grip tightening on my hand. "We have *such* a good time. You know," she leaned close and confided, "they say these small towns are dull."

"Oh. Do they?"

Betty's eyes, which I had taken initially for merely glassy, I noticed now to be glittering with evil, and suddenly I wanted my hand back worse than I had ever wanted anything.

"But we have *such* a good time . . ."

Finally she left, and rather than let the issue fester I addressed it head on. "Chester," I said, "was that woman being deliberately *sinister*?"

"Mm?" My husband was gnawing the cellophane off an electric foot massager. "Oh no. That's just how people are round here. Friendly."

On an impulse I sprang to the window and swept aside the plastic curtain. At the far end of the road an ambulance had backed up to a house, and floating faintly on the air you could hear a woman sobbing hysterically . . .

"'Friendly'?" I muttered to myself. "Or sinister."

"Hey, hey, now. What's that you say?" Having dropped his appliance Chester came up from behind to hug me.

"Mm? Oh nothing."

[28 AUG--1:52 A.M.
this whole fifties section is hackneyed and ridiculous and pathetically unbelievable]

Reaching behind me, I pinched Chester's buttock affectionately. "Really. It's nothing."

June 28th—Monday

And, reader, it really *was* nothing. After continuing to creep about the place for a few days as if I were the heroine of some particularly terrible modern novel about a middle-aged female detective probing the shocking underbelly of a superficially pleasant little town, my jet lag wore off and I was able to see the place with clearer eyes.

Fordham, Wisconsin, actually wasn't that "sinister" when you got to know it. Betty Olsen, I heard from people, just happened to speak in a repetitive, rather drugged-out manner. As for the psychotically waving man with the lawnmower, fifteen seconds, when you think about it, isn't actually *that* long to be waving at a person who has come to a standstill in the roadway and is staring at you like a lunatic. As for the ambulance and the person sobbing . . . well, welcome to human existence, reader. Occasionally people have accidents, and when they do, then it's other people's duty to call an ambulance.

No. I decided upon reflection that I had been discomfited those first few groggy days by something far, far subtler:

Fordham, Wisconsin, *wasn't actually modern*. All those gadgets and conveniences, the bells and whistles that had reminded me initially of me grand-da's modern paradise, were on closer examination entirely ornamental. Our car, for instance, a sporty lime-green number provided by Chester's work, had an impressive set of seemingly aerodynamic fins running along the rear of the fuselage, and yet the thing could hardly top fifty miles an hour—let alone actually *fly*. Same situation with our hi-fi system in the recreation room. Despite nine speakers and a whole battery of complicated-looking knobs and switches protruding from its sleek, black housing—including one toggle switch labeled CLASSICAL/POPULAR—the quality of the sound was terrible and there was nothing you could do about it. And then there were those lawnmowers. They all looked fantastic from a distance, the most ostensibly hi-tech pieces of equipment I'd ever seen and yet, to a machine, those lawnmowers were about as efficient at cutting grass as me mam used to be with a rusted and buckled old hand scythe, as evidenced by the fact that the good men of Fordham had to spend all weekend, every weekend, mowing their blessed lawns.

I was rather pleased with this observation, that suburban nineteen fifties America was something of a sham, though obviously a little disappointed that me grand-da's vision of an ultramodern utopia where me and my little blue dress could finally feel at home had still not come to pass. One evening, in fact, to test my grim hypothesis, I put on my little blue dress just to see how Chester would react to it—and sure enough he completely freaked out.

"Jeepers criminy" Chester said from the foot of the

stairs as I hove into view on the landing. "What are you wearing?"

"Dab of perfume," I curtsied playfully, "little blue dress, hoop earrings. *¿Qué es el problema?*"

He jingled his car keys in agitation. "You can't wear that. I . . . I will not be seen with you looking like that."

"*¿Porque no?*"

"Because it's a goddam . . . freak show . . . costume . . . and the Olsens are decent people." We were supposed to be having dinner with Betty and Dale at a local fondue restaurant.

I pouted. "You don't like it?"

Chester went white and his veins stood out. "No," he mouthed.

"Jesus. What's your problem?" I put my hands on my hips and frowned at him. "You're acting like it's got holes cut out for my nipples or something. Can you please relax?"

But, Chester didn't want to relax. Quickly he was on his knees on the swirly carpet, covering his face and peeking at me through his fingers as if I were the Virgin Mary and he were some Portuguese goatherd who'd encountered me in the hills. "Modern?" he quavered hysterically. "Are you *nuts*? That's like something out of the eighteenth century . . . or the twenties . . . or . . . oh yeah, you know what?" He jumped up and jabbed his finger. "It's like something from the twenties *and* the eighteenth century. There's like five different styles in that goddam dress and that's why I suddenly gotta puke so bad!"

"Okay fine. Don't pop your cork. I'll go and change."

Which I did. I went and changed, and in fact I was privately rather glad Chester had hated my little blue dress and that we weren't living in the Future me grand-da had predicted after all. I had forgotten how much it made my head hurt to think about all of that, forgotten how little sense it all made. The simple fact was, as I had perhaps known in the back of my mind all the time, that grand-da's whole theory about how there was some sort of cosmic difference between the Past and the Future such that a person could be "allergic" to one and perfectly comfortable in the other was a steaming pile of nonsense. How could there be a difference between the Past and the Future? Surely it just depends on where one stands. Now it is always the Present. Everything that's already happened is the Past. Everything that hasn't happened yet is the Future. End of story.

Pretending to sulk and clad in a tight pink dress that made my hips look big, I accompanied Chester to Heidi's Fondue World where we all got fairly squiffy on gin and ended up having a pretty nice time.

The next morning, while Chester slumbered, I crept out of bed and down to the garage where, with a pair of "electronic" garden shears, I snipped my little blue dress into three pieces and stuffed them in the incinerator. As the flames took hold I shed a tear. But only one, reader. Because for all its sentimental value, and despite everything we had been through together, there was just no getting round the fact that my little blue dress was possibly the most headache-inducing and downright irritating piece of clothing that any young girl had ever had the misfortune to be . . .

Actually, hold on a minute.

Stop the text.

I think I may have just had a major revelation, possibly of Nobel Prize–winning caliber.

Chester's criticism of my dress that evening back in the

fifties, that it seemed to be haphazardly paying homage to multiple different fashion traditions simultaneously: That's how people dress *now*. In fact, that's the *only* way they dress now. Turn on the television right at this moment, reader—seriously, go and do it—and I swear to god you'll see a young man wearing a gas-station-attendant's shirt from the nineteen fifties above a pair of nineteen thirties German golfing trousers, or something. That's the *style* now. That's the fashion. The only clothes anyone ever wears these days are clothes from the Past, and if you tune into the Fashion Channel you'll find that all they ever talk about is how such and such a style is "making a comeback" or some supposedly ground-breaking avant-garde designer is cheekily trying to *repopularize* flared trousers or the ten-foot-diameter hoop skirt, or chain mail, or loincloths, or the figleaf. No one invents anything *new*, do you see what I'm saying? It's all from the Past.

And my revelation is this:

What if that's because *the Past is over*?

What if the reason everyone's running around in wildly mismatched historical clothing is because we're no longer embedded in any particular era, because history itself has stopped happening? Back in twenties Paris, even if you thought you were the most free-thinking, rule-breaking rebel in the world, it would still never even *occur* to you to combine a military jacket from WWI with a pair of turn-of-the-century riding boots, because you knew that rather than making you look glamorous or creative it would just make you look like you didn't have any money. So like everyone else you wore the most up-to-date clothing available, which at the time was long skirts and floppy, bell-shaped hats.

But now . . . well, it's like people getting dressed in the

morning have the entire history of human clothing stretched out before them for the plundering. They can choose clothes from whenever they like: a shirt from one era, a pair of trousers from another . . . because they're *not in an era themselves*. Eras are *finished*. And so is the idea that everyone has to dress appropriately for their "role." Take Bruno's Housing Department T-shirt. I don't know if I mentioned this but the boy doesn't actually work for the Housing Department. And his basketball shoes. He *doesn't play basketball*. He doesn't even know what a basketball looks like, as far as I know. But do Bruno's clothes cause confusion? Does anyone ever stop him in the street and demand that he come provide shelter for them and their kids, or ask if they can get tickets to his next game? *No*. Because the people in the street, who are all wearing exuberantly mismatched clothing themselves, understand that nobody's limited to being any particular type of person anymore, to any particular role. Back in the past, a village blacksmith was a village blacksmith. Whenever you saw him he was wearing a leather apron, and if you asked him what he did with himself he would look at you like you were crazy and then say something like, "Um . . . I'm the village blacksmith. I work with metal." And if you ever went to a new village? One you'd never visited before? And you saw a man wearing a leather apron and banging on an anvil . . . ? Well, then you knew that this man *too* was a village blacksmith.

But not now, reader. Not anymore. See a man in a leather apron on the streets of Twenty-first-Century Manhattan, reader—even one holding a steaming red-hot horseshoe in a pair of tongs—and good luck guessing who he actually is. Oh sure, he *could* be a blacksmith, I suppose, but he's a good deal more likely to be a screenwriter doing research for a movie about blacksmiths or bass player for The Blacksmiths or an extra from a fashion show or a millionaire en route to a fancy dress party. And if he actually is a blacksmith? A fully trained one with metal-working experience who isn't planning to ever do anything else? Then you can bet your bottom dollar he spends most of his time driving out to fancy suburbs to make wrought-iron garden gates and accept huge checks in his sooty hands from bored rich women who will immediately get on the 'phone and tell their friends about how they just had a blacksmith—an actual blacksmith! in a leather apron!—come to their house, do you see? He's the exception that proves the rule. History has ended and we don't *need* people to have fixed identities anymore because the world is now *finished*, there's nothing more that needs doing. We don't need anyone to make any more horseshoes. We don't need any more soldiers to fight any more wars. Finally, this is the end state, and we're going to celebrate that fact by going to parties in leather aprons and military helmets. In fact we're going to throw parties where everyone dresses up in clothes from a particular decade, and gigglingly dances to popular music from that same era to express our relief that we no longer have to live like that, embedded in one particular time. Oh, and you know what? We're going to design bars and nightclubs that look like toasters or golf courses just to acknowledge the fact that this is no longer the past and nobody, and nothing, is under any obligation to actually be how they seem, but rather . . .

Look, I'm rambling. Let me just state my revelation once again, very clearly and quietly, and then never fuss with it again. All I'm trying to say, reader, is that I now think that maybe in a sense me grand-da was actually telling the *truth* on that bizarre afternoon back in 1905. Maybe a person can be "allergic to the Past" and only comfortable in the Future, because it seems to be that there is an actual concrete difference between the two time periods. The Past was the process of the world coming-of-age, very slowly, by trial and error, during which everyone had to dress ridiculously and only have one job. The Future *is* that finished state, in which you can dress and act and be however you want, and in which everything new is recycled from the Past.

There.

June 29th—Tuesday

Once again I want to say how truly sorry I am about yesterday's sudden foray into metaphysical navel picking. As yours was, probably, my first thought was that there's really no place for that sort of material in an old woman's memoir, even a clever, fancy one like this.

But on reflection you know I'm not so sure.

What about this:

What if Bruno Maddox never had Caregiver's Syndrome in the first place?

That would make sense, because to be honest with you I was never wholly convinced that Bruno Maddox had Caregiver's Syndrome. Dr. Hearne states pretty unambiguously in *The Caregiver's Bible* that it's the awfulness of watching *someone you love* deteriorate on a daily basis that gives you the syndrome, and Bruno's affection for me, from the outset, has been as strong as a cup of weak coffee into which someone has poured an entire gallon of water.

So if he never had Caregiver's Syndrome, why has he been such a mess all these months?

It's going to sound slightly bogus but I'll tell you.

Because he's a Citizen of the Future, reader. Because Bruno Maddox was born to participate in this crazy whirling endless era where the old rules of who a person can or can't be have been retired. That's why he came here to New York. He was driven here by his soul, which had recognized in the televised images of this teeming, chaotic city the backdrop for its liberation.

But instead what happened? A few short hours after his plane hit the tarmac? That's right: a horrible old woman came along and denied him his destiny, ripped it away from him just as he was about to sink his teeth into it, and all these months, these cramped and tedious months, he's had to watch the Future dance and frolic through a grimy set of windows, close enough to touch but utterly unattainable because of a certain disgusting old woman. Do you follow? It hasn't been the strain of looking after me that's made him so miserable. It's been the frustration of having all this Futuristic Chaos so close and not being able to just . . . dive in. Freedom, freedom everywhere—as a poet might say—but not a drop to . . . have.

I know this new theory sounds somewhat abstract and unconvincing but sometimes that's how truth is, at first glance. And it really does make sense. Think about the night of the *come hither* party.

Up there beneath the dome of the sky, having high-speed and largely meaningless conversations with wild, exotic people . . . women in long flowing gowns of the Past . . . a muscular Negro in an "I [heart] My Cat" T-shirt . . . three men who weren't lumberjacks but who were *dressed* like lumberjacks . . . Bruno was finally among his people, his environment. . . . What if he finally got in touch with himself? What if all at once it clicked into place?

What if he really is cured?

I think he might be.

And that's good news.

I mean obviously if something were to happen to *deprive* him of his new freedom at this stage then all bets would be off. His reaction would be extreme, sudden and completely understandable.

But . . . maybe that doesn't need to happen.

June 30th—Wednesday

I conclude this turbulent month of entries with the news that today I ate some beef with gold oh and, reader, you may want to read this sentence again.

Yes, that's right.

Beef with *gold*.

The beef with gold was an appetizer from a Japanese restaurant called F2 that Bruno and Hayley seem to have visited last night and it arrived at my swingable side table in the smallest and most delicate paper bag I had ever seen. In fact, so entranced was I by the flimsy lustrousness of the bag that I barely noticed as Bruno tipped its contents onto my scratched, plastic plate.

But then came his words: "Oh, that shiny stuff is gold." My eyes swung to the dark-red blob and my mind got blown clean out the back of my skull. For minutes I lay there in the midday heat, staring at the little moist mound of redness with the yellow metallic flakes.

You see, we never used to eat beef with gold in the past, reader. Beef was a meat, and gold was a metal—a *precious* metal no less. Whole nations fought *wars* over gold . . . and now here people are eating it as a garnish? Not even as a main course but just as an *appetizer*?

I mean, do you see? It's like everything else in this crazy, fluid culture called "the future." Everything's out of context, forming wildly playful combinations with everything else . . . taking on new functions . . . laughing at all the old functions . . .

Life is crazy, here in the Future.

Crazy, reader, and pretty damn beautiful.

[28 AUG--2:04 A.M
rein it in, motherfucker. long way to go.]

July

July 1st—Thursday

When the 1960s dawned I was teetering on the edge of Manhattan's Fifth Avenue in a whirling blizzard awash in a complex set of emotions that stemmed, in large part, from the fact that just the night before, New Year's Eve, as my husband, Chester McGovern, and I sat in matching recliners, with matching gin and tonics, listening to the world welcome in the new decade on the radio, I had sent the words "I just can't keep on living like this" spinning across the gilded tile-and-ormolu coffee table. Chester, to his credit, had merely nodded. Why? Because he'd seen it coming (my departure). We both had. As the years had disappeared amidst the cocktails, pies and *ffft*-ing garden sprinkler systems of Fordham, Wisconsin, so had whatever smidgen of love it was that had drawn me and Chester together. By 1955, we had basically stopped speaking. By 1957, we were eating our meals at different times, in separate rooms. By 1959, there was a slightly childish strip of duct tape dividing

Chester's side of the living room from mine, if he trespassed over which I would hurl my gin and tonic at the wall and accuse him of being a shitty husband.

Being a typically solipsistic American male, Chester blamed himself—I think—for the breakup of our marriage, but he was only half right. There was an additional factor. On the TV news I had recently been seeing reports from New York of something called the "Beatnik Scene," a half-lit world of drugs and free-form poetry and smoky jazz dives where anyone who liked could just jump up on stage and start hammering away at the bongos. The spectacle was so achingly reminiscent to me of Paris in the twenties, in so many ways my finest hour, that even if Chester had been the least annoying man in the world I think I still would have had no choice but to gather my belongings into a bundle, snick my front door quietly shut in the night, and beat a path once again toward a lawless, enchanted city where people were free to be themselves.

However, that midnight bus from Fordham was cold and uncomfortable, and as I wriggled around on the token upholstery, my suddenly sixty-year-old cheekbone yammering against the frigid pane, I allowed myself to wonder whether perhaps I had made an enormous mistake in leaving Fordham's comforts and security. Mile after sleepless, frozen mile the misgivings intensified until the bus shuddered up over the lip of the Midtown Tunnel and I felt my old womanly chin start to tremble, and when we came to a stop and I dismounted I began to cry.

But then I felt it, the energy, flowing all around me as I stood like a speck of dust in the great jeweled trench of Fifth Avenue, beside the river of groaning traffic, being jostled, and cursed at by purposeful unashamed fat men and gorgeous, scowling young women in fur hats and toughened leather clothing, I had made the right decision. This was where I needed to be, and not a moment too soon on that first day of the sixties, because there was something in the air. Something big. Just like back in Paris, I was in at the start, and right at the heart, of something truly *massive*.

And why am I telling you this, reader?

Why do you think? Because that exact same feeling is abroad in my apartment these days, the scent of new beginnings. It's a scent, of course, that has been building steadily in strength for the last few weeks, but it attained a whole new level of pungency today, this first day of July when after lunch, around noon,* Bruno Maddox headed off for his daily grocery run and returned an hour later with the words, "Sorry I was gone so long. I took a stroll. It's really nice out there."

Because that's when the weirdest thing happened.

The instant Bruno finished speaking it was like my vision melted away and got replaced by a flood of *pictures in my mind*. I'm not talking about imaginings, reader, or visualizations. I'm talking about *actual cinematic pictures* of Bruno Maddox . . .

. . . *out there on the streets of Chinatown, knifing through the hordes of miniature ethnic people in his gel-cushioned hi-tech shoes like some sort of . . . some sort of space detective in a movie, poking his head on a hunch into a*

---

* Lunch these days is at half past eleven to maximize my digestion time before dinner, which is these days being served at four in the afternoon so that I can be bathroomed and in bed by *five*, so that Bruno doesn't have to deal with me again until he gets back from Hayley's around ninish the next morning.

crazy little aisleless shop where an old Chinese man is selling circuit board by the square foot and old remote controls by the pound . . . then he's back on the street, following his nose, his bliss, keeping pace for a while with a gang of Asian youths, all angular dyed-tuft hairstyles and beepers and pocket 'phones, and then having his attention suddenly seized by the way that boom: *in the middle of a row of crumbling mossy tenements there has violently been inserted an immaculate, dustless nest of automated bank machines . . . in other words an explosive, organic collision of different textures, and eras, and socioeconomic strata . . .*

Then the vision faded, leaving me moist and exhilarated upon the electric bed, staring up at the same old battered tin ceiling and thanking my lucky stars, both for the substance of what I'd seen—a fully realized Bruno Maddox, happy at last, reveling in the futuristic paradise of Manhattan as he was destined to do, I now realize, all his life—and for the fact that I'd seen anything at all. To a younger woman it would probably be pretty disturbing to suddenly develop extrasensory perception; I imagine she would think she was going mad. But to a housebound old biddy such as me it's obviously a godsend.

In fact, it's a godsend for *both* of us, reader, for you and me *both*. If this . . . this *pipeline* into Bruno's larger life remains intact—and I've a feeling it's going to—well then this is obviously going to become a much richer narrative. No longer am I going to have to *guess* what's happening to the chap out there in the world. I'll be able to simply see what's happening and then tell you about it, which with any luck will make this book a substantially easier read—as well as, frankly, an enormously easier write.

As to *why* we've been blessed with this paranormal development I have a theory, a theory in two parts:

a) When two people have lived as deeply in each other's pocket as Bruno and I have these past five months, I think they quite naturally become sensitive to tiny variations in each other's speech patterns, to the extent that when one says, "I went for a walk," the other is able to glean a lot more information about what the walk was like than would an eavesdropping stranger, especially when one party, namely me, has no actual life of her own and

b) Bruno is finally happy. The clairvoyant pipeline would probably have opened up months ago, except that back then I don't think he was even seeing the outside world *himself*. Not properly. He was too depressed. Everything he pointed his eyes at had a horrible old woman superimposed on it. But now . . . well, now he sees, and, therefore, because of a), so do I. Do you see?

It's simple, really. A simple miracle.

In the afternoon, we sat together in silence and watched a movie on television about a small boy out playing in the woods who finds an eagle with a broken wing. Perhaps you've seen it yourself. The boy wraps the eagle in his jacket, sneaks it into his house, and nurses it secretly back to health in a cardboard box in his closet. Guess what, though? On some nonchalant laundry mission one day the small boy's *mother* finds the eagle, prompting a tearful scene at the kitchen table in which she explains to her devastated son that an eagle can never be truly happy living in a closet, no matter how much love it is showered with. Later that day, with the mother waiting respectfully in the car, the small boy unfastens the top of the cardboard box in a field, lets the eagle go free, and then a smile breaks through his tears as he watches his new best friend soar upward to exult against the grandeur of the sky.

That's you, I pulsed Bruno, sitting erectly in the nasty armchair attentive and immaculate in his Housing Dept. T-shirt and his paratrooper's trousers and his bone-white gel-cushioned basketball player's sneakers. *You're the eagle. And I'm the small boy or the cardboard box or the accident that broke the eagle's wing in the first place—whichever fucked up the eagle's life the most.*

And do you know what the sky is?

The sky is modern Manhattan, your natural habitat. Welcome home, Bruno Maddox. Welcome home.

Bienvenu à votre maison.

July 2nd—Friday

One thing I forgot to mention about yesterday's small-boy-and-eagle movie was that it had a moving epilogue:

A few weeks later, long after his tears had dried, the small boy walked out of school one day to find the eagle waiting for him on a railing! The boy ran home, laughing and rejoicing, while the eagle swooped deliriously around his head. When they came in view of his kitchen window the boy's mother started to cry happy tears, because she saw what was happening. Her son's relationship with his best, feathered friend was now stronger than ever, because the eagle was spending time with him *on a voluntary basis*.

Which is what I have a feeling may be happening between Bruno and myself.

This morning after breakfast he sank into the nasty armchair and rather than activate the television, the young man actually talked to me. I mean *really* talked to me, using phrases like "you know?" and "if that makes any sense," as if he were conversing with an actual person rather than an insensible old drooling crone.

Things I learned from our "chat":

Hayley Iskender's apartment, where Bruno is spending his nights, is on the other side of the city directly laterally from our apartments and sounds like an altogether higher class of real estate: a spacious, split-level apartment, clean and air-conditioned, featuring—among other items, I'm sure—a big black puffy leather couch and a smooth glass coffee table.

Oh, and in a massive coincidence Hayley shares her apartment with a woman Bruno and I once heard being interviewed on *Rod and Tod in the Morning*. The woman's name is Simon Menges and she's a young nonfiction author, most famously of a book entitled *Taking Us from Behind: The Media Ambush of Women in America*. She was on *Rod and Tod* just after that book came out and it was a fairly memorable interview, I have to say.

Rod and Tod are both very zany and hilarious men, even at six in the morning, and as I recall they were a good deal more interested in discussing whether there was a chapter in *Taking Us from Behind* about Lisa the Weathergirl—a member of their staff—than in actually addressing its themes.

Then they got onto Simon's name. Tod wanted to know why Simon's name was Simon, given that she was a female, and Simon explained rather cryptically that publishing was an old-fashioned industry and that "when walking through a minefield one wears the smallest shoes one can find." There was a pause, broken only by a mysterious *boing* sound effect for which I cannot account, and then Rod chipped in, "Tod has small shoes . . . or so I hear," after which the interview drew to a close.

"Anyway," Bruno finished up, with an adorable little sheepish smile, "sorry to bend your ear. I just thought maybe you'd like to know a bit about what's going on with me."

Like it? I *loved* it. Made me feel human again, reader. Positively *human*.

July 3rd—Saturday

More good news. In fact, in its own strange and traumatic way today was possibly the most encouraging day we've had around here since this whole nightmare began.

Ten in the morning, while Bruno was still in the shower, a man identifying himself as "Theo Bakula" rang up and invited the boy to "some thing for some new thing tonight at a place called . . . hold on, hold on . . . pieces of paper they torment me so . . . Magma."

Mr. Bakula's message continued for at least another minute and a half, but I don't feel able to do it justice in this medium. It was less what he said than how he said it. His tone of voice, for instance, was just *outrageously* decadent and relaxed, like he was lying on some sort of ottoman being oiled up by slave girls, and at unpredictable intervals he would stop talking and yawn, make some percussive noise with his mouth, or strangest of all, which he did several times, simply recite Bruno's name "Bruno . . . *Maddox, Bruno . . . Maddox*," just sort of mulling it over, for no reason.

"So see you there," the message ended eventually, "bring anyone you like. *Adios, mon capitaine.*"

That final phrase stuck with me: "*Adios, mon capitaine.*" I couldn't stop thinking about it. Two different foreign languages thrown together in the same short phrase . . . an exuberant thrusting together of farflung verbal artifacts, like a scuba diver's flippers worn with an old suit of armor . . .

And suddenly I knew in my gut who Theo was. He must have been up on the roof of the *come hither* building that luminous breakthrough evening. He must have been one of Bruno's fellow Future People who had welcomed him into their number.

Thank you, Theo Bakula, I pulsed into the air as Bruno stepped whistling out of the shower. *Thank you for midwifing the spiritual rebirth of a young man about whom I care deeply.*

Bruno was back here at 8 P.M., kissed by the sun after a day spent shopping with Hayley Iskender and with a plastic bag at his side from a place called The End of the World Is Nylon. After briefly ducking next door he reemerged wearing literally one of the best shirts I had ever seen: a tight black nylon number, silk-screened with whimsical barnyard scenes such as you might find in a child's alphabet book: there was a smiling horse poking its head over a stable door;

a smiling sow being suckled by piglets; a rooster on a patch of grass . . . It was a funny, clever shirt and Bruno looked very handsome in it. Radiating contentment the young man sank into the armchair, reached for the 'phone book and in a move that surprised me, used it to call that guy Mark Clark whom he invited to join himself, Theo Bakula, and Hayley Iskender at Magma* that evening also. Clark seemed slightly bowled over by the invitation but Bruno assured him he was serious. "We need to stick together, we N! guys . . ." he said. "See you there in half an hour. Just tell the people on the door that you're with me."

Bruno replaced the telephone handset in its cradle, sighed happily . . . at which precise moment my torso reared up off the electric bed and my chest gave a sound like a ream of paper being ripped in half by a strongman.

I blacked out.

When I came to I was looking at the ceiling, the embossed tin ceiling with the slug-shaped gray patches where the paint has peeled off and I was conscious of a sound in the air like an idling engine, *uhr-uhr-uhr-uhr-uhr*, and a flicking sound as well, like pages being turned. My head fell to the side and there was Bruno Maddox, knees pulled up to his chest in the nasty armchair, and, reader, he did not look good. He looked bad. His hair was fluffed crazily out on ei-

---

*I know about Magma incidentally. I've seen it on television. It's a volcano-themed nightclub on 21st St. with a rock-texture interior, pumice stone ashtrays, a Krakatoa Lounge, and walls inlaid with vast networks of see-through plastic tubing through which liquid representing molten rock can be seen to be gushing. Now are you ready to have your mind blown? Once again? Every inch of Magma is colored a cool, bright *white*, reader, down to the last drop of squirting milky lava. If you will, that's sort of the "joke" of the place.

ther side of his head like cat whiskers and he was staring with round white eyes down into the pages of *The Caregiver's Bible*. "Blood-blood-blood-blood," he was muttering, flipping aimlessly through that volume. "Blood-blood-blood-blood-blood."

What? I wondered, glancing down at my smock.

Oh.

From my hip to the bottom of my rib cage lay a lake of pale gray phlegm overlaid with a web of red filaments, like long threads of saffron. *Red* filaments, reader. For the first time ever I had just coughed up blood.

I was about to offer up a short prayer of thanks to whatever deity it was when I heard a *bonk* and looked over. The *Caregiver's Bible* had fallen from Bruno's hands, and now he was frantically dividing his gaze between the lake of bloody phlegm, my face, my neck and my chest as it rose and fell lopsidedly. He was whimpering, under his breath, looking utterly insane. *Utterly* insane, reader. Not one trace was left of the last few weeks' good feeling.

Okay, now, calm down, I pulsed him reassuringly. *You're overreacting. You lose that much blood wiping your face with one of those hot towels in a Japanese restaurant. Plus I'm not even coughing any more . . . Bruno you can't let this derail your recovery. You have to go out.*

He didn't though. Instead he sort of tumbled forward off the chair in a semi-controlled manner and disappeared from my view beneath the side of the electric bed.

It was a crucial, make-or-break moment, I suddenly knew in my gut.

This was like that moment in a Greek Tragedy when the hero is forced to make a difficult choice that affects his entire future. Was Bruno going to go out into the city and live?

Or stay here with me and merely, as they say on the talk shows, exist?

Get up, boy! I pulsed as hard as I could. *Get up, get up. For the love of Pete!*

Nothing.

And *still* nothing.

And then do you know what happened, reader?

Can you guess?

Bruno Maddox stood up.

The boy's face was as white as cod but his jaw was set like concrete and he was unmistakably on his feet. "Look," he mumbled, not looking at me, fumbling for his jacket. "I have to go out, but I'll be back as soon as I can."

Don't come back at all, I pulsed ecstatically as he staggered out into the night. *You've had a nasty shock. Stay out with Hayley until you feel completely better.*

And that's what he did. He left me here with my joy and my phlegm, which retained its sheen all evening in the humid air, and didn't return until way past midnight.

I couldn't tell if he was pleased to find me still alive (I certainly wouldn't have been in his shoes). In fact, he didn't seem to care. Just wiped up the phlegm like it didn't have blood in it and escorted me back to bed, seeming fine.

So all in all an extremely heartening day. Bruno Maddox bent, reader, but he did not break!

July 4th—Sunday

Oh God.

I think I may be too depressed to even tell you what's happened today, reader . . . oh reader, it's *awful*.

Deep breath. (Lungs are fine, by the way. Completely recovered.)

Okay.

The first thing I saw when I opened my eyes this morning was a man's head and shoulders, over in the main room, framed against the window. I couldn't quite make out the facial features . . . but then came the voice.

"You're awake," said Bruno Maddox, rising to come get me. With forearms that felt to me like bowling pins he manhandled me in silence to the bathroom. Not until I was mounted on the electric bed with my cereal and Bruno had toppled backward into the nasty armchair did I get a proper look at him.

He looked like shit and when he spoke his voice sounded just like mine did back in February; just air and flapping throat parts. "I . . ." he wheezed. "I'm having a problem with my brain and I . . . I don't know what to do about it."

What happened? I pulsed him, fighting despair. *Calm down and tell me what happened.*

Coincidentally, that is exactly what he did do. In the croaking sentimental tones of a mortally wounded soldier recalling the smell of his mother's apple dumplings and the way the sunflowers would wave beyond the kitchen window, blah blah blah now never to be reexperienced . . . Bruno told me what happened at Magma.

"So," he began, closing his eyes, "I went out last night . . ."

And suddenly, reader, my own eyes may as well have been closed because instead of Bruno's haggard features and the appalling interior of my vile apartment . . .

* * *

... I am seeing pictures again, just like I did the other day ... when Bruno came back from his walk.

I'm seeing pictures of Bruno Maddox clambering out of a taxi and dawdling confusedly on the sidewalk outside Magma. The sky is dark, the lights of the city are bright, and he is still upset by the blood from my lungs. His eyes will not settle down. Traumatized, they flit from gutter to street lamp to the faces of the revelers queuing to get into Magma, as if old woman lung-blood might suddenly well from any spot ...

"to meet Hayley ..."

Yeah, I see that too. I see Hayley Iskender approaching from the rear.

"Hey."

Bruno Maddox spins around.

There is Hayley Iskender. She is there right behind him, in her cardigan. Her smile is drawn but warm.

"How are you?" she asks.

"Fucking excellent." He kisses her again.

"Shall we go in ..."

"... at some place, some ... nightclub ..."

Yes.
I see Magma.
The great white volcano.

I see Bruno and Hayley enter with no trouble, for they are on the list, but I can feel the young man's distress holding steady. The nightclub is meant to be white; that is the joke of the place, if you will, but everything he looks at, everything he sees, is overlaid with the same lattice of red threads as overlaid the pool of phlegm I disgorged.

The place is very crowded, and what a crowd it is! Every last man-jack is a Citizen of the Future, exuberantly dressed to the eclectic nines, talking fast . . . phrases from about ten languages whizz past the boy like bullets as he shoulders between nonathletes in athletic clothing . . . nonscientists in white lab coats . . . a non-Hindu woman with the largest forehead dot you have ever seen . . .

Bruno starts to feel better.

He is away from that nasty old bleeding woman.

He is among his people.

". . . and this guy, Mark Clark . . ."

Mm hmm. I see him too.

I see Mark Clark through the lattice of red in Bruno's vision. The diminutive earpiece- and microphone-technician is seated in a carved-out niche.

Bruno tugs the sleeve of Hayley's cardigan. They push through the crowd . . .

"Clark, this is Hayley Iskender, my . . ." he turns to Hayley with a smile that is sly . . . "are you my girlfriend? Officially?"

Hayley smiles, extends a hand to Clark. "Good to meet you."

"Hayley, Clark," Bruno finishes up.

Clark is short, and he is hairy, sitting there in his little rocky sconce, knees pressed tightly together, looking up at them like a baby, with big round guileless eyes, as wide and simple as a lake up in Canada, but not as deep. I examine those eyes for a soul . . . and find only an ambition to one day write a small weekly column for a provincial newspaper entitled "News to Me . . . by Mark Clark."

His clothes too are wrong. With the possible exception of Hayley Iskender, whose cardigan defies all categories, Mark Clark is the only person in the place not dressed like a Future Person. In getting dressed he has not surveyed all of History like a god and playfully selected items from multiple different eras . . . no, he is in some rumpled brown trousers, a gray checked shirt and a scuffed old leather jacket. There is no joke to his clothing. All the pieces fit together . . .

And suddenly I know what Bruno will tell me next . . .

". . . and . . ." Bruno rubbed his face with his hand. "I don't know . . . I just suddenly started to lose it really badly. Clark began to *really* bother me . . . just his very presence. I was getting . . . angry. It made no sense . . ."

Yes it does.

Because Clark is dead weight.

He is in cahoots with the blood from my lungs: both of them are trying to slow Bruno down, trying to stop him having fun, trying to drag him back to the bad old days of caregiving . . .

* * *

189

"... and so I went off to get some drinks ..."

"Time to access a little drinkorama," Bruno is rubbing his hands. "I see beverages on the horizon. Clark? Drinksie?"

"Gee ..." says Clark, thinking.

"Hayley?" Bruno says to Hayley. "Would you like some alcohol?"

She nods. "Beer please."

"Clark?"

His round eyes blink, then he nods. "Beer please."

Bruno nods ... and is off, pumping through the crowd trying to regain a little verve ... a little momentum ...

He succeeds. He makes it to the serving window marked Pinatubo, orders two beers and a whisky, is observed by a girl in a Native American headdress alone on a stool. She watches him slide a twenty across the bar to pay for the drinks.

"There's more where that came from," he purrs to her, feeling almost fully restored ... and is off again, back through the crowd, past a quintet of Japanese youths in matching white suits, one of whom is leaning his head into the stomach of another and pinwheeling his arms while all five of them laugh ...

Bruno smiles at the spectacle ...

"... and I was feeling slightly better. But then I got back and Clark was talking to Hayley about his dead mother ..."

Yes.

Even out of earshot Bruno can see Clark's lips making the double muh *sound of "my mother" ... Muh muh ... Muh-Muh.*

Hayley is nodding in sympathy and this makes Bruno crazy. Because this . . . guy, this . . . stranger Mark Clark is brazenly holding the one conversation with Hayley Iskender that he himself, Bruno Maddox, would like to have more than anything else in the world, the one where he tells her about his own experience of dying older females and the strain of it all . . .

"And . . ." Bruno squeezed his eyes shut even tighter. "For some reason I started freaking out again and so I just gave them their drinks and walked off . . ."

"Just going to check out the art" he says and veers away without stopping. The white volcanic walls of Magma are hung with photographs of men's washrooms, cut up and spliced back together to make geometric patterns with the tiling . . . but Bruno cannot focus. He feels terrible. And eventually he has no excuse not to rejoin his companions.

". . . and then eventually I went back . . ."

Hayley asks him if he is feeling okay. He says he is. Clark asks him about the art. Bruno describes it as "fine."

". . . and everything was fine but then . . ." The young man breathed deeply. Then Clark started *talking* funny."

"Eet iz good to be out in zociety . . ." the small hairy man is saying in a bad French accent. It is as if he is mocking the whole scene, trying to distance himself and Hayley and Bruno from it *"experiencing ze festive and cultural amuzements about ze town. Ze artverks zey are very exqueezite."*

Bruno starts to crumble. *"Excuse me?"*

"Ze use of color."

"The use of color. Yes, what about it?"

"Eet is exqueezite."

Bruno has no choice but to stare at him.

Why is Clark doing this? What is his agenda? Why is he trying to cut Bruno off from his world, his happiness . . .

". . . and then I just sort of snapped, started giving Clark a hard time . . ."

Yes.

I see him, looming above the smaller man and saying, "Look, do you know anyone here, Clark? I mean are these really your people? Are you sure you're not slightly out of your depth?"

And Bruno's limbs get in on the act. Without being asked, they are grabbing the lapel of Mark Clark's leather jacket and fingering it. "Oh these really are excellent threads. So hard to find a good pair of proper farm trousers and a decent graph-paper shirt. Did you make a conscious decision not to dress up at all?"

"... and he left ..."

Clark didn't answer. Just immediately said, "Nice to meet you," to Hayley and departed.

"... Hayley was slightly upset ..."

Yes, I see her.

I see her face go hard and curious, an oft-used psychic shark cage has enveloped her. "What happened there?"

The young man shrugs, suddenly lovable and at a loss, "I don't know. That was weird." He looks at her sideways, tries to join her in her shark cage.

Hayley steps back, just enough to deny him entry, studies him afresh. "Is something wrong?"

He looks away, sips his Scotch, philosophical. She is seeing his noble profile, a captain going down with his ship. "I don't know. Sometimes I find these social situations difficult. Trying to balance the needs of different ... groups."

"What groups? There were three of us."

"Yeah no I know. But that guy Theo Bakula's going to be here any second and you know he's a big newspaper nightlife guy. I was genuinely worried Clark might feel out of his depth. I guess I didn't handle it properly."

"You grabbed him."

"Look, Hayley ..." he turns and lets her see the trauma

193

in his face for the first time. "Can we talk about something else? I'm feeling weird."

Hayley blinks. "No," she hands him her beer, "I'm leaving. Leaving you here with your group."

"Er . . . okay. Can I come with you?"

She studies his face one last time as if considering his proposition, though most likely she is considering something else. "No," she doesn't sound angry, but then she turns . . .

"... and then she sort of left as well ..."

Yes.

Off she goes, slouching quickly away through the colorful crowd of revelers, pale ponytail swinging like a metronome, narrow shoulders barely rippling the woolen whimsy of her cardigan . . .

"... I waited around for a while ..."

Yes.

I see him waiting around, alone on a stool in the Krakatoa Lounge, a quiet whisky, no sign of Theo Bakula . . .

"... and then I came home." Bruno's horrible eyes snapped open. "I didn't sleep well at *all* last night," he croaked. "I just . . . I just think the strain of all this is beginning to tell on me. The last few weeks I really started thinking that maybe all this was manageable but . . . yesterday when you coughed up blood . . . it just all sort of came crashing down again and I'm not sure I can cope anymore. I'm exhausted."

I was exhausted too, I realized. The boy's entire narrative couldn't have lasted more than fifteen seconds but the intensity of my visions had dragged me through the whole grueling evening. Suddenly I could barely keep my eyes open.

"It's time to *do* something about all this," he continued. "This is an untenable situation."

I know, I pulsed. *You should kill me.*

Bruno stiffly unfolded his limbs and stood up. "I don't know why I'm talking to you," he muttered. "I have to call Hayley."

Tell her about me, I pulsed. *You know her. She'll be in here before either of us can say Jack Robinson, taking stock of the situation, inventorying my possessions, supervising the ambulance men as they cart me off . . .*

I closed my eyes, exhausted.

"Hi, Simon, can I speak to Hayley? Thanks." I heard Bruno shift his weight from foot to foot. "Hey."

". . ."

"I'm okay. Look I'm calling to say sorry for last night. Yesterday was not an easy day for me."

". . ."

I felt him glance over at me. "Um . . ."

Tell *her,* I pulsed him as hard as I could. *I'm serious. Tell her about me, Bruno.*

Now.

Do it.

End this.

"Well . . . nothing specific. Just a difficult day. Look, that's not important. What are you doing right now?"

"..."

"Are you sure?" Limply his hand raked his hair. "You don't want to quickly get together?"

"..."

"Okay. I'll call you tomorrow."

He hung up. I opened my eyes. Bruno was *glaring* at me.

Back to Plan A! I pulsed, seizing the moment. *C'mon! Kill me! I just cost you your girlfriend. Get steamed. Just push me off the bed! If the fall doesn't kill me then just leave me on the floor to starve. Tell the police you came back and found me dead! Do it!*

He didn't though.

My only punishment for once again destroying my life was to be sent to bed without any dinner, or lunch for that matter.

Which is where I am now, tired and depressed.

Because you want to know the worst thing of all? The worst thing of all is that my lungs are *fine*. Not only have I not coughed up even a *speck* of blood since the afternoon before Magma but my breath has lost its usual rasp. I guess the material I coughed up must have been the obstruction that was causing the rasp, and now I don't have it anymore. I was dying just long enough to provoke Bruno's relapse, and then I stopped.

It strikes me as the sort of thing the devil might do.

July 5th—Monday

Hayley was, or claimed to be, too busy to speak to Bruno when he called her mid-morning but she rang back just before lunch and agreed to meet him this evening, and he's out there right now, intending to spend the night.*

Around threeish he called Mark Clark, whom he would have to see anyway this evening at work, and apologized. He blamed his meltdown at Magma on "family troubles" and Clark, as far as I could tell, forgave him swiftly and without reservation, which puzzled me initially until it came back to me that Mark Clark was raised in Kansas City, Missouri, part of the great American countryside. As I know from my childhood, people in rural areas grab each other by the lapels about five times a day. Country folk are quick to ire, but just as quick to forgive. It's a different code out there.

Anyway, so where do we stand? How is Bruno? Is he still insane? Did the thing at Magma provoke a full relapse to the agonies of last month or was it just a temporary thing?

All good questions, reader.

The truth, as always, is quite complicated I reckon.

July 6th—Tuesday

I mean he's definitely going through some weird stuff mentally, for which I am obviously to blame.

"Good morning" were Bruno's first words this morning, and I was instantly privy to a picture . . .

. . . *of Hayley having not quite forgiven Bruno, of there being a certain downcast quality of her eyes when they're to-*

---

*He put me to bed before leaving for work.

gether, which suggests to the boy that she has not forgotten what happened at Magma, but has instead filed the information away for future use . . .

Actually look, a quick word on these pictures I've been seeing when Bruno talks.

I think they're just my imagination.

I mean of course they are.

Telepathy and clairvoyance aren't real. They're fake.

I think I've just been imagining I know what's happening in Bruno's life because my own is so drab and impoverished. I'm sure it's something an enormous number of old women do. From here on in if I see any more silly pictures I'm just going to keep them to myself, stick to the facts.

And this evening's fact is that Hayley has to work again and, in a coincidence, that guy Theo Bakula called up and Bruno went to meet him this evening instead, returning here to sleep around midnight. I promise.

July 7th—Wednesday

"So I've got a scheme," said Bruno this morning as I ate my cereal. He was standing between me and the window, his silhouette swaying restlessly in the morning glare. "Last night I went to meet that guy Theo Bakula. He was seeing some friends in a bar uptown. Fancy place. All his friends were sort of prominent media people. There was some eighteen-year-old guy who's just made a film about cripples. A guy who writes a column for *Rogue* magazine. Some actress. And that guy Gordon Gundersson, you know him?"

Yes. Gordon Gundersson's a book author who has his own television commercial. I see it all the time. Gundersson is young and well built with longish sandy hair and he sits at a wooden table on a little swivel stool against a white background poking at a portable computer. "I don't know how this [bleep]ing thing works" is I think what he mutters, then he types a few words with two index fingers, grimaces, types a little more, then more . . . then *more*. And before you can say Jack Robinson the guy is typing *unbelievably* fast, really working himself into a lather until he jabs the return key with a flourish, swiveling to the camera and saying, "But it knows how I work."*

"Anyway," Bruno swallowed and started idly pushing me back and forth like you do a baby in a pram, "they all had quite a lot of money . . ." he broke off and regarded me, wondering if I was taking any of this in, ". . . and none of them work in an office. They all work from home. And what I was thinking was that maybe if I started doing something *similar*, doing journalism or something, bring in a few hundred extra dollars a month . . . maybe things would get easier around here. I mean we could get an air conditioner," he gestured at the window, "and I could install some railings to maybe help you get about the place on your own if I'm not here. . . ." he blinked thoughtfully down at my legs, "or even get you an electric wheelchair, even a *nurse* . . . if I made enough money."

*I always perk up at commercials for portable computers, possibly because I covet one so badly. It makes me feel really *old-fashioned* writing out "July 8th—Thursday . . . July 9th—Friday" by hand when I could just touch a button and generate a whole summer's worth of dates in a nanosecond and then just fill them in . . . fill them in . . .

My lips moved and no sound came out.

"Anyway, that's my scheme," he said, turning to leave. "I'm going to try to make some more money. And if it doesn't work out then I'm probably going to have to do something else." He was out of sight now, through the door, and added as an afterthought: "Because I can't keep living like this."

Fair enough, I pulsed as from next door came the sound of the 'phone being raised, the beep of dialing.

Look, I'm sorry if this narrative is getting slightly thin. I'm *tired* is the truth of the matter. Really really tired.

It's been creeping up on me for a few weeks now.

I didn't mention it before because it's hardly newsflash material that a woman in her early hundreds has an issue with fatigue.

But I'm mentioning it now because I fear it's about to affect my performance. If I start to disintegrate then I want you to know exactly why it is that you have to forgive me. And now you do. Old womanly fatigue.

July 8th—Thursday

Bruno started his new job today (the working from home, the writing) and I am pleased to report the spunky young chap really hit the ground running.

9:00 A.M. He called all those magazine editor 'phone numbers Hayley gave him last week. None of them answered, perhaps because he called too early.

9:15 A.M. He settled down to work next door, scratching away at his yellow legal pad with an intensity I hadn't heard since my first boyfriend, whose name escapes me right now, came home injured from the First World War and started spilling his guts in verse.

1:00 P.M. Nearly four hours later we had lunch: a can of tunafish on a bed of Chinese lettuce. Very healthy.

1:20 P.M. Bruno called Hayley at work. His voice on the 'phone was very soft and tender, like a doctor in an emergency room speaking to a beautiful little girl who has fallen off her bike and sustained a concussion. By the sound of it, their relationship has entered a second golden age.

1:30 P.M. He went back next door and the scratching sound resumed.

5:30 P.M. The scratching stopped, Bruno readied himself for work, fixed me a bowl of guacamole with a protruding spoon and disappeared to his other job, the one at N!.

It was all very impressive. Reader, you'd be impressed yourself if you knew how hot it was here in Chinatown without an air conditioner. Myself, I hardly moved a muscle all day and did only limited thinking, yet from 8 A.M. onward I was as slick and slippery as an eel.

July 9th—Friday

Good news. Over dinner last night at a popular new Malaysian restaurant called 112 West 13th Street Middle Buzzer Bruno Maddox told Hayley Iskender about the intolerable conditions down here in Chinatown and she generously extended him the use of her quiet, dustless, artificially cooled apartment to work in during the day.

He's over there now, slaving away, forging us a brighter tomorrow.

And I am here alone in my bedroom, with a whole day's

worth of food and water weighing down the swingable side table, which has been detached from the electric bed and propped up beside the . . . the acoustic one.

Feeling tired.

July 10th—Saturday

Bruno out with Hayley all day. Nothing to report.

July 11th—Sunday

Gordon Gundersson's *Black Current*, which I dipped into today, is more than twelve hundred pages in length and tells the story, according to its back cover, of a freak, once-in-a-millennium river swelling several years ago that resulted in the deaths of eight weekend canoeists in the Pacific Northwest. For prospective readers worried that Gundersson might not be qualified to handle this material, the inside back flap informed us that not only was his first book *The Slowness of Rapids* also about watersports gone horribly wrong, specifically a loner friend of his who canoed out to sea and didn't canoe back, but he has a bronze medal from the 2000 Olympics as a member of the Canadian kayak team. The author photo shows a wet-suited Gundersson in a field of waving swamp grass, his ringlets damp, scowling like he wishes the camera would go away so he could get back to his writing.

What Bruno was doing with a copy of *Black Current*, or why he discarded it this morning on the foot of my electric bed, I do not know, but after reading the flap information I was glad he had done so. It so happened I was utterly in the mood to lose myself in a classic "tale of adbenture" such as me grand-da used to read me.

But then after wrestling with the giant volume I successfully opened it and discovered *Black Current* to be the following sort of gibberish:

Vontroni:
Fir! When the Tide furges white beneath my paddle this hull muft be ftiff.

The Manchild:
Ftiff? Nuncle, this is no common plaftic fhell, you know. This have thirty percent more Compreffive Ftrength than the ftandard urethane fhell you are ufed to—+plus I have fupplemented it with extra core material in high-impact areas . . .

Page after page after *page*—if you can believe it—of two seventeenth-century adventurers arguing in screenplay format about modern canoe technology on the banks of the St. Lawrence River! *Christ*, it was bad. And then just as you've resigned yourself to that, suddenly, *boom*. Everything changes. The prose gets all dense and italicized and a teenage babysitter is having her intestines shoveled out with the blade of an oar while trying to watch something called the *General Motors Jack Benny Hour* on television in the nineteen fifties. No suspense. No human interest. The only jokes are of the "darkly, profoundly comic" variety. Just a total lack of value, reader, clever-sounding nonsense spun out to inordinate length. In fact I found myself pulsing the words, *What a steaming pile of shit*, at Gundersson's author photo and then slamming the book shut with as much force as my withered arm could muster prior to falling back into my pillows, depressed to my core about the state of modern letters.

July 12th—Monday

Bruno stopped by for twenty minutes this morning to feed me and drain me of waste before heading back to Hayley's and I'm glad he did, because on the way to the bathroom I caught a glimpse of his yellow legal pad, which he had tossed onto the nasty armchair, and was pleasantly surprised by what I saw thereon.

All this while I've assumed the boy's been working on journalism or something but it seems instead that he's set his sights slightly higher and has in fact broken ground on a *theatrical* piece entitled *Shades of Manhattan*.

As far as I could make out—Bruno has that wild, sexy sort of handwriting—*Shades of Manhattan* is a stage play about a woman, Amanda, who has lost her sunglasses and is hunting for them with the help of her boyfriend, whose name is Orlando. The action takes place on a scale model of snow-covered Manhattan, twenty feet long by eight feet wide and for all sixteen hours of the performance Orlando and Amanda lie sprawled gigantically on top of the buildings, facedown, fumbling through the canyons of a cold, deserted city for a pair of sunglasses that they never find. The dialogue is mumbled and banal, the action slow, but in time the audience comes to understand that the real subject of *Shades of Manhattan* is not in fact a pair of missing sunglasses but rather the relationship between two emotionally stunted protagonists. For Orlando the search is his way of proving to Amanda that he loves her, without having to actually say so. Amanda realizes this and resents Orlando accordingly. As far as *she's* concerned, the hunt for the sunglasses is a chance to do something on her own for a change without Orlando muscling in and taking charge, as is his style. They are *her* sunglasses. Why can't it be *her* search?

Do you see? They aren't really looking for Amanda's sunglasses, they're looking for something bigger. Possibly themselves—though having said that let me also make the obvious point that they *are* looking for sunglasses, if by sunglasses you mean the masks we all wear to disguise our true feelings, and/or the filtering devices we interpose between ourselves and reality to shield ourselves from its intensity . . .

All right, I need to calm down. I'm getting overexcited. Let me just say this. Bruno Maddox's *Shades of Manhattan* is one good fucking play.

July 13th—Tuesday

It doesn't bother me being here alone, perhaps because I was alone in the early sixties too, to start with, tramping the streets in a threadbare old housecoat, sitting in coffeeshops with steamed-up windows, reading the paper. The Scene was nowhere near as vibrant as it had looked on the TV from Fordham, and what there was of it didn't really appeal: a few bald old men taking speed pills, wearing sunglasses, performing bongo poetry, etc. To be frank, it felt more like the tail-end of something than a beginning.

But still I was optimistic. Out there in the street I kept bumping into people with whom I felt a kinship. Like me, they were small-town dreamers with their collars bent up against the January chill, pacing the crevices of downtown less to *find* something than to kill time before it arrived.

By February 1962 we were a legitimate "band of friends." Every evening that month found me climbing the stairs to a loft in Soho, easing out of my icy boots, turning to find that there was a fire going, wine mulling on the stove, long-haired girls in turtleneck sweaters stretched out like cats on the cushions and the ottomans, exhaling jets of clove smoke, eyes closed, breasts rising and falling as they allowed their minds to be transported by one of the men, who'd be plucking at a classical guitar and using free-form cosmic imagery to weave fantastical tales of magical lands that were peopled with exotic characters . . . What dreams our flickering line of windows must have conjured for the overcoated masses shuffling home in the snowy streets below I can't imagine. But if they were picturing a cozy and transcendent world of gentleness, art and comfort . . . well, they were to be commended for their accuracy.

July 14th—Wednesday

Still tired as billy-o, reader, and still alone, but I'm feeling a strange contentment, possibly occasioned by how well this memoir's suddenly going. I'm getting into a rhythm now. I feel I'm marshaling my material very effectively. With my memories of the sixties plus my occasional glimpses of Bruno's legal pad when he stops by in the morning I think I have more than enough material to sustain both of us, reader, for the foreseeable future.

July 15th—Thursday

For instance, *Shades of Manhattan* is really coming together. It's *really* coming together. This morning I glimpsed the following in the margin of Bruno's pad:

> Amanda: Don't worry . . . it's no big deal . . . I'm sure they'll turn up . . .
> Orlando: Yeah . . . [then to himself]: I remember when I was a child [long monologue].

Jesus. I'm getting chills just remembering it. So much being said without *actually* being said, do you know what I mean?

Seeing those jottings really cheered me up. It's so easy, when you're caught up in a situation as tense as the one involving me and Bruno and Hayley Iskender, to forget that the people involved *are* real people, with fully blown interior lives. All this time I've been worrying about what Bruno's going to "do," how he's going to "behave" . . . whereas the fact of the matter is that however this all turns out there will always be a chunk of him that's above the fray, aloof, dreaming of giant figures and white-dusted cityscapes . . .

In fact, you know what?

Actually?

I was so invigorated by Bruno's jottings that I *did something*. I performed an *act*.

To give me a change of scenery Bruno had deposited me this morning on the electric bed, as opposed to the other one. The door had just slammed shut downstairs when I realized he had left his old green suit jacket hanging from the side rail of my electric bed, and that poking from the inside breast pocket was his *checkbook*. I found myself suddenly inspired. Using the switch on the chassis of the bed I whirred myself up to maximum verticality . . . *whirr* . . . and after some flailing managed to grab the checkbook and remove it from his pocket. A narrow-gauge felt-tipped pen was clipped to the front, which I uncapped with my teeth and, steadying the checkbook on my atrophying thigh, carefully wrote, on the Pay to the order of line of the topmost check, "Bruno Maddox." In the Memo box I wrote "For Creative Services Rendered" and then, after resting and thinking, I carefully made the thing out in the sum of "One Hundred Million Dollars Only," prior to signing the thing in a crude approximation of Bruno's own signature, returning it with difficulty to his pocket, then whirring myself back to the horizontal, tired but happy.

In the evening he showed up again to change his clothes and reinstall me in my bedroom. Obviously, I was hoping to actually witness the moment that he found the checkbook and registered how much faith I have in him, how badly I wish him well . . . but sadly, no. He just took the jacket and left.

July 16th—Friday

Genius is a strange thing. Those early years of the sixties when my friends and I were all running around Manhattan making art and music and weird conceptual films it never *occurred* to us that we were doing anything that *mattered*. We were merely pleasing ourselves, following our blisses, and it came as an enormous shock to all of us when we suddenly, in 1962-ish, became massively successful. One day we were happy, penny-pinching bohemians and the next you literally couldn't open a magazine without seeing Andy (Warhol) or Bob (Dylan) or our English friends the Beatles alongside an article about how great we were, the irrevocable impact we were having on Western culture and what "geniuses" we all were. It was flattering, no question, but at the same time slightly mystifying. Did it really take a "genius" to do a giant, perfectly lifelike painting of a soup-can label? How about "synthesizing black music with white music"? Given that both musical forms did already exist, hadn't it always been *inevitable* that someone would think of combining them? Why did the media insist on giving the "genius" label simply to the first person to execute one of these basic, obvious ideas?

"Because that's the way the world has always worked," I recall Bob Dylan hypothesizing at a party in 1963. It was me and him and Andy, and we were drinking in a corner. "They called Galileo a genius just for quote unquote 'discovering' that the world is round, even though the plain, unvarnished fact of the matter is that the world *is* round. Same with Albert Einstein. Everyone just went nuts about him, and for what? That relativity thing? Did it really take a 'genius' to figure out that there's *some* sort of relationship between energy, mass and the speed of light? That's all physics *is*. The genius of Albert Einstein was in recognizing that the first physicist to spend one whole afternoon with a big white piece of paper working out whether it was $2 = m + c \ldots$ or the square root of $m = c$ to the power of e—I mean, how many combinations are there? Ten? *Fifteen?* The first one to do that could spend the rest of his life sitting around signing autographs and getting his knob sucked every night by Marilyn Monroe or whatever."

"You're right," said Andy. "All those people did was just discover what was obvious."

"Exactly," I contributed. "Discover the world is *square* and maybe you've done something."

"*Then* you're a genius," Andy agreed, with an affirmative twitch of his famous white wig.

"I *suppose* what it is," Bob went on, setting his beer on the floor so he could gesture more freely, "is that we're probably just more *intelligent* than ordinary people. We only see these "great discoveries" and "acts of genius" as simple and obvious because we ourselves *are* geniuses. If we were ordinary people then it would probably never occur to us to do a giant painting of a soup-can label. It would be . . . beyond our capacity. I mean obviously I'm not saying ordinary people are stupid . . ."

"Well, I am," said Andy. "I'm sorry, but that's exactly what I'm saying."

We drank in silence, considering his words.

July 17th—Saturday

Pretty tired all day, reader. I should take some vitamin pills or something. Except I don't have any. Is that an irony? No it isn't, is it? It's just a deficiency. A vitamin deficiency.

Ha ha ha ha ha.

July 18th—Sunday

So I'm having a funny feeling—and, reader, it's a feeling about *you*.

On more than one occasion today as I wafted in and out of reverie on the electric bed I could have sworn there was someone else in the apartment: specifically you, reader, sitting in the nasty armchair and *staring* at me. With a question on your lips. Namely:

"If you were really such great pals with Bob Dylan, Andy Warhol, etc., then *how come I've never heard of you?*"

Which is a more than fair question.

So let me explain.

Late 1964. A Friday afternoon. I was dressed very nicely—in tight black turtleneck, short, plaid skirt—because *The New York Times Magazine* was coming to Andy's studio to take a group photo and interview us all for a large feature article on the New York Scene. We all took our places before the big white background, the photographer told us to smile . . .

And suddenly I panicked. I was about to become History. If I stood there and allowed myself to be photographed then I'd be frozen that way for all eternity, in one particular pose, as being one particular sort of person, as an icon of one particular time period, the early sixties. Throughout my life, I couldn't help feeling, my most valuable trait had always been my ability to adapt, to mutate, to entirely change who I was to fit new and challenging circumstances . . . and here I was about to give that all up?

I ducked out of the shot just as the photographer was about to shoot.

"I can't do this."

"What?"

"You're not taking my photograph."

"We . . . we have to. How else are we going to illustrate the interview?"

"There isn't going to be an interview."

"But . . . but this is your big chance to be a famous artist."

"I know." I covered my eyes with my hand. "And that's why I'm going home."

George Harrison tried to stop me but all he got for his trouble were a few strands of gray hair as I sprinted out of there in genuine tears and hurried back to my hotel.

That was a Friday. The following Monday, after a weekend of room service and introspection, I emerged into the world with a plan: rather than be a famous artist myself I was going to become a *manager* of famous artists, behind the scenes, a mistress of puppets pulling the strings of this exciting new culture without ever being seen myself.

It didn't take me long to put this plan into effect. I bought a newspaper, sat in a café, went through the classified ads with the proverbial red pencil and by the end of that week I had a suite of offices on the West Side, and a staff, comprising:

Wendy, a thin, highly competent secretary with a bored, sexy demeanor.

Russell, an unskilled red-headed teenager whose job it was to do all the box moving and package delivery.

And that's why you've never heard of me, despite my being friends with Andy Warhol.

Because instead of being a famous artist I stepped out of the limelight and became a *manager*.

And life was fine after that.

More than fine.

Good.

July 19th—Monday

First day of a new week and Bruno Maddox seems to have laid the cornerstone of a rock opera titled *Cabin Pressure*. As far as I could tell—Bruno was holding the pad upside down—the hero of *Cabin Pressure* is an alcoholic airline pilot who flies a nightly route between two continents that, deliciously, are never named. There is a real family atmosphere on the plane. Its only passengers are a handful of regular commuters who are all on first-name terms with both the flight crew and the Captain. In fact it seems that most of them are in love with the Captain, but their love, unfortunately, cannot save him from:

> a) himself. He spends a lot of time alone in the cockpit, downing those little miniature bottles of spirits, thinking about lost love, the past … and singing songs such as "One Night over the Azores."

> b) Sharifa Mustafa, a sexy female Islamic terrorist—and it is here that things get interesting.

Known to her friends as the Mother of the Suitcase Bomb, Sharifa Mustafa is riding the plane every evening to do reconnaissance for an eventual terrorist attack. Like all great hunters she has to understand her prey before she moves in for the kill. But. As things develop, Sharifa finds herself coming to respect the people she is planning to kill and actually falling in love with the Captain. Sharifa's mixed emotions are one of *Cabin Pressure*'s principal subplots.

Another subplot is the tension between Sharifa, a natural brunette—she's Islamic—and Debbie, the blond flight attendant, because it quickly becomes apparent that Debbie, like Sharifa, *seriously* has the hots for Captain Mazzocks.

Yes, that's right. "Mazzocks." Which sounds a little like "Maddox." The echo is intentional. You can think of it as an "additional layer" to the whole thing. As the audience sits there in their seats, watching the characters intertwine in their inexorable dance of death, they will be conscious all the while that Bruno Maddox, the composer-librettist of *Cabin Pressure*, has chosen to have a main character with a name that sounds like his own. It'll be . . . stimulating for them in a . . . weird sort of . . .

Oh, look. You get the picture.

Fuck I'm tired.

July 20th—Tuesday

[Day off from writing. Old woman's privilege.]

July 21st—Wednesday

Sorry about yesterday, reader, but I've been having more trouble with my health. Neck all of a sudden has gotten very painful and stiff—and so has each of my ten fingers.

I'm actually in an awful lot of pain. If I think about all the different sensations at once . . . well, it makes me slightly want to *die*.

July 22nd—Thursday

Oh, and my head is just a big bag of dizziness.

July 23rd—Friday

But enough about me. Bruno Maddox is writing a novel is the big news. His novel, as yet untitled, is the story of a man who has a video camera implanted in the back of his head. The man is on the run from some policemen who have falsely accused him of murdering his own girlfriend. By day the man roams the glass-and-steel walkways of an antiseptic city in the not-so-distant future, embroiling himself in a seamy lawless underworld as he fights to clear his name, and by night he retreats to an abandoned warehouse down by the docks where he listens to opera, drinks high-protein milk-shakes, and after attaching a special cable to his head, reclines in a huge steel armchair before a pyramid of old abandoned television sets and reviews a day's worth of footage from the camera in the back of his head.

That would be enough, don't you think, reader? That would be enough for a truly good piece of fiction.

But there's more. A lot more.

For instance, when Bruno actually writes the novel he's going to narrate the material captured by the camera . . .

using a different typeface. I'm serious. For instance, at some point Buck Moolox notices . . .

```
    . . . his supposedly dead girlfriend, ap-
proaching from the rear, pale and thin and
hunted-looking. She reaches out to tap his
shoulder but just then she sees something
coming for her from the side. Her eyes
widen in horror and she finds it necessary
to sprint away.*
```

And also there are *footnotes*, reader. Footnotes written by a kindly, futuristic policeman who has come across Buck Moolox's diary and his collection of tapes even *further* in the not-so-distant future, after Buck Moolox is dead. The policeman contributes a preface to the novel, plus the footnotes, *plus* an index, and then at the very end of the book there's a note by the policeman's wife informing us that the policeman *himself* has in fact been killed. The policeman, we learn, has been killed *by himself* because the story of Buck Moolox was so "goddam fucking sad."

The wife note has its own typeface, too, by the way.

Oh God.

July 24th—Saturday

I fucking hate being alive, incidentally—did I tell you this earlier? My entire body itches and the tip of one of my fin-

---

*Note to editor. Hello! Can you . . . can you please set the preceding paragraph in a different typeface? I cannot do it myself because, as you know, I am writing this with a pen. Plus I am an old woman!

gers has started to bleed. You think I'm joking. Ha ha ha ha ha ha ha ha. I'm not, in fact, joking.

July 25th—Sunday

One of the things I sometimes like to do as a writer is use Sundays to address lingering, possibly festering, questions in the mind of the reader. For instance, this one:

"So *what* if you became a fucking manager back in the sixties? Why does that mean we haven't heard of you? We've heard of all the *other* big name managers. There was that gay guy who managed the Beatles, and that other gay guy who managed the Stones, and that incredibly fat and violent guy who managed Led Zeppelin and that nondescript guy who had that club in San Francisco . . . ? I mean who do you think you're trying to *fool*, you stinking and imbecilic old crone? What kind of game . . ."

Let me cut you off there, reader, and quickly point out to you that one overcast Monday morning in 1965 I marched forcefully into our main conference room committed to resolving the problem of my own non-celebrity once and for all. My brain felt like it was seeping blood into the upholstery of my head, but the fact remained: I was one tough fucking daughter of a bitch and I was seconds away from taking care of business, once and for all.

Wendy and Russell were both there—Wendy in a pale blue sweater and a miniskirt with her hair in a ponytail, Russell in a fringed jacket and a big red ball of hair.

"I have something to say," I said, looking first at Wendy, then at Russell, then back at Wendy.

"What is it?" asked Wendy.

"It's that changes are being made," I replied. "Made to the way we do things around here."

"What are these changes?" asked Russell.

There was a tap at the door right then and a man came in, bent on. . . .

Okay, stop the presses! Amusing occurrence! My pen seems to be running out of ink! I'll tell you the rest of this anecdote in a day or two.

July 26th—Monday

Sorry about yesterday. I've got one of those ridiculous old-fashioned pens that dry up if you don't keep switching between the Past and the Present . . . I mean, not *actually*. That isn't *actually* why the pen dries up. That's just sometimes how it feels and I do *actually* find that if I switch narrative modes then the pen relubricates itself, sometimes. Look, just humor me, would you?

Bruno's back, by the way. He's back here in Chinatown for the forseeable future. Simon Menges just kicked him out of her apartment for the crime of "desecrating her psychic space" with his "noise."

"What noise?" you ask, reader?

Well, it's somewhat hard to describe. Place a gun to my head and I would have to say that it's a bit like the sound of a bulky young man standing up and sitting down and standing up and then trying to watch television very quietly and then possibly eating a giant sandwich. In short, a hard noise to put into words, especially with one of those old-fashioned pens that you can't rely on.

July 27th—Tuesday

Tuesday. Fantastic.

I hate you, reader, did I mention this earlier? I hate your fucking guts and I hope that one day you too know what it feels like to have your whole body just *completely itch*. All of it. Every particle. Have you ever felt that way, reader?

I didn't think so.

You've been sheltered haven't you? All your life. Mummy and Daddy resolved to keep tiny little baby Reader all swaddled up and out of harm's way, didn't they? No total-body itchiness for Reader. Nothing bad at all for Reader. Just a comfy upholstered perch from which to judge.

Christ, you've got problems.

You've got *real* problems, reader.

You should see someone.

But not me.

Please don't try to see me.

Because I hate you.

July 28th—Wednesday

"Okay, here's what's happening," I said to Russell and Wendy, back in the sixties, back in the conference room, gesturing with my hands as I sought to explain to that pair of quietly sitting employees why it was that you, reader, have never heard of me. "I started this management company because I didn't want to be famous. It seems that's not possible. All the managers these days are celebrities themselves. So I'm changing the very *nature* of our business."

"Are you firing us?" This was Wendy.

"No." I laughed and laughed and laughed. "I'm *promoting* you. I'm promoting *all of us*. I'm taking this company *up a level*. Instead of managing quote unquote "famous artists" like Andy Warhol and Bob Dylan we're going to manage the careers of . . ." I managed a really rather excellent drum roll on the table with my hands, ". . . *other managers!*"

Wendy popped her gum.

"How will that work?" asked Russell.

"Yes, *do* you see?" I agreed with him. "We'll be like *meta*-managers . . . managers *squared* . . . helping our manager clients . . ." I did another drum roll, ". . . *in their roles as managers!*"

"How will that work?" asked Russell, who I realized now was trying to . . . trying to get more information about my brave new scheme.

But he had missed his chance. I had already exited the conference room and was already sauntering back to my private office with the lockable door, knocking over the water cooler as I passed it, whistling a tune, suddenly not giving much of a shit about anything anymore and man oh man was that a good feeling!

July 29th—Thursday

Oh, hey, do you know who's fat? Do you, reader? Do you know who's a fat fucking fuck? You do, don't you? You can tell by the way I'm saying it. Yes, that's right.

Bruno Maddox is fat

Just this very morning, in fact, he waddled in very fatly arm in arm with an egg-cheese-meat "breakfast sandwich" the size of a large throw-cushion. Using his stubby fat fingers as utensils he pressed it deep into his face hole while flipping chubbily back and forth between *Wheelchair Tennis Master Class* and *Trowel Sports International* and then what he did next was fall asleep. Had to have been at least eleven, reader, before he finally got down to work.

Work.

"Work" is a funny word, reader. Not just the way it's spelled relative to how it's pronounced but the way it can mean so many different things to different people.

For a road digger "work" can mean digging a road.

For a doctor it can mean curing a patient's disease.

For Bruno Maddox, most days, it means staring at his legal pad and with a flick of his pen, relocating the novel about the man with the video camera in the back of his head to the Scandinavian nation of *Finland* in order to capture "that austere, echoey feel." After that he pulls his shoes on in order to scour the city for a reasonably priced Finnish phrase book . . . but what do you know? All of a sudden it's noon, lunchtime around the globe, and so he has to just quickly wolf down three slices of giant pizza from the place around the corner. After a shortish nap the young man tends to be sufficiently rested to field the daily midafternoon 'phone call from Hayley Iskender. "How's it going?" she always asks him. "Good!" he always chirps, expertly expanding his throat so it doesn't sound like he's lying down.

It's been like this for a while, reader, as I suspect you've suspected. Maybe for a *day* or two after that initial session with Theo Bakula and Gordon Gundersson and Theo's successful media friends Bruno did in fact manage to scratch at his pad for the entire length of the morning, feeling good about things, occasionally exploding out into the streets of Chinatown and stride around composing acceptance speeches for works as yet unwritten, that when they were eventually written would be written in weird mixed-media hybrids as yet unsynthesized.

But then of course it all fell apart, suddenly, one morning a few weeks ago, possibly a Wednesday, when for a change of scene, in an attempt to put the spark back, Bruno began his workday at this simply atrocious little place over in the bohemian district that surrounds Hayley's very unbohemian giant purple apartment building. The Dead Dog it's called, somewhat whimsically, and I suppose, to be fair, that it's a decent place to nurse a mug of flavored coffee just so long as you don't mind being penned in on all sides by Bruno Maddox–type individuals with pens in their mouths scouring the exposed brick walls with their eyes and lightly dusting yellow legal pads with partial and illegible schemes for Global Domination.

And all of a sudden, two sips into his ninth cup of coffee, Bruno *did* mind. One moment he was sitting there marveling at what deluded, inferior scumbags the other patrons seemed to be . . . the next he had noticed that the horrible little shit at the adjoining table was quote unquote "using" the same brand of pen as he was, as well as being identically as stubbly and wild-haired. With torrential foreboding Bruno craned to peek at the guy's yellow pad and predictably, although the fellow's handwriting was every bit as free-spirited and romantic as Bruno's own, our plump and irrelevant hero was able to make out the words

> Alison: [nibbling her lip] I don't love you anymore.
> Well, I *love* you. I just don't . . . *love* you [then explains what she means].

and instantly it was all too much. With twenty-five trainee geniuses compiling adjectival clusters with which to perfectly render the passionate, elephantine manner in which he exited the establishment, Bruno Maddox did in fact exit the establishment and lumbered off through the scorching streets in search of any kind of comfort, winding up, ill fatedly, in an enormous chain bookstore where with the urgency of a man trying to clear his name after being falsely accused of murdering his own girlfriend, Bruno Maddox fell upon a display table by the entrance and started ripping open volumes of New Fiction just to quickly, you know, check that there wasn't, you know, any single sentence in any of the books that he couldn't personally have written.

Saturday afternoon and the fairground was full of patrons.

was the first sentence he checked. Could he have written it? Yes. In his sleep. He knew what a patron was. In fact, he'd just been sitting among patrons in the Dead Dog. As for fairgrounds . . . well, he'd actually *been* to one once. Fortified, the boy pressed on. A new volume, a new victim.

They ate as they had drunk: as if compelled.

which with hindsight was where all the trouble started. The problem was that colon. That horrible, brilliant colon. What kind of wunderkind did you need to be, how much classical music did you need to have been played in the womb to be able to think of using a colon in the middle of that sentence there? Who *was* this guy, this . . . "Greg

McEwan?" Surely he at least had a Nobel Prize to his name, or a world chess championship? Bruno scrabbled for the flap copy. "Greg McEwan's first novel, *Gary's Song*, won the Delia Carter Prize for Fiction. He lives in Fordham, Wisconsin."

Now I'm not saying the boy would have been *okay* if he'd managed to prize himself out of the bookstore at that point. He'd already sustained significant damage. People were even starting to stare, reader. In fact, *patrons* were starting to stare, if that's a word in your vocabulary. They were starting to stare at a horrifically deformed young man reaching with trembling eellike fingers for a slim, ostensibly manageable volume of Scottish short fiction.

Mind you, it wisney like the cunt given 'im any *smack* for the fish fingers 'ad 'e? Just *ta'en* 'em, adn't 'e? Bird's Eye, then fish fingers 'ad been. Top of the line. Creme de la fuckin creme. "Fresh from the Captain's Fuckin Table."

Yeah, that was the one that did it. A thin, high cry was briefly audible in the air, and shortly after, for those who cared, there was a large bloated distended young man to be seen shuffling home at high speed through the terrible noontime heat, as close to crying as you can be without actually doing so.

Why?

Because he's one of *them*, reader. One of them, one of them, one of *them*. One of those young *men*, reader. One of those extremely low-quality young men whose entire peace of mind rests on the knowledge that they are a *genius*, not just that they're a genius but also that nobody else is a genius, and that nobody else even thinks they're a genius in the same way they do, one of those *insanely bad* young men, in fact, who are so utterly addicted to the idea of their own genius that—and here's an irony, given what happened to me in the sixties—they loaf about the place harboring a secret confidence that had they been born in any earlier era they would naturally have been best friends with all the *other* geniuses, the ones you've heard of. In third-century Italy, or whatever, they would have been palling around with Michelangelo on the golf course suggesting, as they followed the flight of their ball, that he do a painting of a woman with an enigmatic smile. In Stone Age times he would have been hunting buddies with the guy who invented the wheel and in the sixties of course a young bruno-maddoxy man such as Bruno Maddox would have been rubbing shoulders with Bob Dylan and Andy Warhol. Of course he would have been.

Where else would he be but with the geniuses?

Out there, reader?

Out there with the scum? With the masses? With the people who were *impressed* by the idea of a man's enlarging a soup can label? With the *consumer*, reader?

No. Of course not.

The idea of enlarging a soup can label, to a man like Bruno Maddox, is child's play.

Though his tragedy, of course, is that he wasn't born then back in the Past. He was born *now*, in the Future, when all the good ideas have already been *taken*. When all the world's most dominant geniuses can do is sit tight and wait for inspiration, with the TV on—as long as it's meaningless sport, where there's never any mention of any of those fake athletic geniuses who stalk the globe, stealing all the money, stealing all the girls—maybe a little glass of something, maybe a *sandwich*, and that's why he had a meltdown in the bookstore, reader, and why things have been tough around here lately on the "work" front.

And to my enormous delight it is all about to get worse.

You see, this morning at Hayley's while Hayley was de-linting her cardigan and Bruno was hovering around her like a turd, like some absurd little puppy in the kitchen area waiting to walk out with her, he encountered a sleep-puffy S.J. Menges just emerging from her bedroom in an Extra Large black kimono on a mission to make herself the oblig-atory cup of chamomile tea with which her sort of writers—Eloïse, for one—have historically fueled their morning. Keen to re-ingratiate himself after all the unpleasantness surrounding his Noise, Bruno congratulated Simon on her new book, *The Queen's Pearl Necklace: Women, Pornogra-phy, and the Rise of an American Class System*, into which he had dipped just the night before to quickly check that he could have written all of its sentences. "It was fucking good," said Bruno to Simon this morning, and suddenly it was if he had never made any Noise. Simon thanked Bruno for his compliment and invited him and Hayley to join her and her good friend *Gordon Gundersson* for dinner and a launch party this Friday night. Yes, that's right. Gordon Gundersson of *Black Current* fame. Author, canoeist, spokesperson of a generation.

Bruno's very excited. Here in the apartment all day it was "*Gordon* . . . how are you . . . brunomaddox" again and again and again, sometimes with Bruno shaking the air's hand, sometimes just glowering at it with an appalling we-meet-again-old-foe lift of the chin, which made me want to vomit. Even the *memory* of it makes me want to vomit. In fact I *will* vomit.

There.

I feel much better.

In fact I feel *much* better.

The key to this writing thing, I've discovered, reader, incidentally, is absolutely *not* to hunch over the thing and strain to get it right. The key to it . . . the absolute *key to it* . . . is just to sort of tilt your face back, put as much space as possible between your face and the screen, so the words are so tiny you can barely see them and then . . . and then just imagine you're standing at the top of some sort of metal slope, pouring a jugful of liquid . . .

July 30th—Friday

. . . down the slope the literary liquid runs . . . following its nose, its bliss . . . from Thursday into Friday.

And let me *welcome* you to Friday, reader, to historic Friday evening. I'm here with Bruno Maddox and why don't we say for the sake of argument that we were coming to you live at approximately 1 A.M. in the morning. It'll just be me, unfortunately, because Bruno's passed out in a vomit-slathered heap beside the radiator and will not be able to give us an account of his evening, but the show must go on. Like the professional I am, I shall think on my feet and deduce the events of the evening just passed by examining the evidence at hand.

Exhibit A: The smell of the boy. There is an odor to him this evening, reader, an odor of sweat that has been warmed by the rays of the evening sun, from which, as a genius, I am able to deduce . . .

. . . that at thirty minutes past seven this evening Bruno Maddox found himself exploding into the fancy beige confines of the *Capo di Tutti Frutti* Italian restaurant slick with sweat and hair wings a-flap after maniacally shambling the thirty odd blocks from his lonely, unappreciative workplace. The maître d' of the place will have viewed him, correctly, as something of a Tarzanish figure as Bruno pointlessly shielded his eyes and spotted Hayley, Simon and the large brown bulk of Gordon Gundersson, seated at the very farthest table, a round one.

There was another note in his odor, though, a scent of perfume and irritation, which leads me to the assumption that *Capo di Tutti Frutti* was, rather like the steerage section of an aircraft, the sort of place where the slightest movement of one's muscles places some portion of one's flesh in somebody else's face, something that happened significantly more than once, I have a feeling, as Bruno shambled through the gaps between the tables.

One final thing I smell: a tangy cocktail of Hayley Iskender and the boy's own fizzing neurotransmitter that tells me Bruno's first act upon joining his party, even before sitting down, was to pointedly ignore Gundersson, say "Hey," and plant a firm kiss on the cheek of Hayley Iskender while scraping an unaffiliated diner with his buttock.

Elementary.

Exhibit B: A crease in the muscle above his eyebrow, from which I deduce that what happened next was that Simon Menges greeted him, "How are *you*?" in a weird way that made him raise that eyebrow as he slid heavily into his chair next to Hayley.

"Oh *I'm* okay," he tosses out. "Feeling a little . . . diminished. The, uh, camera seizes my essence and distributes it electromagnetically."

And the table will have fallen silent.

"Bruno . . ." begins Simon.

The young man's head jerks up, cocks.

". . . this is . . ."

Slow smile of . . .

". . . my friend Gor . . ."

Recognition changes the shape of Bruno's mouth. "Oh . . . right. Yeah, we've met. Hi." His fingers flick up. "Good to meet you."

Gundersson is, geniusly, the only person in the restaurant wearing a T-shirt, a gray one. He is similarly the only person drinking a pint of beer, and not just any pint of beer, but a pint of beer so hoppy and authentic that it looks like it's had a tree dipped in it. Gordon sits there bronzed and humorless and muscular beneath his pile of canoeist ringlets. He nods at Bruno then resumes a conversation with Hayley Iskender. "Iskender. That's a Turkish name, isn't it?"

"Mm hmm."

"You're Turkish?" says Bruno to Hayley, grandly unflapping his napkin and looking, for some reason, at Gordon.

"Yes. My father's father was from Turkey."

Bruno winks at Simon. "But you're *blond*."

"I thought you two were together," Gordon comments with a frown.

At this Bruno has to guffaw. "Oh we *are*," wrapping a

thick arm around Hayley's thin shoulders and squeezing. "I suppose it's just that . . . I've been . . . suppressing asking her about her Turkishness."

"What?" asks Simon, failing to make the connection between Bruno's unfathomable remark and the truth: that he is himself a genius.

Exhibit C: The wrinkle pattern of Bruno's horrible green jacket, which tells me . . .

. . . that after a waitress has recited the specials and selections have been lodged, Gordon sets down his beer and addresses Bruno in a fairly amiable manner, "Sorry what was your name again?"

"Brunomaddox," whispers Bruno, leaning forward, wrinkling his shoulders.

"Burn . . . eye . . . ?"

"Bruno, *B-R-U-N-O*, Maddox. *M-A-* double-*D-O-X*."

Gordon has it now. He nods. "Okay. How's it going."

"*Fucking* well, actually, Gordon." Bruno jabs a finger at Gordon, congratulating him on his extremely germane inquiry. "*Fucking* well."

"Why?" wonders Gordon.

Bruno nods. He understands what Gordon is after. Chance for him here.

"Oh, you know. Good day at the . . ." wiggles fingers, miming typing, ". . . endeavors."

"You're a writer?"

"Oh yes." This is Simon, the bitch, and her eyes are glittering in a sinister, almost sexual manner. "Bruno has his finger in *many pies*!" Hayley, all this while, is looking at her plate.

Bruno: "I'm not quite sure what Simon's implying, but

yes I am working on quite a few projects at the moment. I'm doing a rock opera about an airline pilot who has a few problems with the . . ." wiggles fingers, miming drinking, "bottle. *Cabin Pressure*."

Hayley looks up at Simon who is still smirking at Bruno who is staring hopefully at Gordon.

"My friend is an airline pilot." Gordon takes a bite of his beer.

"Oh really? How does he stand it?"

"Stand what?"

"The awfulness."

"Awfulness?"

"Yes the . . . the constant fear, the stress, the little chair."

"What little chair?"

Bruno doesn't know. He unflaps his napkin one more time. "Er . . . don't worry." He dabs at his immaculate lips with the napkin. "Forget it. It's not that big a . . ." and then inspiration strikes, terribly, cheapening and ruining everything that was good, or even acceptable, about the scene around the table, ". . . *chair*," he says.

Exhibit D: A crease on Bruno's thigh that I just *know in my gut* was caused by Hayley Iskender reaching under the table and squeezing his leg to make him rein himself in.

"I'm sorry," Gordon's forehead is knotted like a tree, "I'm not following you."

"Oh there's nothing to '*follow*.' Look, are you okay? I haven't . . . said something to bother you have I?"

Bruno uses this line on Gordon because people are always using it on Bruno, it seems, and it always has the effect of rallying whole tablefuls of people against him.

The line does not work in reverse, though, it seems. Simon and Hayley both stare at Bruno. Gordon shifts comfortably in his chair, scrapes his stubble with the backs of his fingernails. His watch is nice. "No. It's just you seem kind of . . . unsocialized. I don't mean to be rude." For an instant Bruno considers bursting into tears, but just then the food arrives. "Ah. Food," he says and steeples his fingers like some weird old German man or something.

Exhibit M: An oval smooth-patch the size of a melon on the back of his jacket, which I can't help feeling must have been caused by Bruno spending the rest of the meal on his absolute best behavior, dominating conversation with his contrition and his increasingly drunken silence. Simon engages Gordon in a somewhat stilted discussion of the difference between Public Space and Private Space, likening the answering machine she shares with Hayley to a *valve* in the skin of her Private Sphere, through which Public Space intrudes in the form of people calling her up and asking her to do things because she is a famous author.

"Like in a dome," squeaks Bruno, voice sticky with disuse, they all agree, not wanting to set him off. "It *is* like in a dome," all three of them chime, not knowing what they're saying.

Exhibit O: A stretch mark on the front of Bruno's Housing Department T-shirt presumably caused by the massive sigh of relief he gave when it all, finally, seemed to be over. "Eighty each," I detect Simon saying, after studying the bill. Three credit cards appear, and Bruno's checkbook.

"Looks like you have a check already made out," says Simon, squinting, her strange glow returning, forgetting to worry about setting Bruno off.

Gordon, being a canoeist, having constantly to be peering into the distance for semi-submerged rocks, has better eyesight. "Wow," he observes. "I like the 'only.' "

Exhibit Z: And finally: a great crust of milky yellow vomit down the forearm of one of Bruno's sleeves, from which I infer that within an hour of his checkbook appearing Bruno is crouched inside a brushed-steel stall at Aluminum Bertrand regurgitating six quick whiskeys and his penne with Tuscan meat sauce, which tasted like cat food anyway, into the brushed-steel toilet bowl. There is a good deal of banging on the door, much of it official—barmaids, barmen, bouncers, managers, owners, local councillors, congressmen, presidents, kings—and a majority of the remainder coming from Simon Menges, who is having the time of her life. "Bru-no!" roars Simon in a sing-song. "You need to get out of there so that other people can get in!"

"Is he vomiting?" asks a stranger.

"Yes," choruses everybody.

" 'Kay!" Bruno shouts, the syllable echoing in the bowl like the foghorn of a ship.

"You guys shouldn't bang on the door," comes Gordon's voice, an ally all of a sudden, now that Bruno has all of the shallow, wine-drinking Manhattan nightlife belle monde ranged against him. "It's not cool. He may really be ill."

And then it's Hayley Iskender. Her voice is sad and tired and sober and would have preferred not to be heard . . . and yet it cuts through the tumult like a knife made of paper. "Hey. It's me. Bruno if you come out of there we can go home."

"'Kay . . . ay . . . ay . . . y."

Hayley again. "It's okay." The crowd grows absolutely silent to listen. "Nobody cares about the checkbook."

"I 'idn't write that!" he thunders incorrectly. "I id *not* write *that*!"

"Nobody cares. Just come out."

The Chinese have a saying, you know, reader. Be careful what you wish for because blah blah blah. And all of those people who wanted Bruno out of the bathroom should have been careful what they wished for because when he *did* come out into that sea of dim open-mouthed faces he immediately vomited in such a way that it affected nearly all of their shoes, apart from one Chinese guy who'd seen it coming and climbed on a chair.

July 31st—Saturday

Message from Hayley Iskender around noon, an inexplicable one: "[pause] Hi. It's me. Bruno? Are you there? I know you're there. [pause] Look . . . I'm sorry if . . . I'm sorry about last night. You obviously had a difficult time and I want to know you're okay. So if you get this message call me. Please."

I hear Bruno shift in his sleep next door.

You've got the wrong number, I pulse the machine in the fraction of a second before Hayley disconnects. *You've got entirely the wrong number. This is where that young man lives, the one from last night. You should exhibit more care when dialing. Dial more carefully in future and you will*

reach other residences, where other, better people live. Please.
For your own sake. Please. While you're still young.

And that's all I have to say to you, reader.

I'm done.

I've shot my load.

I'm passing out now.

Goodnight.

Sorry if you wanted more. There isn't any more. There was August of course but you're not going to hear it from me. Not, I suspect, that you need to hear it from anyone at this point because August

August

_____

August 1st—Sunday

you can figure out for yourself. Obviously, the boy being
the boy, he didn't call Hayley back that Saturday.

Why?

Don't know.

I can tell you that in his *mind* it was the hangover. The
revolting little lad's bad insides had a pole through them and
even through when he went to vomit he necessarily passed
the 'phone it seemed to him no more than common sense
that he should wait till he was out of the vomit stage before
calling.

He stayed in it though, the vomit stage, all through Saturday, and then Sunday he was in a new stage, just as debili-
tating in its way, all trembly and braindead,

August 2nd—Monday

and then on the Monday just as he was *probably* about to
call her, standing by the 'phone in his bedsheet toga that was
practically translucent with sweat and tears and other classic
male effluvia, the blessed thing *rang*, and that guy Theo
Bakula started purring through the answering machine and
then into the boy's ear directly that what Bruno was going
to be doing that evening was meeting Theo for drinks and
then accompanying him to "some thing for some new
thing."

Reader, Theo wasn't *asking* . . . he was *telling*! And as
I've either mentioned or you've gathered there are these
phases Bruno goes through when he's feeling rather *flimsy*
and anyone whose vocal tone has a certain amount of au-
thority and *zing* to it can in effect just order him around like
some sort of robot puppy.

So he went. Bruno met Theo for drinks and then moved
on to the thing for the new thing, and there was a great number of whiskeys and banquettes and fun girls who seemed
able to appreciate basically *any joke* even if it was just a noise
and a hand movement, even if the joke was just you becoming extremely drunk, and the upshot of it all was that

August 3rd—Tuesday

come Tuesday morning not only was the young man in even
worse shape physically than on the morning after the Night
of the Checkbook but as he knelt to the toilet bowl, taking
an unflinching look at what had recently been inside of him,

the quiet realization took hold that he now needed an excuse for having not returned Hayley's 'phone call for four days.

Should he tell her he had food poisoning? Try to explain away some of the Checkbook Night's vomiting as well as his subsequent disappearance?

Mmm . . . no.

August 4th—Wednesday

Food poisoning doesn't stop a person using a 'phone—in fact quite the contrary, in many instances. To a victim of food poisoning the 'phone can be a lifeline. He or she uses the thing to liaise with family and friends, to contact medical professionals, to build and maintain support networks, both emotional and whatever . . .

Maybe something grander was required, such as . . .

Oh wow.

Oh his God.

What if he called and explained that he had been so *disgusted* with himself that he'd rented a car and gone to sit beside a cold clear lake in some random unpopulated state with his knees drawn up to his chest taking an *unflinching look inside himself*?

Jesus.

That was an excuse and a half. With material that strong maybe he could get away with not calling her back until the end of the week!

August 5th—Thursday

Right?

August 6th—Friday

Mmm . . . no. *Un*right. Wrong.

Hayley knew he couldn't drive, so that scuppered that.

Damn. But was it . . . was it stretching plausibility to tell her he had learned to drive? What if he had learned to drive on the Sunday, then driven out to the lake on the Monday? Doesn't intense self-disgust sometimes give a person super-human powers of . . . learning?

No.

No it doesn't. That whole direction was just completely stupid and useless and pathetic and disgusting.

Besides, what if all this while Hayley had been tuning into *Thirty UN!der Thirty* in the evenings? What then? That fucked up every excuse imaginable. A guy who can go to work can use a 'phone. A guy who can contribute meaning-fully to a discussion of nuclear proliferation on the Asian subcontinent—even if his meaningful contribution is only "You can't really trust a Pakistani . . . not really . . ."—can surely be expected to at least *contact* his supposed girlfriend just to tell her he's alive . . .

What a fool he'd been for going to work. What a . . .

Then it came to him, in a rush of warmth, the perfect excuse.

Shame.

Was that not brilliant? He hadn't called her back all week because he'd been *ashamed of himself*.

Not only was it brilliant, *it was true*. In fact . . .

Oh wow. Maybe his shame had been so intense that he'd spent the last seven days composing some sort of *statement* for Hayley, an apology, a *confession* . . . maybe not just on his own behalf but on that of his entire *generation* . . . an epic *poem*, even a *novel* . . .

And maybe the thing to do, just to really add some flesh to the excuse, was for him to just quickly whip off a *first draft* of his generational apologia novel before call . . .

August 7th—Saturday

Bruno finally called Hayley Saturday morning around ten-ish. He had to.

Only eight hours previously, in the back room of the This Is Not A Bar Bar, all the way uptown, the Sports and Fitness Editor of *come hither* magazine—Jane, the redhead, the one who'd taken him under her wing the night of the rooftop party—had witnessed Bruno poking a cocktail napkin into the bra strap of a consenting plus-size fashion model. Just as he'd straightened up . . . there she'd been, on the far side of the lounge, peering at him evenly as a team of furrows jogged out onto her forehead and arranged themselves into the words "You have, at most, twelve hours before news of where you just poked that cocktail napkin reaches Hayley Iskender."

So he made a preemptive strike and called Hayley himself, around tenish, as I say. The first part he ad-libbed.

"Hayley? Hi, it's me."

And the rest he read from a sheet of paper. "Sorry I've

been out of touch all week. I've been a bit depressed. That guy Theo Bakula tried to cheer me up by taking me out last night but . . . [pause] well, it was just a whole bunch of weird *fat* women playing party games with cocktail napkins and frankly it just made me feel *much* worse. Anyway. Here I am. Sorry I didn't call. How are you?"

"Um . . ." This syllable was vastly reassuring to the boy. It was neither the pause he'd been expecting, nor one of those high-pitched, slightly nasal "ums" people emit while they check with their conscience that they really want to make the particularly hurtful remark that's on their mind. (Do you have any idea what I'm talking about?) "I'm okay. I've been worried about you though. I kind of assumed you'd taken some time out to . . . reassess things. But it would have been nice if you'd called. I might have been able to help."

"Yeah. I'm sorry. Like you say. I just needed some time."

"I know. It's fine."

"No. I should have called."

"It's time. Do you need *more* time? Or should we meet?"

I was staggered, reader, by these words from the girl. In fact the whole tenor of the conversation was literally blowing my mind. Hayley seemed almost prepared to . . . *forgive* Bruno for everything, sweep it all under the rug, offer him a twenty-fifth chance . . .

The boy was stunned as well, and not entirely pleasantly because, reader, you see the fact of the matter was that he had already agreed to go meet that guy *Theo Bakula* that evening to attend a thing in the uptown showroom of a top person's perfumerie, a thing sponsored by a whiskey, and so rather tragically and inevitably he responded with the words, "Okay. That's fine. I'll call you in a day or two."

August 8th—Sunday

One.

August 9th—Monday

Two.

August 10th—Tuesday

Three.

August 11th—Wednesday

Four.

August 12th—Thursday

Five, and obviously by this point if Bruno was going to call Hayley then yet again he needed an excuse for not calling.

Which is where, reader, this whole thing just gets terribly terribly sad.

Because, you see, he had one, reader. He had an excuse, a terrible, shitty, disgustingly sad excuse that I wouldn't be telling you if I didn't suspect you of already guessing it.

You see, as I can't remember whether I mentioned, Bruno was passing all these evenings out there in upscale

Manhattan with that guy Theo Bakula going to various openings and celebrations and though the evenings were tending to end up identically, in vomit, in loneliness, in a cab ride he couldn't afford back to a stinking Chinatown sweatbox he could hardly stand looking at, they could be counted on, the evenings, to contain certain *moments* in which the tiny little mite felt calmer and more centered than he *ever had in his life*. Watching some other little fuck get turned away or better still *ejected* from the VIP lounge ... informing a high-quality waitress that his cocktail was too warm and nodding graciously at her *apology* ... surreptitiously stroking the hair of the world's third richest fashion model with the back of his forefinger when they coincided in line for the bathroom ... moments of shallow, vain and utterly insubstantial glory, reader—and he knew this—which nonetheless provoked a Feeling in the boy that could not have been more wholesome. A feeling of clarity. Sanity. The power of reflection. It was the darnedest thing, but it was only when sprawled in some cool-to-the-touch VIP banquette with a lurking paparazzo eyeing him from across the lounge trying to remember who he was, that Bruno was able to remember who he was himself. Only then could he *think about his life*. It would all just snap into focus. He drank too much; he didn't do any work; he was going to lots of stupid meaningless parties at the expense of what he had with Hayley Iskender. Hayley Iskender was excellent, possibly *the one* ... it all came clear.

But, tragically, also clear was the fact that his only hope was to *hold on to* the Feeling. If he had to go back to being just another little man, just another speck of scum, of plankton, back to being the same haywire little man that Simon and Gordon had failed to embrace as an equal on the Night of the Hundred Million Dollars, the same minuscule nonentity that Mark Clark, that proud irrelevant, *had* embraced as an equal that night at Magma, then nothing he tried was ever, ever going to work. Because it was the feeling of being a little man, he now knew, that drove him crazy.

So that was Bruno's Plan for getting back in touch with Hayley: just quickly make the Feeling *permanent*, just quickly get to the stage where the men on the doors let him in because he was Bruno Maddox rather than because Theo Bakula was Theo Bakula, then retire from the Scene, stride directly into Hayley's place of business, scoop her away from her keyboard and then whisk her away to some better place where he'd make her the happiest slightly tired-and-stringy looking blond woman since they started keeping records.

He knew it was a pathetic strategy but the thing seemed doable. The waitresses and doormen were starting to recognize him, possibly. The drummer of a rock band was very friendly to him at the bar one evening, though there were visible grains of cocaine in one nostril. And when finally he did see Hayley, when she saw, when she felt who he'd become, she'd understand that in a sense all his senseless partying had been for her benefit, and she would surely forgive him one last time for everything. Even if the senseless partying were to drag on several days longer than he expected,

August 13th—Friday

for instance six

August 14th—Saturday

or possibly even seven,

August 15th—Sunday

or even *eight*.

August 16th—Monday

Didn't matter, ultimately, because by the time Bruno finally did call the girl the Plan had been discarded. He came awake that Monday morning in darkness with an abdominal pain of the stabbing variety that was stronger than anything anyone had ever felt and the *bad* news, reckoned *The Caregiver's Bible*, was that it was definitely either diverticulitis—an exclusive disease of elderly people like me—or stomach cancer, probably stomach cancer. Skipping the traditional sequence of Denial, Anger, Hiding Under Doctor's Desk, etc., the microscopic little shit went straight to Crying. In his bedsheet toga on the creaking predawn floor Bruno rocked back and forth and grieved the unfairness, and yet the inevitability, of his having been struck down only a day or two—three at the most—from his ultimate becoming.

By mid-morning he was bravely appreciating the irony of it. Ironic that it would take something like this to finally make the Feeling permanent—remember the Feeling, reader?

The future was simple now, and obvious, and eerily similar to the one he'd been planning in the VIP lounges: his diagnosis was the occasion to renounce the Scene, renounce everything and spend what time remained to him making Hayley Iskender happy. It was the obvious foolproof move, which is why it was so distressing to him when she seemed reluctant to play along.

"Why do you think you have stomach cancer?" was what she asked through the 'phone, after a short bored pause.

"It's the ... aaugh! ... It's the *symptoms*. I've got them exactly. Hayley ..."

"Do you have a hangover?"

"No."

"Well, I'm sorry to hear that. I hope you'll be okay."

"Um ... thanks. Um ..."

"Is that it?"

"*No*. Hayley ..."

"Yes?"

"Is something wrong? Are you mad at me? I'm really picking up a tone."

He really was, reader. Hayley was using a tone. Even when she wasn't speaking—like now—she was pausing—there was palpable hostility coming through the 'phone.

"Bruno, I'm sick of this."

"Sick of what? What? Are you sick of *me*?"

"Yes."

"*Hay*ley. *Listen*. Are you listening?"

"I'm working. I have a deadline."

"So do *I*! But Hayley ... look, listen. I'm sorry. About everything. I've been a moron. But I'm not fucking joking about this cancer thing." He gave one sob. "I am dying. Even if you don't want to be with me anymore ... I need you. Look, I'm not from around here. I'm a traveler alone in a foreign country with a fatal disease. I just need someone to talk to. Just for five minutes. Just for *one* . . ."

And Bruno Maddox began to cry, like a tiny little girl, faux-stifling his sobs until Hayley, as she had to, relented and agreed to meet him. Let me tell you, as a woman myself, it's very hard as a female organism in Nature to refuse the requests of a grown man who is actually crying, even if he's the sort who basically cries all the time.

So they met, in the evening, at Midnite Xpress, a twenty-four-hour Turkish take-away franchise with exactly one plastic table. Bruno chose the venue. It was his stupidly clever way of paying homage to the tiny drop of Turkishness apparently rolling like a marble down Hayley's bloodless, echoey veins—the one that Gundersson had so cunningly zeroed in on that night of all the nonsense at *Capo di Tutti Frutti*. Precisely what subliminal effect this was meant to have on the girl he didn't know—the same way he didn't know how the *Shades of Manhattan* audience member who discovers Amanda's sunglasses beneath his or her chair was supposed to feel—but he found her hunched above the plastic table looking tired and bothered and even a good deal *older* than he remembered her. The eight Turks behind the counter thought Hayley looked good though, they were lusting at her visibly, speculating in Turkish about what fun it would be to penetrate her in a special tent during a sandstorm.

Bruno's conversation with Hayley Iskender went like this:

"Hey," said Bruno.

"How are you?" said Hayley.

"Fine," said Bruno. "How are you?"

"You're fine?" said Hayley, the legs of her plastic chair creating a barking sound as she stood.

"Ye . . . oh oh oh oh," said Bruno. "The stomach thing. Yeah, it's the weirdest thing but it's actually feeling much . . ."

Hayley didn't wait to hear about his miraculous recovery. She exited at that stage, reader, and stalked away into the hot night and the crowds of people with her usually limp ponytail swinging like a stiff and unfeeling pendulum.

How did Bruno feel about her sudden departure? Oh come on, reader. You know how he felt. There in that glaring cube of aromatic space? Under the glittering eyes of those terrible Turks? Having just been jettisoned by the woman on this planet who most precisely fit the definition of his "girlfriend"? He felt like the Turks were *judging him*.

"She's . . ." he announced, rubbing his chin like an adventurer. "She's an untamable stallion, that one." And then he laughed, "No problem, though," and resolved not to deal with the larger issue until he'd made it back to Chinatown, downed his massive Turkish sandwich, and watched a documentary about some scientists examining a corpse in order to determine who had killed it.

By morning, though, of course,

August 17th—Tuesday

The thing had become a proper crisis. He couldn't *believe* it, reader, couldn't *believe* that he'd actually been fool enough to exchange his one shot at finding love in this appalling universe for . . . for what? For the transient cool of a supermodel's hair against his forefinger? For the hollow, ephemeral clinking of cleverly shaped, complimentary ice cubes? It hardly seemed worth it.

Oh, and also summer was ending, reader. Another thing to spark regret. That end-of-Summer atmosphere was fully noticeable in the air: the one where you step outside in the morning and notice that the air is fractionally cooler and the light fractionally more orange and more angled than you remember, as if the Earth has tilted slightly on its axis while you've been asleep, which I suppose is actually pretty close to the scientific truth of the situation, and some pieces of paper are blowing around in a circle at the corner of the street and you think you might even smell a distant *woodfire* ... and possibly even hear the bonging of a distant *churchbell* ... and all of a sudden it's like your mam calling you home for your tea or something because you get all overwhelmed with poignancy and regret and a strange *nostalgia* that isn't for anything in particular. I mean you're nostalgic for the summer just ending, of course, but when you try to actually put your finger on it you find you're merely nostalgic for the day you went to the Post Office and bought stamps, and for the day you saw a dog with a set of small wheels instead of a set of hind legs, and for the day you did laundry ...

The young man felt *old* all of a sudden, reader, slightly. Venturing out for his morning sandwich he caught sight of his clothes and could no longer see the point of them, get the joke of them. No longer did his clothing make him feel like a *god*, reader, a god reaching languidly down from a cloud and plucking the trousers off a nineteen forties paratrooper and the shirt off the back of a 21st Century Housing Department worker ... no, instead they made him feel like a man who lacked either the money or the basic common sense to dress appropriately.

And so he acted. Bruno bent his steps west and at a vast discount clothing emporium on the huge wide street that runs the length of Manhattan Island he conducted a transaction and emerged not long after wearing two of the *plainest* items of clothing that you ever did see, reader: a gray collarless shirt so utterly unremarkable that one of those puppeteers who usually perform in black clothing against a black background with their head in a black cowl could have worn it in a pinch without ruining the audience's experience, and a pair of black denim trousers, reader, so spectacular in their featurelessness that even a writer of my own demonstrated *excellence* has absolutely *nothing* to say about them.

His next move was to fix his hair. At a giant mechanized barn of a barbershop the protagonist Bruno Maddox maintained perfect unwavering eye contact with himself in the mirror while an elderly Italian soccer fanatic relieved him of the appalling hair wings upon which he has been propelling himself all summer and left with what can only be described as "a very poor haircut indeed." His head now resembled a potato, and truth be known Bruno *felt* rather like a potato as he made his way back through the teeming, steaming streets. He felt like a knobbly old gray spud rolling lumpily home between the weightless, gallivanting strawberries and kumquats that people the streets of Manhattan. He felt stupid, ugly, and miserable . . . and it felt good to feel that way. After months of juggling all those glamorous, unfeasible identities? To be able to let them all thud to the ground and just for better or worse be "Bruno Maddox"? A humble normal man with a name and a telephone number and a troubled past and a difficult recovery and a new, hard-won appreciation of his limitations? A solid citizen who if you called out "Hey!

Bruno Maddox!" from across the street would probably lift his face to see if he could be of any assistance?

It felt fantastic.

He'd finally got it right.

After one of the longest periods of trial and error in the entire history of the phrase, Bruno Maddox had finally *got it right*.

Bruno pinged Hayley's bell at eight o'clock that evening after a day of housecleaning and vegetable eating, to say good-bye, and possibly do some more suffering. She opened the door and looked at him. "Hello," she droned inscrutably. "What do you want?"

"Can I come in?"

She blinked up at his head. "What happened to your hair?"

"I took care of it," said Bruno Maddox. "Do you think I could come in?"

" . . . "

Reader, the word she was groping for was "No." It was right on the tip of her tongue. Knowing the boy as well as she did, Hayley had been braced all day for a surprise visit, but this . . . this she was *not* prepared for. The tragic haircut, the unspectacular clothing, the quiet yet forceful vocal tone . . . Curiosity alone would have probably made her stand aside and bid him enter—even if there hadn't been something else, something she couldn't quite put her finger on.

Sitting with him on the black leather couch Hayley stopped trying to put her finger on what else was different about Bruno and switched her attention to the sensation in her *genitalia*, reader. For the record Bruno was pouring his heart out in a long, unstructured ramble about his family, his childhood, a recurring dream of his in which he's dangling irrelevantly from the undercarriage of a plane . . . but Hayley was seeing past his words to the big picture, to the man himself, and having a response that was largely physiolog . . .

"Do you want to stay?" she heard herself interrupt. "Simon's at a writer's retreat till the end of the month. You could stay here till then."

"Um . . ." The young man chewed his lip and gathered his thoughts, then launched into a whole new speech about how *careful* he was going to be about making decisions like that from here on in, and what a fool he'd been in the past for just rushing into . . .

Hayley prodded him with her toe. "I think I need to be naked with you" were her exact words and trust me, reader, you would have said the same. *Anyone* would have done. Any man, or woman, or child. Any rock, or stone, or tree. Reader, a *jar of mineral oil* seated next to him on the couch that evening would have also started to fizz and steam and tilt slightly in his direction. *And I'm not being sarcastic.*

Because the thing was this:

Bruno Maddox was *magnificent.* He really was. All those horrible defects that were all the *old* Bruno Maddox really had in the way of a personality were beginning to look an awful lot like *virtues* now that they were organized around this soulful, clear-eyed core. The megalomania was a nice balance to the crippling low self-esteem, the compulsive socialite glibness—when you thought about it—worked rather well with his occasional spasms of clinginess . . . just as long as at the eye of the storm there was a self-awareness and a goodness and a *reason* for it all . . .

Look, I'm sorry, reader. I'm not being clear. The hour is late and I have been losing focus for some time now, truth be told. The only point I'm trying to make is that you too, in Hayley's position, would have informed Bruno Maddox of your need to be naked with him, and that you too, frankly, would have also allowed him to pump himself empty inside you with the power and sincerity of an early steam train and would probably, just like Hayley Iskender, have melted off to sleep with the warmth of his magnificence still dying on your tongue like the warmth in a spoon that you have used to stir your coffee and are using now to eat your cereal. His magnificence, reader, was just that intense. As

August 18th—Wednesday

it tends to be on that first day after he's reinvented himself. Sometimes even the second day.

But by the following evening, though when Hayley got back from work evidence of the boy's enduring magnificence was strewn all around the apartment—the floor had been swept, he had paid some bills with his notorious checkbook and stacked them neatly on the entranceway radiator, he had visited the hardware store and cut himself a copy of Hayley's keys, and her, sweetly, a set of his—hairline cracks were already visible in the newly cast monolith of "Bruno Maddox," a nervous glow around the eyes, a restless springiness to the legs . . . And by that Thursday evening Bruno

August 19th—Thursday

knew it himself. He knew he was slipping. He managed to muddle through the sex act well enough, no complaints from the girl, but there in the dark postcoitally Bruno tried to *cradle* the nude Ms. Iskender in the same wholesome, brunomaddoxy way that had served him so well in recent nights . . . and just couldn't remember how it went. Was it mainly wrist . . . or largely forearm?

By Friday he

August 20th—Friday

had deteriorated to the point of asking himself, "What would Bruno Maddox say under these circumstances?" whenever the situation demanded he say something, and over the ensuing weekend, to be perfectly frank,

August 22nd—Sunday

he wasn't particularly magnificent at all. Hayley took him shopping in the sun and though the girl isn't usually a big fan of couplesome hand holding, she found herself having to do so, because otherwise Bruno tended to grind to a halt in front of random shop windows and scour his reflection for clues as to what it was about being "Bruno Maddox" that had so recently seemed so revolutionary. Back at the house he hit the couch and watched the television, hoping Hayley wouldn't notice him there as she vacuumed unhappily around.

Mid-morning Monday Bruno's answering machine back here in Chinatown picked up the sound of that fellow Theo Bakula inviting Bruno to join him for a quiet after-work drink "avec certain amigos," which was all very confusing to the boy when he retrieved the message remotely using Hayley's 'phone. There was a sort of *warm anticipation* in Theo's voice that suggested Bruno *would* in fact be meeting him . . . but then there was also the fact that *not* going out and having drinks with Theo Bakula was practically the only tenet of his new, wholesome personal doctrine that he was currently able to remember. In the cool of Hayley's apartment, the fragmenting young man actually *whimpered* slightly, reader, under the confusion of it all, then put a call through to Hayley at the office to get her take on the whole thing.

"So there's something I need to tell you," he said to her. "Something bad."

"What?" Hayley worried.

"A few weeks ago I stupidly made plans with that guy Theo Bakula to go to have drinks this evening."

A pause while she digested. "That's it? That's the bad thing?"

"Yes."

"Why is that bad?"

"Um Because you and I were going to cook dinner this evening."

"And you don't want to go and meet Theo?"

"No, I . . . Look, if I do go do you want to come?"

"Mm . . ." Yawny yawny girly girly. "No. You should go, though."

"Well I think I might *have* to go."

"You should."

He *did* go, reader, and was back before midnight drunk off his face but in a rather upbeat frame of mind having stumbled, if you can believe it, across the Secret of Existence. The Secret of Existence was Moderation. It had been staring him in the face all along. The absurdly monkish and sterile regime he'd been trying to pursue since the day of his haircut, the day of summer's starting to end—and it was continuing to end, reader, continuing apace—was far too severe. Maybe for a simpler man, a man of fewer parts, such a lifestyle was sustainable, but for a man of Bruno's obvious complexity it was not merely *okay* to go get a drink occasionally with Theo Bakula, it was *essential*.

Hayley he found asleep on the couch with an architecture documentary still blaring. He snuffled her awake and rather devilishly proceeded to make her his—right then and there, if you must know, reader.

But it was a fleeting little uptick, by which

August 24th—Tuesday

I mean that he wake up the next morning long after Hayley had left for work and lay there literally for an hour, just blinking up at the immaculate ceiling and failing to remember anything at all: where he was, what the Secret of Existence was, what he was like as a person, any of that. By 6 P.M. he had called in sick to work and was huddled beneath a blanket on Hayley's couch. As the hour of her return approached, he leapt from the couch several times and ran to the hallway mirror where, miming a handshake with himself, he attempted the act of speech. "Ho ho. How's it going?" he inquired of his image. "Oh really? Man. Wow. Sorry to hear that. Um. Gotta run."

And run he did, reader, all the way back to the couch where he languished all evening, pretending to be asleep-slash-unwell so as not to have to answer Hayley with anything more than a grunt when she addressed him, which wasn't often. He genuinely did not feel well, for the record. His sinuses or something had snapped shut in his head and he was overpowered by the taste of his own saliva, just like back in the bad old days, a condition that

August 25th—Wednesday

persisted all the following day, not dissipating one iota, getting worse and worse, reaching its nadir when he got to work. The topic of *Thirty UN!der Thirty* that Wednesday evening was The Scourge of Gun Violence in America and the only thing Bruno could think of to say was:

"In England, where I come from, there's a . . . a chinchilla of random violence always lurking under everything."

Which didn't make any sense, a chinchilla being a fur or an animal or something of that sort.

"Er . . . not a chinchilla, obviously. A . . . skein."

Which made even *less* sense, impressively, and to anyone floating a foot or so behind his head as I was, bodiless and suspended by cosmic-slash-literary forces above the trading floor of the American Stock Exchange, peeking over Bruno's shoulder into the great black funnel of the camera, there were audible snickers bleeding from his earpiece from a) Kelly-Ann from Minnesota and b) bow-tied-black-guy Pierre, as they took his measure in their orderly, employable minds.

Cabbing back up to Hayley's Bruno stuck his head out the window for air and I found myself watching with enormous pity, reader, as the very last shred of personality fluttered briefly in the gale and then detached.

Hayley was in her cardigan, leaning against the abutment of her kitchen counter, drinking a bottle of beer. She smiled, when Bruno entered, and nodded over toward the couch where, sure enough, there sat a stranger, a third organism: an older man with a ball of frizzy gray hair, wearing a scuffed old leather jacket and round little sixties glasses. Bruno blinked at him, not knowing what to do.

"Dad, this is Bruno Maddox. Bruno, this is my father, Orson Iskender."

Oh yes. Oh dear. Hayley had mentioned something about . . . oh dear.

Did I tell you about Hayley's father, reader? I have no memory of doing so but of course in this stage the memory thing is ebbing in and out, in and out. . . . Anyway. Hayley's father Orson Iskender is "Orson," the brains and the pen behind one of America's least enjoyable syndicated daily cartoon strips, a three-panel nonsense of a thing called "Bring Out Your Dead" detailing the exploits of a squat moronic nobleman in a funny hat and his taller, cleverer manservant. For the last twenty years or so this pair has been wandering pointlessly around plague-stricken sixteenth-century London, engaged in banter that is only superficially *not* about twenty-first-century American politics. "Tell me, Face," the nobleman says every day in the first panel, "why do the wealthy landowners who grow tobacco give bags of gold coins to the Members of Parliament? Is that not corruption?" Nothing ever happens in the middle panel. The servant just looks down at the master. Then in the third panel the servant says, "Maybe so, sir, but . . ." and then the supposedly amusing and satirical part, which I apologize for not being able to remember here. No, no, I have to. I have to. I should take a stab. ". . . they say there's no smoke without bribery!" Literally. It's that bad. Or it can be.

Anyway, that's Hayley's father, and there he was in her apartment, on that fateful Wednesday evening. The legendary cartoonist stood and with a craggy, socialist smile offered Bruno his hand from twenty feet away.

And Bruno merely *waved*, reader, limply. "Hello," he called back in a quiet voice. "How are you? Nice . . . nice *daughter*."

No one said anything for a second. Hayley stoically sipped her beer.

"Thanks," said the man, a certain hesitancy in his voice as he wondered whether perhaps his daughter had accidentally landed herself a boyfriend of *low quality*. "Hayley says you're from London?"

"Yes . . ." Bruno nodded, then cleared his throat and chuckled. "I'm . . . I'm *from* there."

For a second, reader, no one said *anything*. Bruno Maddox broke the silence. "And . . . and you're from . . . someplace else, Hayley was saying."

"Yup. Philadelphia."

A glassy bonk from Hayley's direction as she set down her beer upon the pristine countertop. "Shall we go?"

"Sure. Where?" This was the great cartoonist standing up.

"Anywhere you want. What do you feel like?"

"Somewhere close by. I'm starved."

Oh dear.

It was flooding back to the boy that he'd agreed to go have *dinner* with Hayley's father, ages ago, literally days beforehand, and the sad thing was that that, for the boy, was simply not feasible. He'd had a really tough day. He wasn't sure anymore where he was exactly coming from, what his stance was, and going to dinner with Hayley's father would almost certainly involve certain *questions* being asked, questions about jobs and hobbies ... maybe even about ambitions ... maybe even about *preferences for one thing over another,* and right now Bruno just simply didn't have access to that sort of information. No, he just ...

"Um ... Hayley?"

The girl was at the fridge, reader. The fridge was open, the girl's hand was inside, storing her beer. She didn't turn. Just kept looking into the fridge, staring at a concrete vision of the near-term future.

"I'm afraid ..." said Bruno, pausing to clear his throat before every syllable. "I'm afraid I can't come out to dinner. I've stupidly agreed to ... I've accidentally become thin. I mean I ... I've accidentally gone and *spread* myself extremely thin."

"That's too bad," said Mr. Iskender relieved. "Are you sure?"

"Fuck," said Hayley into the fridge.

"I'm really sorry. I just ..."

"Bruno likes Manhattan," Hayley said, then she turned and the troublesome thing, the unexpected thing, was that she was actually *crying.* Her face was uncontorted, reader, don't get me wrong. She wasn't *crying like a little girl.* She was crying more like a statue, a statue that's also a fountain, like one of those big black blocks of marble in the plaza outside an investment bank where the water flows down the front and gets pumped back up to the top and then flows smoothly down again . . .

"Ah . . ." Bruno casually started tilting backward.

"Baby?" Orson was up and moving toward his pale bony offspring. "What's the problem?"

"I'm very unhappy."

Mr. Iskender's progress toward his daughter was interrupted by the kitchen counter.

"You should leave," Hayley said to Bruno as he struggled successfully to remain upright.

"Leave?" He nodded, nodding nodding nodding like so many times before, fading. "In what . . . in what sense?"

Reader, I shan't trouble you with the rest. The scene with Hayley's father in her airy apartment that terrible Wednesday was merely the latest in a long line of distressing human scenes, and I offered it up within these pages—I realize now with hindsight—primarily by way of *semi-apology*, semi-apology, reader, for having wasted so much of your time.

You see, for close on a million pages now I have been dragging you endlessly through scene after scene to try to show you Why What Happened Happened, why Bruno Maddox is the way he is, and I began, I remember, by trying to fool you into thinking that Bruno's behavior was excusable because of his having Caregiver's Syndrome, and then, when that stopped making sense, some four, four and a half thousand pages ago, I started trying to tell you—much more bogusly—that his problems were more complex, that it was all a matter of me *cramping his style*, that he would be a happy, productive member of society if the ugly-slash-poorly smelling old lady in the apartment next to his weren't denying the chap access to his *true nature*, which

was either to be a Citizen of the Future, a futuristic urban cowboy swashbuckling his way in hi-tech mismatched
clothing through the glamorous, seamy underbelly of
Twenty-first Century Manhattan, or a Creative Genius, remember all that?

Well, none of it was true, obviously. As you will have realized yourself if you have half a brain—even *half* of one,
reader—the only thing wrong with Bruno Maddox is that he
is one of those standard young men who Doesn't Really
Know Who He Is—except of course on those days when
suddenly *boom:* he *does* know who he is, and everything
clicks into place, for about forty-eight hours, before he for-
gets—which is not, to be frank, a terribly interesting thing to
have stayed up all night writing an entire book about. That's
what all the other books are about: young men not knowing
who they are. *Gary's Song,* by Greg McEwan, in particular, I
suspect. In other words, I have wasted both our times.
Which is why I am offering you an apology.

Or rather a semiapology.

It is only a semiapology, reader, because I am also aware
that for the last hundred thousand pages you have been sitting there in your little reading chair with your piped-in
classical music and your nearby strokable cat, *hating* Bruno
Maddox for the way he is, when the truth of the matter is
that you yourself are just as bad. Of course you are. We all
are. Don't even *try* to tell me that you're so sure and settled
in your personality that you don't occasionally get seduced
by some shiny New Way To Be, even if it's just a resolution
to be nicer to animals or eat nothing but fresh fruit each day
for breakfast, and don't even try to tell me that within the
week you aren't back to whipping your donkey and wolfing
down great slabs of blood sausage with bolognese sauce be-

fore you've even stepped out of bed. That's just the way we are, reader, all of us, as human beings. Even you.

Even you, reader. Which is why it's such an unappetizing spectacle to see you squatting there in your chair and detesting Bruno Maddox. For God's sake. The only difference between you and him is that Bruno possibly tends to try to reinvent himself on a slightly larger scale, his entire personality, from soup to enchiladas, but even that has its precedents.

In fact, I call your attention to years 1967–69, during which—if you consult your history book, reader—you will find that an *entire generation* of young men *and women* suffered a somewhat brunomaddoxish episode: deciding, in 1967, that they finally had it all figured out, that the unimpeachable secret of life was to renounce all human values but Love; managing, throughout 1968, to keep the dream alive despite the novelty wearing off slightly, despite a drip in the roof of the teepee; succumbing, in 1969, to pent-up hatred and recrimination, drowning en masse in a sea of mud, brown acid, and recrimination.

But perhaps you hate them too, reader. Perhaps you hate the hippies. Perhaps you're the sort of person who dons a long-haired wig for Hallowe'en, who allows a hint of a wry smile to mangle the corner of their mouth as they watch old footage of some sun child placidly inserting a flower into a soldier's gun.

Jesus, you're vicious.

How can you hate the hippies, reader? *How?* They were only trying to do the right thing, just like Bruno Maddox. It wasn't their fault that they came of age in an era of unprecedented peace and prosperity that led them to the utterly understandable, though false conclusion that the boring and interminable process of the World's coming of age was over and that it was time for mankind to see to the business of living for all eternity in peace and love and harmony.

Which, now I think of it, and at the risk of saying something frighteningly intelligent, may be Bruno Maddox's problem as well. *He* thinks the Past is finished and that we're all living in the Future. Of course we are. Why else, as discussed, would everyone be dressing up ironically in mismatched clothing from earlier decades? Why else would this entire culture so proudly consist of nothing but recycled, reanimated artforms of yore? How can you blame Bruno Maddox for constantly trying to transform himself into a god, reader, when he gets reminded at every turn that he's living in a futuristic age without limitations in which anything is possible and divinity is not merely attainable but his *birthright*? Hmm?

You can't.

You can blame me, though.

Because, if you think about it, *I* am Bruno's sense of history. It is because he thinks the past was as quaint and cartoonish as the early sections of this book, the early sections of *my* life, that he has such high expectations for the world he lives in.

So it's all *my* fault.

In *fact*, reader . . .

(And I refuse to call you "reader" anymore. We're beyond that now, reader. We can put down our masks. No need to stand on ceremony. We're closing in on something. I'm sorry I yelled at you earlier. I . . . I was angry. We should put that time behind us. What if I just call you "Michelle"?)

In *fact*, Michelle, if you've been teetering on the edge of your seat for the last thousand or so pages waiting for the next installment of my memoir, then why do we not just say that all throughout the period of Bruno Maddox's growing-up, throughout the nineteen seventies and the nineteen eighties and the nineteen nineties, I had my mouth jammed to his ear and was telling him telling him the same steaming pile of nonsense I was telling you earlier, Michelle, that the Past was quaint and ridiculous and small-minded and unambitious and inward-looking, and most important, that it was very, very different from the glorious golden Future in which he was very, *very* fortunate to live? He believed me, too. Perhaps because the television was saying the exact same thing.

And perhaps, Michelle, from time to time, if ever we found ourselves alone, I would dig out the old Super-8 movie projector that I had salvaged from my sinister nineteen fifties living room back in Fordham, Wisconsin, and show the young Bruno Maddox a *movie*, Michelle. Any old thing would do: a thrilling old war film with a stubbly hero mowing down hundreds of faceless Germans with a gun made out of his shoe . . . maybe a flick involving a modest, thoughtful scientist in the fifteenth century getting roundly ridiculed by a panel of kings and queens in large bulbous hats for having dared to suggest that the world is round or that grass is green . . . or maybe just one about a young boy with nothing but a guitar and a dream, growing up in a little rural village where everyone thought his music was shit. Didn't matter, as I say, because when the film was ended, when the tail end of the celluloid was flapping round and round in the projector, I would infallibly turn to the very young Bruno Maddox and demand to know where his sympathies lay. "Do they lie with the ordinary, clear-thinking hero?" I would ask. "Or with the stupid faceless masses?"

"With the hero?"

"I'm . . . I'm sorry?"

"With the hero?"

At which point, Michelle, I would pretend to fall over. Well, I actually *would* fall over, but it would all be a sham, and when I regained my footing, after a minute on the floor, I would lean into the face of the tiny little guy, my features white and sharp with urgency, and inform him of the following: that he was a genius, just like the man in the movie; that unlike the man in the movie he wasn't living in the drab and piddling Past, but the sparkling, unlimited Future and would therefore be rewarded for his genius, not with millions of dollars, but with *billions* of millions, if not in fact more.

"But . . . but what'll be my field, my . . . zone of expertise?" the little tyke would bleat, regurgitating vitamin-fortified pear mash onto his plastic bib with the picture of the cow on it.

"'Field'?" I would thunder. "Did Albert Einstein have a 'field'? Was he paid his measly million dollars for being quote unquote 'a physicist'? No. He was paid those monies in return for being Mr. Albert Einstein, for allowing the world access to his *personality*. And it will be the same way with you, as long as you don't fuck it up."

"How might I do that?" he would wonder aloud, his tiny forehead crinkling.

By failing to keep his options open, I'd explain. By allowing the hordes of little people to define him as one of them, as a particular sort of person, with a particular sort of job, from whom a particular set of behaviors could be expected. That was not how geniuses had behaved. Geniuses were limitless. They didn't join the army. Or get a job. Or marry some moderately attractive woman at the age of twenty-four. Geniuses stayed true to themselves, doing nothing that required any effort or compromise, until they woke up one morning and found that their entire personality had been smoothly converted into a glittering mountain of money and renown, sitting there at the foot of their bed.

And that, Michelle, is why Bruno Maddox is the way he is. That's why he just keeps starting again ... starting again ... starting again. He's waiting for life to feel like I told him it was *supposed* to feel. He's been keeping his options open, Michelle, all this time, wide, wide open. Nobody knows how to keep his options open like Bruno Maddox. Jesus, Michelle, he won't even let you *take his photograph* for fear it might establish irrevocably that he was in a particular place at a particular time. If you approach him at a party and say "Hello. How are you?" then *no way in hell* will he respond "Fine. How are you?" Because he's wise to your little game, Michelle. He knows what you're up to. How dare you assume he's just like you, some tiny-minded nobody who plays by the rules and engages in the standard small talk. No, Michelle, you can expect the unexpected if you ever try a stunt like that. You'll get a "*fucking* well, actually," for your trouble, or an "I have a brain tumor, thank you, and I'm *dying*." And if you're working behind the checkout counter, Michelle, of an emporium that happens to purvey gentlemen's toiletries, and an extremely stubbly Bruno Maddox approaches you to purchase a bag of disposable safety razors, well, then brace yourself, because as he slides his cash toward you he's going to mumble something like "These are for my goldfish," thereby puncturing the arrogant hypothesis you were quietly forming that you knew what he was going to do with them.

Yes, Michelle, bad things happen to people who think

they know what "sort" of person Bruno Maddox is, or what to expect of him, or what he's capable of.

Case in point, one Ms. H. Iskender of Manhattan Island, who called us up in Chinatown that

August 26th—Thursday

Thursday morning to leave the following supposedly devastating message, which I shall embolden for emphasis:

> **Hello? It's me. Um, I'm . . . I've decided to go to England for two weeks with Mark Clark, starting today, and I don't want you using the apartment, okay? Pause. I guess pause I guess I'll speak to you in two weeks. Mm . . . 'bye. Click. Buzz. Click.**

Bruno didn't think much of Hayley's message. In bed, beneath a greasy sheet, he frankly didn't *understand* the bulk of it. All that stuff about Mark Clark . . . and going to England for two weeks . . . and that whole subtext about her and Bruno not being an item anymore. It all seemed pretty opaque.

No, the only solid information he was able to glean from those few seconds of staticky droning was that Hayley Iskender was clearly under the impression that Bruno Maddox was the sort of person for whom she could safely leave that type of message. The sort of person who will just lie back and take it. The sort of person, frankly, whom she could count on *not* to roll commando style from his bed, squat above the 'phone, ingeniously consult with Directory Assistance in Kansas City, Missouri, and place a call to **Clark's Quality**

Optical Frames to extract the flight information that he knew in his gut all members of the super-intimate, recently bereaved Clark family were routinely filing with one another, then jump into his nasty green suit, ride via cab to the airport, wander about feeling completely insane, lurk behind a nest of 'phones while she and Clark—exhibiting to his relief no obvious signs of intimacy or even affection—checked their bags and disappeared into the bowels of the airport, and after suffering a moment of intolerable hollowness and desperation, consult the screenful of Departures and book passage himself aboard a flight that was due to reach England before her own.

That was a big mistake on her part, Michelle, thinking he wouldn't do that.

Because it meant that that was what he had to do. A genius cannot let himself be defined by others, can't let them make him small like that. Or so I told him.

Which is what I've been trying to tell you, Michelle.

That it's all *my* fault.

Mea culpa.

Whatever the German is for "It's all my fault."

And that's why *everything* . . .

That's

PART III

Why Everything, *Michelle*

August 27th—Friday

Why everything.

Michelle, . . . as I examine you this morning I find myself overcome, by all the usual fondness, obviously, but also by a degree of concern. Are you doing okay? Are you bearing up? Not crumbling a shade around the edges after all this terrible reading marathon? Sentence after sentence after sentence . . . paragraph after paragraph . . . chapter after chapter after literally chapter . . . ? Mm? Michelle? Are you okay? Can you hear me?

No no actually no *shhhhhh*, Michelle. *Shhhhhhhhh*. Don't try to speak. No fuss. Don't buck and heave. You're the tiredest little sausage in all the land, Michelle. Lie still, lie still and rest now. Nothing more is required of you. You just lie there and be still, you hot little slip of a reader. I'll do all the work, just like I've been doing it all night. I've done it all for you, Michelle, think about it. I've been your eyes, your ears, your walking stick, your nose, your fingertips, your sixth sense, your seventh, your ninth, your twelfth, not to mention, of course: your eyes, your ears, the hairs on the back of your neck, your metal detector, your smoke alarm, the thing that alerts you to wind shear . . .

Your *dawn module*.

I am your dawn module also, Michelle, in which capacity I have news:

It's dawn.

Michelle, *dawn* is coming up. Michelle, a filament of tiny pink is breaking far away in the chilly eastern sky as I make these very words. Let the record reflect that this day began at

28 AUG--4:29 A.M.

from where I stood, when I saw the dawn and reported it to you. This moment is never to be repeated and I am wasting time.

Michelle, I was telling you why everything.

I believe I left off with Bruno Maddox sitting in an air-o-plane in the sky pointed back toward England feeling utterly, utterly sane, despite his situation. He is on his absolute best behavior, Michelle, and it is paying massive dividends vis-à-vis his state of mind. They have told him to keep his seatbelt fastened if he isn't moving about the cabin and he has done so. They have encouraged him to eat a meal and swallow multiple beverages and he has willingly complied. Slightly above him, slightly in front of him, a drawing of a cigarette has a line through it and, Michelle, he has not smoked. Life, Michelle, has not been quite this easy and obvious for the microscopic little fellow in quite some time and as we tunnel on backward through the black of night he finds himself growing saner still.

For he has, it dawns on him, no obligation. Though Clark and Hayley are also in the air, also bound for Lon-

274

don's Heathrow Airport, and despite the agony and the madness of the day just exited, there is no pressure on the boy to do *anything at all*. He is merely going home. As people do. Hayley and Clark do not *know* that he is hunting them. Should he choose not to make an ambush at the airport, but instead to slip away, to become one with the crowd, to visit family, and/or friends, frequent old haunts, he is *perfectly at liberty to do so*.

And so, Michelle, the young man sleeps, with no decision made.

28 AUG--6:33 A.M.

Awakening, Bruno finds that dawn has broken for him, much like it broke for us, Michelle, you and I, oh so recently. His neck is stiff but his heart is light. England can be seen below, through the clouds, that misted island of the viscous Past. Excited and bodiless I float to the porthole and peer to catch a glimpse of Murbery . . . ! But alas! The clouds are too thick, the village of my birth too nonexistent, for me to properly make it out. Captain Mazzocks prepares the flight crew for our final descent, the air-o-plane sluices this way and that for what seems like several minutes and then all of a sudden . . .

Eep. We do land. *Rumble*. We taxi to the gate. All is serene, but with the *ping* of the seatbelt sign that serenity is broken. As all around him stand to collect belongings and he has none of his own to collect, the boy feels fear for the first time in hours, fears the old fears storming the beaches again, fear about what he might be about to do, fear about what he has already done might mean about how sane, or not, he really is. At Immigration and then Customs, the young man yearns to be stopped, to be taken aside and have the sense kicked into him by officials . . . but no, as a lifelong Caucasian he glides through like a ghost and is borne through sliding doors into the body of the airport where he ambles down the boulevard of broken chauffeurs with their hand-lettered signs:

LORD KING

MULTIZONE

"MR SKINNER"

SPRUCE

But he is none of these. There was a time, Michelle, when he might have stopped to wonder, might have stopped to wonder whether he *was* in fact Spruce, whether this was the clue he'd always been waiting for . . .

Not today, though, Michelle.

He is in England.

This is his *home*, his turf, his demesne, his veldt. His sanity and poise resurge to hitherto unseen levels and in low-vent ash-colored embrace of his native land Bruno Maddox remembers who he is.

He is the Hunter.

And, Michelle, why not? Why not be the Hunter? Nowhere is it written in the laws of Nature that a Hunter must necessarily *confront* his prey. A Hunter's mandate is solely to hunt, to stalk, to spy, to *know* . . .

Thinking on his feet the Hunter establishes himself in the Café Metro, a faux-French bistro-oasis amidst the madness of the world's busiest airport. With burnished wooden dais and railings of brass, the Café Metro is a little slab of nineteen twenties Paris installed in twenty-first-century England and the Hunter quickly sizes up the place's elements and bends each one to his purpose. An upholstered booth becomes the Hunter's lair and a cappuccino his binoculars. Through its steam he scans the fresh Arrivals as they are borne through sliding doors: the weak-chinned English, sunburned in their cowboy hats and mouse ears, the Americans slick with moisturizer in their unwrinklable travel trousers . . .

Flicker flicker flicker.

Flicker flicker flicker.

The large mechanicized board emits a *flickering* sound, Michelle, as it cycles through points of departure and flight numbers and arrival times . . . Oslo, Hungary, Paris, Arabia . . . the names *become* one other, Michelle. Letter by letter they slowly transform, like the identities of characters in a dream . . .

And then suddenly boom.

By the looks of her, Hayley Iskender has had a sleepless, uncomfortable flight, and possibly a sleepless and uncomfortable couple of years. Her ponytail is all bulging out one side and her skin is more lined and gray and papery than usual. Her cardigan clings to her waist like an exhausted child in need of love.

Clark of course is fine, as stubby and indestructible as ever in what seems to be a *new* black leather jacket—though perhaps he has merely oiled up his old one with some secret rural unguent. The pair of youngish elopers—the *Prey,* Michelle—are trudging several yards apart, but the short, hairy Man is towing *two* sets of luggage—which *irks* the Hunter in his lair, Michelle, irks him *considerably* . . .

And yet he keeps cool, in fact sinks fractionally back into the upholstery of the Lair. Observing them, the way they are, tired and unsure in a strange new land, the Hunter feels something approaching pity for Hayley Iskender and Mark Clark. This day will not be easy for them. Soon jet lag will gnaw at their connective tissues, strange money will scramble their brains, new standards in food preparation and general service will give them the sensation of stepping off a cliff into ice water. Hard as he is—and, Michelle, he is jungle toughened—the Hunter knows that there are times when it is wrong to pounce, when the hunting gods would prefer the prey to live to die another day. The Hunter is not the sort of person who

Quickly he is up, and moving, supple as water as he flows along and off his banquette, away across the burnished dais and into the crowd. The Prey are passing down the boulevard of chauffeurs and the Hunter matches their speed, so that when the railings dwindle, when it is all just unstructured and formless milling, the Hunter is right there with them, close enough to touch.

"Hey" is his quiet line. Nothing comes of it. They cannot . . . they *will not* acknowledge the Hunter, though he is inches close.

"Hey."

Michelle, it is the girl who stops first. She stops and she turns and she sees. The other one, the Man, just keeps bareling ahead, increasingly dimly aware that over his shoulder lies a developing situation, but refusing to let it stop him. He's got the bridles of two rollables wrapped securely around his fingers and he seems to have made it his mission to keep tugging them, no matter what, much like Olaf Ver Olafson used to drag parked cars crammed with bimbos to world's-strongest-man glory from 1978 to 1984, or like how the wise old carthorse used to tug his cart home in the dusk from Brapton up to Muffly Forge oh so many years ago. Now even he stops, though, and turns and sees.

"Welcome to England." The Hunter's voice is cool and dark. "I have followed you here."

And nothing comes of it, not immediately, or hardly anything. There's a very quick flash of emotion visible in the girl, a moment of rage and frustration, though it is not directed at the Hunter, necessarily. Indeed a person walking past at speed might think instead that Hayley Iskender has rage for the ten-member family of Africans loitering behind the Hunter, for it is them the rage is pointed at, but very very quickly it leaves, the rage, and like Clark she studies the Hunter, waiting for direction.

"Er . . ." says the Hunter, making a face.

His embarrassment is contagious. Hayley Iskender actually blushes. The man Mark Clark looks away and scratches his eyebrow. It feels strange to them, I reckon, the embarrassment. Is this what it feels like being English? Mark Clark might be wondering. Though then again . . .

"What are you doing?" Hayley wonders out loud.

Aping Clark, the Hunter scratches his eyebrow. "I'm having a coffee. Over there."

"Do you need to talk to me?"

"Um. No. Yes."

"I'm going to talk to him," says Hayley to the suitcase man.

"Okay."

And with a jerk of the Hunter's wingless head they are off, tunneling through the crowd like a colonial expedition through the jungle: the Hunter in front, seasoned and ma-

279

chete wielding; Hayley Iskender in the middle, hot and bothered white woman, titillated by all the wildness; then of course the miniature little hired native bringing up the rear with the suitcases. Reaching his lair the Hunter pulls back the mosquito netting, shepherds Hayley inside, and gives Mark Clark a look that seems to say *go wait over there,* which Mark Clark does. In a booth across the dais the smaller man wedges his precious cargo of luggage beneath the table and sits sideways on the edge of the banquette, hunched over, fingers all multipled over his mouth, just staring. The Hunter slides into the lair and treats the girl to a toothless smile.

She just looks at him.

He looks at her back.

"I'm going to leave now," says the girl.

The Hunter nods, then catches himself and shakes his head. "No, come on. Don't."

"Why not?"

He thinks. "I don't know. You know. Final conversation. Or something."

She just looks at him.

"How are you, for instance?"

She ceases looking at him, drops her eyes to his steaming binoculars.

The Hunter speaks again. "Look, I hope you don't think I'm following you. I just wanted to see if you were okay."

"I'm not okay."

"Sorry?"

"I'm not okay. I don't know what I'm doing anymore."

The Hunter nods and sips casually at his binoculars. "Can I ask a stupid question?"

"Yes."

"What *are* you doing here?"

Michelle, I hate to interrupt but I feel I really have to point out that there is something about the Hunter's demeanor that is just *undeniably* suave and intoxicating. He seems to be changing again, Michelle. He is still the Hunter but no longer is he savage. He's just a hunter of information now, a man who crossed an ocean because he was curious, a global thinker . . . and it suits the Hunter, this new reasonableness, sipping his binoculars like that and calmly blinking. In fact, he's magnificent.

Not so the girl, whose mouth has become literally an upside-down *U* of unhappiness as she stares down at the Hunter's souvenir Café Metro napkin which she has taken upon herself to rend into a thousand pieces with her long, unfeeling fingers. Oh, and periodically she is swallowing with her long throat. "I'm here with Mark. He's been offered a job and the company paid for him and a companion to fly over for an interview. He called me up at work yesterday and asked me if I wanted to come with him."

"Oh *really*?" The Hunter sounds fascinated. "Now why would he go and do something like that?"

"He's had a thing for me, apparently, since that night at that volcano place." She bites her lip.

"A-*ha*."

"And I said yes because I needed . . . I needed to get away from New York and from you and from everything."

Hayley says this last part quickly, with no particular emphasis on any particular words, but of course the Hunter did not get to be the Hunter by allowing people to slip things past him.

"From me? What are you talking about?"

Oh, *now* she looks up. Hayley Iskender ceases her examination of the Hunter's tattered napkin and indeed glares at the Hunter full in the eyes.

Does he crumble, Michelle? Does he crumble and look away?

No. He meets her glare and holds it. Because, of course, he's the Hunter now. The Hunter, Michelle, with eyes as deep as jungle watering holes, eyes as dark and green as an outsize sail of shiny leaf being toted along a branch by a tiny ant on television, eyes shot through with the sadness and wisdom of the coconut as it plummets from the hairy crotch of the palm tree, the only home it has ever known. Bruno Maddox is the Hunter now, and these are the eyes Hayley Iskender must deal with now, if she can.

"You know, I, uh . . ." The Hunter's neck hurts suddenly and he has to look away, in order to grimace and rub it. "I'm sorry about what happened with your dad. I really . . . dropped the ball on that one. I was having a tough day."

And this, Michelle, turns out to be the wrong thing to say.

"Tough day?" is how Hayley begins and it's awhile before she stops. Methodically, starting at the very beginning, she reexamines her entire unfortunate relationship with the Hunter, building a fairly convincing case that it is *always* a tough day for the Hunter. It was a tough day for the Hunter, she reminds him, when they first met, that night they went out for drinks and he had to bolt home unexpectedly after blurting something about wanting to live in an undersea dome. There then ensued approximately *twelve* tough days *in a row,* if he recalls, lasting the length of their ill-conceived probationary period. And who could forget the tough day in whose later hours the Hunter unloaded in Mark Clark's face for no reason whatsoever at Magma, plus of course the tough night out with Gordon . . .

"Well actually," the Hunter interrupts, sounding an awful lot smaller, "you're not being one bit fair. I really had just had a particularly tough day. I'm not trying to make excuses but I was having . . . having real trouble with my work."

"You don't do any work."

"Yes I do."

"No you don't. You don't do anything. You never even called those numbers I gave you."

"Yes I did. No one was in."

And she begins again, Michelle. She begins to savage him afresh, cracking the cellophane on a whole new *ream* of facts he didn't know she knew about his working habits, and the holes in his personality, and his private, secret opinions about the world, leading him literally to the brink of *tears*, Michelle, before finally, stopping. "I'm sorry. I'm tired. I'm going to leave now. We shouldn't be together."

"Yes we should," Bruno squeaks.

"Why? I don't even remember why we were together in the first place."

But I do.

Michelle, *I* remember. Or at least I have a theory.

It was the *dome*. That first night when Bruno stammered that nonsense about how his ultimate, overweening ambition was to live in an undersea dome . . . well, I reckon something clicked inside the girl. She'd been thinking the same herself, Michelle, it occurs to me now. She'd been thinking it was probably about time to flee New York, long past time to flee the booths, the banquettes, the towers of zany conceptual food, the parties, the synergy, the speed . . . the terrible media jobs like flypaper once they got you . . . and the men. The men most of all. The endless sequence of men beneath whose surfaces, if you scratched, you found a fermenting plan to one day soon whip off a quick rock opera and funnel the proceeds into a pair of interlocking swimming pools in the shape of their own initials. I reckon she was probably done with those men, Michelle, and wondering where she might possibly go to hide, at the moment that Bruno Maddox came along, that night, with his talk of domes and solitude. Clearly here was a fellow sufferer. I mean just look at him. Shambling and twitching . . . unable even to stand up straight for the sheer tonnage of fraud and meaninglessness. And listen to what he's mumbling! A dome beneath the sea! Away from the awfulness.

What she failed to appreciate was that the dome Bruno Maddox had in mind could not be built for less than ten billion dollars and that, if everything worked out, the color supplements of the world's newspapers every Sunday would feature double-page spreads of Bruno Maddox and Companion in the dome's master bedroom, wearing matching white terry-cloth robes, sipping freshly squeezed guava-pineapple blend shipped in via trained dolphin from Florida, opening his fan mail while just beyond the toughened picture window sharks and plankton cavorted. Hayley never realized, Michelle, that there was room in Bruno's dome for a staff of Filipinos. But she appreciates it now.

"You're just like the rest of them."

"What do you mean? The rest of who . . . m?"

"The rest of the twenty-seven-year-old guys who write themselves checks for a hundred million dollars and want to rule the world."

Hayley's jaw has gone all square. The Hunter blinks at a loss.

"Are you finished?"

"Yeah." She swings her eyes vaguely in the direction of Mark Clark, though not with love, or interest, or even recognition. Just because things are less cluttered over there.

"Can I speak?"

She has no opinion.

"Okay. Well, to start with, that first day I met you at that . . ."

"No."

"What?"

That head of hers swivels back. "Don't. I'm not going to sit here and listen to you make up excuses for every time you fucked up.

"Why not?"

"Because that's what you always do."

"Oh." The Hunter is hurt.

"Well in that case I won't say anything."

"Okay. I'm going to leave."

She tries to. Tries to exit the booth but her long limbs get tangled in the strut work beneath the table, and now she looks confused, frightened. This is not an ergonomic *American* booth like she is used to. This is a very poorly designed *English* one, and Hayley, for a moment, is stuck in it.

Michelle, to the best of my recollection it is right about . . . *now* that I make my entrance. I'm in a place called Books Plus, a standard-issue airport newsagent. An extremely old woman, I am hunched painfully over a stack of newspapers, presumably *The Irish Times* or *The Sporting News* or *Old Women's Wear Daily*—speaking of which, I am in: a clear plastic head scarf, a beige-gray old-woman coat of low-cost lightweight tweed, and some flat brown shoes, lusterless and clunky as hooves. I'm nowhere near a hundred years old, Michelle, but then again, like a fine wine, I am very old indeed. I feel the young man's eyes upon me. He blinks.

"You can't leave," mutters Bruno to the trapped young lady, not trying to be funny. "You don't have enough information to leave me. You have no idea who I am."

"Yes I do." She stops struggling.

It is the Hunter's turn to glare. Hayley's long limbs are still entangled. It's her turn to be uncomfortable. "No, you don't. You've only seen the edges."

"The edges?"

"The tiny . . ." He clenches his jaw. "The tiny residue."

"What?"

Michelle, I've reached the cashier. In my hand, my gnarled old hand, is a little red leather change purse that I have had in my possession for simply years. A line is forming behind me as I poke for coins.

Bruno Maddox lifts a hand to his eyes and in a single gorgeous sigh exhales the entire pain of all the summer. "You don't know what I've been through." He sounds serene.

"No." She starts to struggle again, makes some headway.

"I should have been more open with you."

"Yes."

"Is it too late?"

"Yes."

"No. I mean is it too late for me to be open with you?"

"Yes."

"I've been having some family trouble. All summer. It's been really difficult. I should have told you."

She stops. "Someone's ill in your family?"

"No. Not my actual family. Felt like family."

"Sorry?"

"She . . . felt like family. Hayley?"

"Yes?"

"The thing is this. I've been looking after an old woman all summer. In the apartment next to mine. I should have told you about her obviously but . . . well, she really didn't want me to. It's been very . . . stressful as you can imagine, and I'm sorry I've been such a freak."

Michelle, if you were to put a gun to my head and force me to go with an adjective, I think I'd probably end up saying that Hayley appears . . . *interested* by Bruno's statement. Her entire face retreats fractionally on its chassis. Her eyes narrow. Her lips part. An involuntary sound makes it past the various medical structures of her long throat, a little preliminary "ah" of comprehension . . .

Because for the briefest of moments she knows it's true.

Not *actually* true of course. She's not a moron, Michelle, as she would surely have to be to believe that Bruno Maddox had been an old woman's caregiver all summer, but true in the following way: that if you were to take a proper, complete young man—a *really* proper one, the sort whose hair doesn't vary wildly in length, who dabbles in sport, who calls his parents occasionally, who has given at least fleeting thought to joining the army, who looks you in the eye when he shakes your hand, who impregnates, at twenty-two, his averagely attractive childhood sweetheart . . . Mark Clark, I suppose. Take Mark Clark, force him to look after a hundred-year-old woman for a while, and you'd end up with Bruno Maddox: a miserable creature whose mind is always elsewhere, whose stamina and sense of purpose have been eroded by months of toil and futility, who seems clearly to have at some point *been* complete—why else would he keep trying to exercise those inner muscles, and be so dismayed to find them missing?—but is now just a ravaged·and grieving mess.

So yes. Hayley does, for a moment, know that Bruno is telling the truth, but then, understandably, allows herself to be sidetracked by the fact that he isn't.

"You're lying."

This remark is very hurtful. Bruno Maddox, the Hunter, call him what you will, was just about to have a full-blown epiphany—and now here Hayley is messing the whole thing up. Why does she have to be this way, always? She knows as well as he does—he can see it in her face—that there clearly *is* a sense in which he's been looking after a one-hundred-year-old woman all summer, but rather than help him work out what it is, thereby making everything okay, she's making a conscious choice to be difficult. Why? Why are other people always so difficult? Bruno sighs. "I wish I was."

"The apartment next to yours is empty. I looked in there once."

"I know. You were looking right at her. You just didn't see." The young man speaks quietly, grimly. He does not enjoy being forced to lie.

"That's not true."

"Yes it is. Why do you think I kept the fire door open? That was how I tended to her."

Actually, Michelle, Kevin Lee broke the fire door, exploded its latch that day he charged through to assault my radiator.

"Can I call her?"

"Who?"

"The old woman."

"No."

"Why not?"

"Because she's dead. She died yesterday."

(Big mistake, Michelle. Big mistake killing me off. Leave me alive and maybe I just didn't feel like answering the phone—sorry the 'phone—maybe I just wandered off as oldsters are wont to do. But a *dead* old woman . . . well, she's fixed data. Somewhere there has to be a 'phone number, or a birth certificate, or dental records. Something. No, Michelle. Never should have killed old woman in first place. Stupid stupid stupid.)

"I'm sorry for your loss," says Hayley, who isn't believing all this I've-been-tending-to-an-old-woman-type material.

"Thanks. It's fine. She was at peace. Her affairs were in order. She'd finished writing her memoirs. She lived to see the new millennium. She was ready to go. But anyway, this is why you can't leave me."

"What was her name?"

"Mm?"

"Old woman's name. So I can call Directory Assistance to see if she exists."

That's when it all got absurd.

Bruno didn't know my name, he explained, because I couldn't really speak.

That was ridiculous, Hayley told him.

No it wasn't, he replied.

Why?

She didn't have any bills lying around?

Nope. Bruno paid for everything. That's one of the reasons he may have seemed not to have very much money.

What about the memoir he mentioned? The one she finished prior to dying. That didn't have her name on it? Or in it?

Maybe. He hadn't read it.

But he did *have* it, the memoir.

Yes. Not on him, obviously, back in New York. In part, why didn't Hayley just quickly fuck off and do whatever she had to do with Mark Clark and then when she returned to New York there would be Bruno Maddox waiting for her with the old woman's memoir in hand ready to watch her eat an entire humble pie?

Actually, Hayley had a better idea. Why didn't she call her colleague Jane, get Jane to use the spare set of keys in Hayley's office drawer to access Hayley's apartment, retrieve the keys to *Bruno's* apartment, then go round and ascertain whether there was or was not an old woman's memoir lying around.

Because it . . . it probably wasn't there anymore. Owing to the author's advanced age, her publishers had insisted she give *them* a set of keys to the apartment so they could retrieve the manuscript on the appointed day, which happened to be today.

Oh really.

Yes.

That was an unorthodox arrangement, Hayley reckoned.

Bruno agreed. In fact, he couldn't agree more. It really was unorthodox. Unorthodox was a fantastic word for the arrangement. But it made sense if you thought about it. The publishers were keen to protect their investment. They'd dumped an entire million dollars on account of my having been born on the first day of the Twentieth Century.

How did Bruno know all this?

How? Because he'd found a copy of my publishing contract.

And the contract didn't have my name on it?

Didn't . . . oh, come on. Surely Hayley knew how contracts were written. The party of the first part, as defined in subsection twelve. The Author shall do this . . . the Author shall do that . . . Presumably my name was in there somewhere, just not on any of the pages he happened to have glanced at.

Did he still have it?

What?

The contract.

No. He'd left it on top of the manuscript for the publishers to collect. But look, this was all getting stupid. If Hayley genuinely didn't believe he'd been caring for an old woman all summer, then he would go to the bother of contacting the publishers, whose Chief Executive happened to be a good friend of Theo Bakula's and a really nice guy, incidentally, and get him to send a copy to England. Why didn't Hayley go fart around with Mark Clark for a few days and he'd meet her in central London at the end of the week, old woman's memoir in hand. At which point she could jettison Mark Clark and return to Bruno's side, no questions asked, no grudges borne.

Scotland.

What.

Clark's new job was in Scotland and they were flying there tomorrow.

Where in Scotland, exactly? wondered Bruno.

"Okay, I'm leaving."

And she did this time. Effortlessly Hayley slid from the booth and slouched across to where Clark was. Clark was

pretty gracious about everything, refrained from even looking in Bruno's direction, let alone taunting him with any
kind of hand gesture. Bruno watched as Clark extricated the
baggage from the bowels of his rival booth. "You don't believe me," he shouted at Hayley's back.

She ignored him, but he could see that she didn't, and
that, Michelle, was troublesome to a man like Bruno Maddox. Had Hayley even *slightly* believed his story, well, then
he would have been comfortable letting it slide. He could
have gone about his business, never seen her again, secure in
the knowledge that in her mind he remained an enigma. A
complex, unknowable man. A mysterious stranger.

But this . . . intolerable. She was doing it again. Making
assumptions about who he was; in this case that he was a
shabby and predictable liar about whom many things were
knowable, chief among them the fact that he would *not* in all
likelihood be there the next morning at the airport to confront her with the entire text of an old woman's memoir.

"You don't believe me," he called again as the pair of
them set off. They turned, they both did, at which point
Bruno Maddox literally reared up in his booth and without
pausing for breath, without even pausing between words, informed young, pale Hayley Iskender at volume that everything was going to be okay because he had just remembered
that Theo's publishing friend was also co-owner of a technology company specializing in handwriting recognition
software and it was all going to be okay because Bruno was
certain in his gut that by this point the old woman's memoir
would surely have been run through a machine and converted
into incredibly immaculate electronic text which Bruno
would persuade the publishing man who was really nice to

transmit to him somehow over the airwaves and that he too, meaning Bruno Maddox, would also be at the airport tomorrow with the whole thing printed out and she was making an enormous mistake going off with Mark Clark but within twenty-four hours she was going to be rueing that mistake and begging him to take her back.

"Fine," she said, not caring. "Nine thirty."

The rest, of course, is history: the sinking back; the minutes of peaceful heroic reflection; the downing of the dregs of Hunter's now room-temperature binoculars as if they were the finest champagne; the quiet acceptance that this probably wouldn't happen; the pulse of self-disgust; the sub-table fist pump and the vow to self that no, no it *would* in fact happen; the springing to feet; the thinking on feet; the helpful woman at the info desk; the bureau de change; the complimentary shuttle bus to the business traveler's lodge; the room rental; the forceful conversation with the reptiles in the 24-Hr Business Centre; the way they just folded; the laptop computer; the elevator; the shower; the magnificent emergence; the arrangement of the desk and armchair; the little bit of television; the passing out; the coming-to in Hell with darkness already falling, at least the cars had their lights on and a hideous low-wattage exterior screaming in through the soundproof window and Bruno unable to remember who or when or where he was except that he had once had a girl, a nice one, in fact the best, but that he didn't have her anymore and that meant he was going to go mad and die; the crying; the starting . . .

Anyway, that's it, Michelle. That's your lot. I've told you everything. As promised. Everything.

Except that there's a dead bird on the concrete, unreach-able balcony. And a black-and-white photo of some blurry ferns in a bent tin frame that in a different world, a different world, might warrant further investigation. And an unmiss-able heap of quivering young man with a bleeding finger and a back that hurts so much it actually feels *unbelievably pleas-urable*. Oh, and there on the floor is the notepaper. Look, it's right there. The notepaper with all the provisional titles on it.

A Backwards Glance
Me, Looking Backwards
Me: A Life
Me and My Big Life
This Is My Life
Crazy Little Thing Called Life
Things My Mother Told Me
My Mother's Little Enameled Music Box Thing
My Father's Leather Apron
My Little Blue Dress
Memories
Reflections
The View from Here
It All Went by So Fast!
That's All Folks!
What?? You're Telling Me That's It? But . . . But I
    Was Only Just Getting Started!
Reflected Memories

Wow. Really takes me back seeing that. Seems like ages ago that a hysterical young man with his heart in the right place scribbled all that down, circled the middle one, committed himself to becoming Queen of the May in a miniature little village, then just dove in. *Ages*, Michelle. Incidentally, do you have the time?

28 AUG--8:32 A.M.

Thanks.

Wow.

So still doable then. Business Centre's just downstairs, ready to go with the good old laser printer.

The airport's shockingly close as well, Michelle. *Frighteningly* close. Five minutes. If that. More like four.

This book's a pile of feces, though, obviously. Is that a problem? That it's a glistening pile of implausible feces, steaming in the thick morning light?

No.

Not at all.

It isn't like Hayley's actually going to sit down and *read* the thing. The existence of a massive pile of paper, text on each page, chapter headings referring to decades, would probably suffice, for as long as it took her to ditch Mark Clark, whom she doesn't really like . . .

Actually, no.

You're not thinking, Michelle. Look at the boy. Look at how he looks. He's got blood on him, Michelle. Blood blood blood blood blood.

Plus he's visibly insane. Just think. He'd come galumphing through the crowd with his hair all everywhere and his skin all sick and gray like that, knocking people over, papers flying. . . . She'd know, right away, what he's done.

But maybe that would touch her. I mean, how could it

not? That he . . . *he,* Bruno Maddox, who can't ever do *any-thing* . . . stayed up all night and did all this? That's called Evidence of Deep Emotion, Michelle. Or something. She'd be *touched*. She'd be *moved*. She'd *relent,* and then . . .

Then it would all start up again.

Which would be bad.

The last thing he needs is a fresh start. It would all start up again . . . and then it would all go wrong again. Because you can't become a better person in a single night any more than you can fake an old woman's memoir in a single night. Just can't be done.

So Hayley, you are not reading this. These words? That I am writing? You are not reading them.

Or if you are it's because it's now years from now and you just ran into Bruno Maddox at some party or something, fuck knows where, and conversation turned inevitably to yesterday morning and you both had a good laugh and when the laughter died down he told you about tonight, about this, about how much, in a way, he conceivably cared. Then printed you out a copy.

But you are not reading this now, Hayley Iskender.

Not this morning.

Because this morning it is time for bed.

The wheel has turned full circle.

The cows have come home to roost.

The chickens have . . .

Sorry, What's that, Michelle?

Oh.

Yes, I know I know I know.

All of a sudden this is reading like the end of a book: the short sentences, the one-line paragraphs, the bittersweet stench.

I'm sorry.
What do you want me to do?
There's nothing.
It's out of my hands.
All I can do is say, Bye.
Take care of yourself.
Thanks for bein' lasses wi' me.